Ev[illegible]n 1949 and before turning to spy thrillers she wrote a succession of ten highly successful historical novels, all of which were widely translated and two of which became Literary Guild Choices in America. Married to the director of a mining company she has six children and runs two houses, one in Belgravia, the other, a beautiful Elizabethan mansion, in Essex.

*Also by Evelyn Anthony and available from Sphere Books*

THE ASSASSIN
ELIZABETH
VICTORIA
THE POELLENBERG INHERITANCE
VALENTINE
FAR FLIES THE EAGLE
IMPERIAL HIGHNESS
THE FRENCH BRIDE
CLANDARA

# *The Tamarind Seed*

**EVELYN ANTHONY**

SPHERE BOOKS LIMITED
30/32 Gray's Inn Road, London WC1X 8JL

First published in Great Britain by Hutchinson & Co Ltd 1971

Published by Sphere Books 1973
Reprinted April 1973
Reprinted March 1974
Reprinted February 1975

To Bobbie Neville
with love

TRADE
MARK



Printed in Great Britain by
Hazell Watson & Viney Ltd
Aylesbury, Bucks

ISBN 0 7221 1171 1

# PROLOGUE

He had sent his secretary off duty; she was a conscientious girl, who loved her work and never minded staying after hours. He had often described her as invaluable, but that evening her eagerness to stay late and help him was a maddening attribute. There had been a little battle between them, which left him victorious and alone in his office. He waited for a few minutes till he was sure she had gone. Then he went and turned the key in his door. It was dark and the windows were spattered with snow; he pulled the curtains and switched on the desk lamp. There were papers on his desk; it was their untidy presence that had worried his secretary, who felt it was beneath his dignity to wander through the building and return them to filing. These were of no interest to him. He pushed them aside, and unlocked the centre drawer of his desk, using a key that hung on a chain attached to his waistcoat. It was the only key to that particular drawer. He took out a file, with a red sticker across the top left-hand corner.

He placed it directly under the desk lamp, and then, page by page, he began to photograph the contents, using an object that was in fact a miniature camera.

At one moment he had stopped, frozen to immobility by the sound of someone walking down the corridor past his office. His eyes were fixed on the door handle. He had a moment of crazy panic, common to the fright experienced in a nightmare, that he might have broken the habit of years and forgotten to lock the door. If the footsteps stopped, if there was a knock on the door and then it opened . . . But nobody knocked, nobody turned the knob. The feet went past and the sound of them grew muffled, until he knew that what he was hearing was the bounding of his own excited heart. Within five minutes he finished taking the pictures, rearranged the papers, closed the file; only then did he permit himself to go to the door and make sure that disaster could not have overtaken him. He tried it, and he smiled. It was secure. He had not forgotten.

When he left his office, the desk was clear, the middle

drawer locked, the unimportant documents returned to their place in the filing room, and the file with the top security red sticker lodged in the safe on the floor below.

## CHAPTER ONE

'Ladies and gentlemen, we are now approaching Barbados. We shall be landing at Seaways Airport in approximately ten minutes.'

The pilot sounded bored; a small child in the rear of the tourist class stopped crying for the first time in two hours. Judith knew because she had timed it by her watch; the irritable weeping rose in pitch and then just as abruptly stopped, as if the disorientated baby understood that the journey was at an end. It couldn't have felt less enthusiastic than Judith Farrow. The other passengers were leaning towards the windows, craning to see the island in its cushion of bright blue sea. She glanced across her neighbour and saw the small landmass, incredibly green in what must be burning sunshine. In spite of herself, a little interest, even a suggestion of excitement, stirred at the sight. It was said to be very beautiful. Very peaceful, remote from the hustle of the larger Caribbean islands, a sleepy paradise, where someone like herself could re-assess the chaos of her life and try to create some kind of order. At twenty-eight her pattern of living had disintegrated into a sordid undignified mess. Take a holiday; that was the advice given by her boss Sam Nielson. Get right away from UNO, New York, your friends, the whole background. He was a kind man and they had a pleasant relationship in which he was able to indulge a harmless paternalism towards a woman only a little older than his own daughter, Nancy, with whom Judith shared a flat.

Nancy, tough, determined, as unemotional about her numerous love affairs as any male sophisticate, had suggested the same remedy. Flight.

And without wanting to or really caring, Judith did as they advised. They assured her she would feel better after the first few days. She would begin to see it in proportion.

She saw the island slip from view behind the aircraft's wing as it banked before the final descent to land. Like hell she would feel better. Like hell a holiday restored lost faith, illusions, self respect. And yet the Nielsons might be right; when real tragedy struck her four years earlier, she had pulled up all her roots from England and gone to a new life in the United States. The death of her husband had been a tragedy in the accepted sense of the word; certainly in the conventional sense. The loss of the man she loved and had been living with for six months was only a trifle by comparison. Her affair with Richard Paterson didn't deserve more than fourteen days' healing time.

The landing was smooth; the passengers were filing out towards the exits, the baby had begun to cry again. Judith had been married for two years, but she had never had a child. Never even started one. She had married Patrick Farrow when she was twenty-two; he was a rich man, with the charm and humour of the Irish, an unappeasable appetite for travel, for trying out new places and collecting new people. He had collected Judith during a trip to Morocco where she was staying at the British Embassy. Her uncle was counsellor there, and she had met Pat Farrow at a dinner party given by the Ambassador. He had married her a month later and they began a two year paper chase across the world. At the beginning Judith had insisted that she was happy, that living their kind of life was fun. It was fun to go to Kenya, to fly on from Mombasa to Nepal, where Pat was bored after a week or so, and besides somebody had suggested a trip to Tokyo to see the cherry blossom.

Farrow was generous and affectionate, but there was no settled home, and even the most luxurious hotel suite looked much like the last when the novelty wore off. But certainly he was happy. He was the luckiest man alive, as he often announced at yet another all night party, with a glass of champagne in one hand, and his arm around his wife.

They were in London for a short spell which would take in the first major meetings of the Flat Racing season, and Judith had gone down to see her father, leaving Pat Farrow to go racing without her. On the way back from Newmarket he crashed his Jensen into the back of a stationary lorry and was killed instantly.

Her father had been kind, but he was a dry, withdrawn man, whose wife had left him early in the marriage, and he had expended too much feeling on that old calamity to have much left for his daughter. So Judith arrived in New York, with an introduction to Sam Nielson from her uncle, who had exchanged Morocco for Ottawa.

She missed Pat Farrow; it seemed impossible that so much vitality and enjoyment of life could be snuffed out for ever, but there was less grief than guilt, for she knew that she had fallen out of love with him by the time he died.

He had left his estate equally divided between Judith and a woman living in Ireland who had borne him an illegitimate son. There was no shortage of money, but there was less substance than his style of living had implied. Judith had applied for, and got, the job as personal assistant to Nielson, who was Director of the International Secretariat at UNO. That was four years ago. A number of men had tried to have affairs with her, a charming but serious-minded lawyer in Nielson's department had asked her to marry him. Judith said no to everything. And typically, when she did say yes, it was to the wrong man. She hadn't been any better at choosing a lover than she had a husband.

The heat when she stepped out of the plane was like a blanket, out on the tarmac she blinked in the blinding sunshine. There was a balmy sense of warmth, of penetrating heat, relieved from any feeling of discomfort by a gentle trade wind which kept the temperature constant and took the burn out of the tropical sunshine.

It was a very small airport; there was none of the sense of urgency and frustration which she always associated with flying. The bags were unloaded at leisure, the passengers filed through Customs and Immigration, passing a burly coloured policeman in white tropicals, with campaign medal ribbons on his chest, and a village constable's air about him. Nobody seemed to mind that they were waiting, even though there were no duty free shops or tourists' gimmicks worth looking at. Suddenly, miraculously, the frantic pace of American life had slowed to a near stop.

Judith passed through the Customs, and stood waiting for her bag. Unlike most women she preferred to travel light; all she would need was in one suitcase, and that was made up of last year's summer dresses and two bathing suits. She wouldn't know anybody and she wasn't planning to go anywhere outside her hotel.

Richard Paterson had tried to telephone her the day before she left. Nancy Nielson had answered. Judith had gone away for a while, she said. The receiver went down on him before he could even ask where Judith had gone. Now, walking through towards the exit, with a black Barbadian carrying her case, Judith felt an overwhelming feeling of relief. It was all so different, from the first moment she had landed at the airport. A policeman in a bright white uniform looked at her and smiled. He was young, and it had never occurred to Judith before how magnificent a coloured man could be as a physical specimen.

He wasn't very dark; though not as mixed as other islands, Barbadians had mingled, and the beautiful youth in his Colonial inspired uniform was the result of some integration a generation or more before his birth.

'Welcome to Barbados,' he said. 'The taxis are just here.'

'Thank you,' Judith said. It was the first time she had smiled for days. 'Thank you very much.'

The island was ablaze with flowers. Hibiscus, pink and white oleanders, the glorious purple bougainvillaeas rioted over walls and rooftops, and most beautiful of all, the scarlet poinsettias, usually seen as a spindly plant in a florist's at Christmas time, flared in a great bushes, hedging the roads with banks of blazing colour.

The taxi driver talked throughout the journey, but with an accent so thick it made him unintelligible. Judith couldn't understand more than a few words. And then the sea was visible; sapphire blue with snow-white running surf. Palm trees soared into the sky. The hotel was another surprise. It was a series of small cottage bungalows, surrounded by the rich tropical gardens she had seen everywhere during the drive from the airport.

An aquamarine swimming pool shimmered in the centre of a paved patio, banked by brilliant flowers; small tables clustered round it topped by striped umbrellas, blooming like crazy mushrooms, and a coal-black barman stood behind the bar, rattling a shaker as if he were playing the maraccas.

She registered; now she was feeling very hot. Her

clothes were sticking to her, and when she saw herself in the glass across the reception desk, she realised with surprise that the pale, exhausted face, framed in lank brown hair, was how she really looked.

She looked round the little bungalow; it was bright, with white walls and brilliant chintzes, a balcony overlooking the beach, and a bedroom with an air conditioner. She was pleased to find a tiny kitchen, completely equipped. She went into the bathroom, stripped and got under the shower, letting the water soak her head and body. Her skin was unattractively white, compared with the brown figures she had seen lying round the pool. The water beat against her, battered her face and poured in a torrent between her breasts. The sense of nakedness brought unwelcome memories back. She wrenched the tap to 'off' and wrapped herself in a towel. Making love to Richard Paterson was the last thing she could afford to remember. She dried, and wandered into the bedroom. The sun was going down, and the sky had a deep, grey line coming up as if someone were slowly pulling a blind from below. It would soon be dark. She felt so tired that she dropped back on the bed; remembering the wet towel, she threw it off, and covered herself with the sheet. Later, she could ring down and have something sent up, a sandwich, some coffee.

She was still deciding what to order when she fell asleep.

When she woke, it was pitch dark, and the luminous hands on her watch said 2 a.m.

There was a man in the adjoining bungalow, but he had not been sleeping. He saw the light flash on from the dark windows on his right, and stay on, making a yellow beacon in the night. He had given up trying to read, long after he had abandoned the attempt to sleep, and gone out to sit on his balcony and smoke. It was noisy outside; the sea pounded on the beach only twenty yards away, and a small, persistent noise shrilled from the trees growing along the sandy shore line. It sounded like a kind of bird. He identified the crickets, with their tiny chirping roar, and the prosaic hum of outside air conditioners. It was the second night he hadn't been able to sleep. Sleep always eluded the pursuer. All his life he had suffered from periods of insomnia; without warning, and unassociated with stress, he would find it impossible to sleep for several days. Just as abruptly the cycle would break. He had learned to accept these occurrences without recourse to drugs.

He had never been to the West Indies before; it amused him to choose what was described as a capitalist playground, sustained by the sweat of the black proletariat, because he had an ironic twist of mind. It was a choice which was certain to offend others, only too eager to criticise. He had always thrown bones of contention to his enemies, and walked away while they fought over them. He sat in the darkness, smoking and waiting, staring upwards at the glittering fragmentation of stars in the sky. Men had travelled through the infinite space and proved it finite; they had hurtled past the stars and found them empty, ugly. The enormous white moon had been violated by the spaceman's boot. He thought that it would never be the same again. Nothing remained immutable in that old phrase applied to the stars. Everything changed; the wise welcomed it and stuck out to swim with the stream.

Others resisted, damming progress with human bodies. It was no less true, because it was so bitterly ironic, that the children of revolutionary change, became the stiffest of reactionaries. Backwards. That was where the current was turning, and he felt it taking this direction, well below the surface, but with increasing force. He could have taken a woman with him; he hadn't wanted one. At thirty-nine his body was as tired as his sleep-starved brain. He could have women whenever he wanted them. Too easily, meaning nothing. The bungalow adjoining his was empty; he hadn't realised until the lights went on that there was someone in it. He heard noises; he had well tuned ears. They picked up the sound of someone moving round inside, a door opened and shut. Light broke out, turning the balcony yellow. The doors slid back and a woman walked through and towards the rail, where she leaned for a moment, looking out over the black sea where the broad, rippled track of moonlight narrowed into the horizon. The figure was straight, with young lines; long hair hung down to the shoulders. He couldn't see her face. He stayed still in the darkness, watching, keeping the red glow of his cigarette hidden at his side. She turned, still with her back to him, and went inside. He was sorry. It made his insomnia less lonely knowing that at that hour someone was awake and near.

Then he heard the door of her bungalow shut, and thought in surprise that she had gone outside. Minutes later there was a splash. Of course. She had gone to the swimming pool.

Down by the patio one yellow light was burning over the shuttered bar. There was no need for it. The huge white moon hung in the sky, surrounded by stars. Looking up, Judith found every cliché speeding through her mind. The moon was like a pearl, the stars like diamonds; the palm trees waved and the crickets sang. It was all so corny and impossible until one saw the reality. Then it could never be described without using a coinage of words which had become debased. She dived into the pool, and started swimming, up and down, very lazily, her mind occupied with playing the game of metaphors, trying to think of ways to describe the night.

'Evenin'. Lovely evenin'.' It was the same odd accent, less exaggerated than the taxi driver's speech, but unmistakable. She turned and saw a man standing by the pool's edge. He wore a cloth cap, which he took off.

'Good evening,' Judith said. 'Are you the night watchman?'

'Yes, Mam.'

'I'm staying here,' she said. 'I couldn't sleep. It's so lovely and warm.'

'Yes, Mam,' the man said. 'Right warm it is.' He put his cap on again, saluted her with a torch and moved away. Judith went on swimming.

The man had come quietly round the edge of the building, where he could see the figure slipping through the lighted water, without being seen. He stood and watched her, until she climbed out, and then he got a look at her under the yellow light, as she dried her legs and rubbed her body with a towel. She was young. She had a pretty face. He went back and let himself into his bungalow before she came up the path. He had a bottle of whisky in his sitting room. That was one American habit he had picked up. He drank Scotch in preference to vodka. Some people would have said that was when the rot had started. He smiled to himself, filled a glass half full and went back to his balcony. The light next door went out.

. . . . .

In a specially equipped dark room on the lower ground floor of the Soviet Embassy on 1125 16th, Washington D.C., a roll of microfilm was being developed and enlarged. The process took some time, and it was watched by two Embassy officials. The film covered thirty pages of typed foolscap, with some handwritten insertions; the enlargements carried headings in thick type, and some of the letters were from the State Department, others originated in the British Embassy, and there were several copies of memos from the White House. The shorter and older of the two officials leaned over the developing tanks and read a little of what was on the print.

'Excellent,' he said. 'Another one of major importance.'

The second man was his junior assistant, a lieutenant in the Army, who was officially an attaché. He was very junior and he stayed three paces to the rear of his superior.

'It'll be copied out and assembled in the "Blue" file, General.'

'Excellent,' General Golitsyn said again. He looked at the luminous watch on his wrist. 'I must go. I have an appointment with the Hungarian Ambassador. You will stay here until all the prints are ready. The "Blue" file must be on my desk in the morning, at nine.'

He went out of the room; the lieutenant saluted him, an assistant rushed to open the door to let him out. The General went upstairs to his rooms to change into his uniform. Unlike the Western diplomats who wore civilian clothes, the members of the Soviet Embassy who were serving officers declined to follow this custom. The General liked his uniform; there was a patchwork of medals across the left breast, awarded for a life of service to his country, and including several foreign decorations. He was thinking of the 'Blue' file as he got ready to go out. Nominally he was the head of the Mission; he held the rank of General, he was an old, revered member of his country's political hierarchy. But because of the absence of his section's real superior, he had got the first look at the information passed to them by the most important Soviet agent in the Western Hemisphere.

. . . . .

'Good morning.'

'Good morning.' Judith was used to finding her neighbour on his balcony when she came out to eat her breakfast. For the first two days he hadn't spoken; she had hardly noticed him, and spent most of the time lying on the beach, or reading on her own balcony. The hotel was full of people enjoying themselves; couples paired off with others and became noisy little groups who clustered round the bar and monopolised the swimming pool. Judith had resisted several attempts to draw her into joining them. She avoided the pool except at night; she still woke in the small hours and went out alone in the dark to swim. She had talked more to the night watchman than to any of the hotel guests.

She had never seen her neighbour standing in the shadow by the bungalow every night, watching her. The fact that he hadn't said more than good morning established him as harmless. He didn't mix with anyone either. He took his meals at a single table; she had resisted the manager's attempt to put her with another pair of women, Canadian matrons staying on a hen holiday.

Until that morning Judith hadn't really looked at him.

'It seems hotter this morning.' It was quite unexpected when he continued the conversation.

'Yes,' Judith answered. 'I think it is.'

'Perhaps we will have rain. I see some clouds over there.'

'Perhaps. It doesn't matter, it never lasts long.'

'You know not to shelter under those trees?'

She put her book down. 'No? What trees?'

He was younger than she had supposed. Dark and thin featured; it was a nervous face, with light coloured eyes and a mouth that twisted at one side.

He was looking at her with an intentness that made it impossible to pick up her book without being rude. 'Those dark green trees there. They have a curious name, I can't pronounce it. But if the rain comes and you stand beneath them, the water will burn your skin. They are very poisonous. They should have told you about it.'

'I haven't given them much chance,' Judith said. 'I haven't spoken to anyone since I arrived.'

'The same for me,' he said. 'I came here to get away from people. And you also?'

'Yes,' Judith said. 'I'm afraid the last thing I've felt like was a jolly gathering at the bar.'

'You are not American? Canadian, perhaps?'

'I'm English,' she said. 'Maybe I have a slight accent; I've been working in the States for three years.'

'What is your work?'

'I'm with the United Nations,' she said. 'You're Russian, aren't you?'

'Feodor Sverdlov.' He got up; his body was tanned a dark brown. He was a long, lean man in a pair of shorts, his feet in old-fashioned lace up canvas shoes. He leaned across and held out his hand. Judith stretched and shook it briefly. She had met with the Russian mania for shaking hands. It was a sign of goodwill if they pumped your arm at intervals, before doing it all over again as you said goodbye. If they didn't shake hands with you, as Western diplomats knew, it meant the knives were really out.

'I am also in America. I'm with our Embassy in Washington. You must know Washington.'

'Oh, yes,' she said. 'Yes I know it.' It was as if her mind were a stage and all this time, for four days and nights, Richard Paterson had been waiting in the wings. At the mention of Washington he was right on centre. She got up quickly.

'I'm going to swim,' she said. 'Before it rains.'

'That is a good idea,' the Russian answered. 'I will come with you.'

There was nothing she could do to stop him.

When it did rain they stayed in the sea, swimming out and coming back on the crest of the frothing little waves. There were patches of coral which could cut the feet to ribbons. He warned her about them, and she found herself obeying him and swimming clear. Judith began to tire; the man swam like a professional, with long strokes of great power. He was obviously very fit. She lay on her back and floated. The brief shower slackened and died off. Immediately the sun poured out, the sky turned back to a hot blue, and the sunbathers reappeared on the beach like wasps coming down on a picnic.

'Machineel,' Sverdlov swam up to her. 'That is the name of it.'

'The name of what?'

'The tree that is poisonous. Will you come back now, and have some coffee with me?'

As they stepped out of the water, he got hold of her arm and pulled her to one side.

'That is coral there. You must buy some shoes. I will drive you into the town before lunch. There is a shop where I got mine.'

'No thank you, I'd rather sit on the beach,' Judith said. He had let her go, and was walking beside her. He was taking too much for granted. She needed shoes, but she wasn't going into Bridgetown with him. She hadn't come to Barbados to pick up with another man.

'I'll order the coffee,' Sverdlov said.

She was lying on the canvas lounging bed with her arm up, covering her eyes against the sun. She didn't hear him come back on the soft sand and he walked slowly, looking at her. He had never liked big women, or women with the motherly breasts which were considered so erotic in his own country. It occurred to him that his people were as obsessed with the mother figure as the Americans. Perhaps neither societies gave enough security at the start of life, hence this mania for suckling that disguised itself as a sexual stimulus. To Sverdlov, the body of the English girl was truly beautiful. It had shape and delicacy, a warm brown colour, with a line of white along the pelvic bone, where her bathing briefs had slipped. He stood looking down at her.

'If you will tell me the size of your shoes, I will go and buy them for you,' he said. She sat up; he stood over her, not moving.

'I won't intrude on you,' he said. 'I will get the shoes, but I won't intrude. You mustn't cut your feet. It would spoil your holiday.

'Please sit down—they're bringing our coffee now.'

'Thank you,' he said. 'I would like to drink it with you. If you are sure you don't mind?'

'No,' Judith said, 'of course not. It's very kind of you to worry about the shoes. I'm sorry if I sounded rude.'

He was not a handsome man; the slight twist of his mouth to one side gave his face a dour aspect, which completely altered when he smiled.

'You were not rude,' he said. 'You were telling me I went too fast. I understand. Here is the coffee. Will you give me three spoons of sugar please?'

'You have a very sweet tooth,' Judith said. She realised that she had relaxed with him. The assumption of authority had been disturbing; more so because she had responded to it so naturally. He was used to giving orders.

'What do you do in the Embassy?'

'I am a military attaché. I work with General Golitsyn. Does his name mean anything to you?' He had been looking out to sea when he answered Judith's question; he turned and the light grey eyes had the same intent expression that made it difficult to look away.

'No,' Judith said. 'Why should it?'

'He's been in America for nearly three years. You said you knew Washington.'

'I know someone who lives there—works there, I mean. I used to go down for a weekend sometimes and stay with friends. I don't mix in Embassy circles.'

'They're not exciting,' Sverdlov said. He sipped his coffee. 'The same faces all the time. I would have remembered you if I'd seen you. What do you do in the United Nations? Or is your work a secret that I mustn't know?' The twisted smile was mocking her, but with friendliness. He had followed her thoughts so accurately that Judith reddened.

'I'm a secretary, personal assistant. My boss is Sam Nielson, he's with the UNO International Secretariat. There's nothing secret about what I do.'

'I know him,' Sverdlov said. 'Canadian, Director of the Legal Department. Very clever. He is usually able to prove that one side is more in the wrong than the other.'

'He's the most impartial man I know,' she spoke up quickly in Nielson's defence.

'You think it's possible to be impartial?'

'It's an absolute necessity in *his* work. Sam would never take sides.'

'You are a very loyal assistant,' Sverdlov said. The steely look was gone; he was making fun of her for getting on the defensive.

He was really enjoying himself. 'Would you like a Russian cigarette?'

'No thank you,' Judith said.

'I promise you, it isn't drugged,' he said. The amiable tone rebuked her.

She shrugged. 'So long as I don't wake up and find myself in Siberia . . .'

He leant across and lit her cigarette.

'Or a prisoner of the K.G.B.,' he said. 'If I go away now and leave you in peace, will you sit at my table for lunch?'

'Well,' Judith hesitated, 'well, yes, if you like . . .'

'It would be very pleasant for me,' Sverdlov said. 'Now I am going into Bridgetown. I will wait for you by the bar.' He made a little bow, and shook hands with her again. She lay back in the sun, stretching her body in the sensuous heat, and finished the strong-tasting cigarette. It was an extraordinary situation. He was the first Soviet Russian she had ever met. She found her book in the beach bag, and opened it; she had forgotten to mark her place, and she admitted that it wasn't very interesting. Military attaché in Washington. He would know Richard Paterson. So the less they discussed that the better. Now that he had gone, Judith wished she hadn't agreed to have lunch with him.

The shoes he brought back for her didn't fit. He was waiting by the bar when she came down from the beach, with a paper bag in his hand. 'Please,' he said, 'try them. Then we can walk out over the coral this afternoon.'

Judith had put one on, and realised immediately that it was too big. 'How stupid!' the Russian exclaimed. 'How stupid to try and make it a surprise for you. I should have asked. Those are no good at all. I will change them this afternoon. I am so sorry!'

'Oh don't bother, please. It was so nice of you to go all that way . . . I wouldn't dream of letting you go back again. I can change them tomorrow.' He looked at her and shrugged; he seemed irritated by his mistake.

'You must not swim far out,' he said. 'There are sea urchins in the rocks; they are like hedgehogs, very poisonous. You must have shoes.'

'If you go on much longer, I won't go into the water at all,' Judith said. It was oddly fussy and obsessive; unless she changed the subject he could go on about it through lunch.

He seemed to anticipate what she was thinking. 'I should not lecture you,' he said. The smile returned for a moment, he touched her arm, turning her towards an empty table by the pool. 'I am going to buy you a drink first.'

The waiters were slow; Judith had noticed the easy pace that people moved, the lack of tension and the pervading sense of hustle which ran through American life like an electric current. The Barbadian indifference to time didn't worry her; she waited for meals, for her coffee, for her breakfast tray in the morning, and it never occurred to her to feel irritated. It surprised her that as soon as the man beside her raised his hand, one of the staff came over immediately.

Sverdlov ordered a double Scotch whisky, and a rum punch for her. She watched fascinated, and a little alarmed, as he drank it straight down.

Again the same waiter appeared, with a second glass. Sverdlov raised it to her. 'I learned to like this in America,' he said. 'It is a very good drink. Better than vodka.'

Judith couldn't resist it. 'Isn't that treason?'

'High treason,' Sverdlov agreed. 'If you report me I will be sent home and shot. How is the punch? Do you like rum?'

'I like it out here,' she said. 'It tastes different. I think it needs to be drunk in sunshine.'

'It improves most things,' Sverdlov said. He hadn't enjoyed himself so much for months—more—a year . . . It didn't matter what he said to this girl. He could make jokes, he could sit in the shimmering sun and say whatever came into his mind. Within limits, of course. She was a pretty woman; now, after the drink, she looked less miserable than in all the time he had been watching her. She had a self containment that interested him. She hadn't wanted to talk to him; he had made her do so; it would amuse him to go on making her do things she didn't intend doing. He had plans laid for the rest of the week. An excursion across the island, a trip deep sea fishing, dinner on successive nights at two other hotels, where there was a barbecue and a cabaret.

'That is a very pretty dress,' he said.

'It's a year old.' Judith offered him a cigarette. He shook his head; he preferred his own. 'I just packed and came out. I must say, it's lovely here. The people are so nice.'

'Nicer than on the other islands,' Sverdlov remarked. 'That's one of the interesting things about slavery. It either makes them hostile and violent, or it takes the spirit out of them. They become passive, easy to manage. Like here, in Barbados. The Jamaicans are not the same at all.'

'Whatever it does or doesn't do, it was a revolting business.'

'Our people were slaves until 1861,' Sverdlov said. 'I wonder what effect serfdom has had upon us—a sociologist ought to make a study of it. One of those clever Americans who know all the long words and none of the answers to their own questions . . .'

'You might find,' Judith said, 'that they wouldn't be interested. They'd probably say there wasn't any thesis, since nothing had changed.'

He leaned back in his chair, and laughed. 'Very good. You argue well. I enjoy that very much.'

'I nearly didn't say it,' Judith said. 'But if you crack at the Americans and the West, I warn you, I shall crack right back.'

'No,' he held up his hand. 'No, peaceful co-existence. That is the way now. Please don't declare war on me.' The eyes were fixed in that demanding scrutiny; they insisted that she look at him and give her full attention.

'I've never declared war on anyone,' she said. 'I'm the kind that runs away.'

'Ah,' Sverdlov said. 'I don't think so. I think you would be a brave and beautiful capitalist heroine.'

It was the first time he had heard her really laugh. They ate their lunch at the table by the bright blue pool; he drank a succession of whiskies, and bought wine for Judith which she didn't want. The afternoon grew very hot; for a brief period the ubiquitous breeze dropped and the air hung still and brazen. Most of the lunchers had gone to their bungalows to rest; a couple of small children splashed in the tepid waters of the swimming pool, watched by a sleepy mother lying in the shade. Suddenly, Judith couldn't keep awake. The rum, the wine, the intense heat all combined to make her head weigh like a lump of lead. Her limbs ached. 'I'm going to lie down,' she said. 'I'm just tired out.'

He got up and held out his hand. 'I am so sorry about the shoes. Will you sit at my table for dinner tonight?'

'Only if you promise not to apologise about those shoes again.'

'I promise. I will be at the table. Unless you wish to

make friends at the bar? All the Canadians will want to buy you a drink . . .'

'No thank you,' Judith said. 'I'll come to the restaurant.'

He watched her walk away, climbing the short flight of steps towards the bungalows. He decided not to follow her. The mother of the two children had lifted her head and was watching Judith Farrow. The husband had come down to join her, he was settling down on a lounging bed beside her, rubbing sun oil into his over-weight body. Sverdlov stripped off his shirt and moved into the full sun. He leaned back with his eyes closed. He liked her; an intelligent woman, with a sense of dignity. Her reserve amused him, he couldn't help sniping at the prejudices which he knew were there, bristling like anti-tank traps in her mind. It was a temptation to prod and tease the enemy. Enemy. His eyes opened for a second into the burning yellow glare. She was a pretty girl, who made him feel like making love. Enemy . . . That was how Golitsyn would have seen her. He hadn't thought about Golitsyn once, since he had gone swimming with the English girl that morning. And he hadn't thought about his wife either.

The Canadian couple were drowsing in the shade of beach umbrellas; their children called to each other from the safety of the swimming pool. The man watched Sverdlov as he passed them on his way down to the beach. He saw him go into the sea and swim out.

'You notice those two at lunch,' he muttered to his wife.

'Aha,' she said, not looking up from her book.

'Didn't take long for them to jell.'

'Yeah,' she answered. Her husband was a talkative man; she enjoyed long, explicit sex novels, with laboured anatomical descriptions.

'It's so hot, honey,' she said. 'Why don't you go to sleep?'

# CHAPTER TWO

'Rachel, if you don't hurry we'll be late.' Richard Paterson tried to keep the irritability out of his voice. They were going to a reception at the French Embassy. His wife always took hours getting ready, and it was a trait that infuriated him. He thought it was rude to be unpunctual, an indication of a sloppy routine and careless thinking. He came to the bedroom door and watched her. She turned round from the chest of drawers where she was hunting for something, and smiled at him. She was a pretty girl, fair haired and fresh skinned, very English in type. She looked very good in country clothes, and nothing fancy really suited her. She had an unfortunate feminine love for the inappropriate, which she indulged when they went out at night. Richard had good taste, and the gleam of bead embroidery on the baby blue cocktail dress made him wince.

'I'm coming, darling. I'm just getting a handkerchief. It's only 6.30.'

'The Ambassador likes to get there at seven,' he answered. 'I just don't want to sweep in at the same time. Look, come on for Christ's sake. Haven't you got a tissue?'

She struggled into her coat, and followed him down the stairs and out to the front door. In the days when they were living in London and he was at the Air Ministry, the exchange would have ended in a row, with her staying behind in tears. But things had changed since she came over to the States and made the effort to keep their marriage going. After the first two years they had begun to grate on each other; when they weren't bickering they had drifted in different directions, she relying more and more on her own family and friends, he absorbed in his career. When he got promoted to Group Captain and was offered the post in Washington, the prospect of leaving home and living with him in a strange country was too much for Rachel. She had misjudged badly, by giving him a straight choice between going to the States and staying married. He had chosen to go to Washington.

When he had gone the atmosphere in her own circle was disapproving. Family and even friends made pointed remarks about poor old Dick being lonely, until she began to feel miserable with guilt. Also she missed him. As the months passed life seemed very aimless, without a husband, and their smart little London house more like an empty box than ever.

So Rachel sent him a cable, with her family's approval, and took flight for Washington.

And it worked. Now, carrying the baby, beginning to meet people in Washington and make a few tentative friends, Rachel sailed through his bad moods, and tolerated his weekly absences in New York with gentle complaisance. She had learned her lesson. He was a difficult man. Selfish, irritable, distant; but she loved him and in a few months she would have the baby to look after.

He couldn't have provoked a quarrel with her if he'd deliberately set out to do so. And of course she knew nothing about Judith Farrow.

'Sorry I kept you, darling.' She turned to him in the car and squeezed his arm. 'Doesn't everything look pretty in the snow?'

'Yes,' he said. 'Very pretty.'

'Mrs. Stephenson's asked me to lunch next Tuesday,' his wife said.

He had been surprised and pleased by the way the people liked Rachel. Even the stickiest of the Embassy wives, including the Minister's wife, Mrs. Fergus Stephenson, accepted her and pronounced her charming until he felt he ought to take a closer look at her himself. The trouble was he kept thinking of Judith; every time he saw Judith, his wife seemed more insipid by comparison, as superficial and fluffy as the frightful pekinese he had made her get rid of after they were married.

'You must be very nice to her,' he said. 'Stephenson's tipped for the Paris Embassy. He's a brilliant chap.'

'Don't worry,' she said. 'I won't put my foot in it. Don't forget, I was brought up in the senior wife tradition. Here we are, and it's five to seven. That's all right, isn't it?'

'Yes,' Richard said. 'But just drop your coat and don't start powdering your nose!'

The French Embassy was housed in a large elegant building on Kalorama Road; Richard and his wife passed the reception line, shaking hands with the Ambassador and his handsome wife, and then merged in the throng of people in the main reception room. They had hardly moved through the first thin crust of the crowd, before the British Ambassador was announced. Richard made his way to a group of people Rachel didn't know by sight. A huge Dutchman, one of the First Secretaries at his Embassy, heaved into sight, his pendulous chins bouncing against his collar, as he shook his massive head from side to side.

'Ah, Group Captain, I was looking for you earlier. I want to introduce my new military attaché to you. He's a fine fellow—you'll be friends. Come along, he's over there, standing near the West German Ambassador.'

As they moved through the groups of people he spoke over his shoulder.

'By the way,' he said, 'I can't see Sverdlov here. Have you seen him?'

'No. I don't think so.' Instinctively Paterson stiffened. He avoided all the Russians and Eastern bloc people. Nobody would ever be able to dig up some acquaintance-ship and point their finger at him.

'Does it matter that he isn't here?'

The Dutchman shrugged his huge shoulders. 'No. I just noticed because where General Golitsyn goes, there one finds Colonel Sverdlov. Like the Heavenly Twins—perhaps that's not a very apt description of them! Ah, there is Jack Loder over there.'

'I'd like to meet your attaché,' Richard Paterson said. 'Come along, darling.' He caught Rachel by the arm. He had no wish to talk to Jack Loder or to inflict him upon his wife. In Paterson's view that type of man should never be allowed to rise above the rank of chief filing clerk in a top grade Embassy.

Loder had been in Washington for a year. He had arrived the previous February, in freezing weather, to take up an appointment at Liaison with Plans. His former post had been in Delhi, where he was listed as commercial adviser to the trade commissioner; before that he had spent six months working on a cultural exchange programme with the Embassy in Bonn. In all his jobs the other members of the staff had avoided him.

Nobody liked spies; Loder had discovered that very early in his career. Like policemen they were only at ease in each other's company.

Unpopularity didn't worry Loder; he loved his work and you couldn't have both. He was not a prepossessing man to look at; he was short and wiry, with a roughly assembled face, and the poor teeth associated with a working class background. He was unfortunate in having ginger hair, his lumpy features sprinkled with freckles, puffy pink lids cushioned his sandy eyes. He looked as if he drank heavily. In fact he was a teetotaller. In Delhi, after his wife left him, he had begun to drink to an extent that qualified for alcoholism, though nobody ever suspected or could say they'd seen him drunk. For months he was never sober. He hadn't minded too much about his wife leaving; they had drifted apart after the war; like so many marriages undertaken in a hurry, the foundations were shallow, and when she went he didn't miss her. But he missed their children. He had a son of twelve and a girl of ten, and he had begun to enjoy them, with a sense of rare companionship.

The distance between them made it worse; they were in England, there was no contact except occasional, inarticulate children's letters. He had never appreciated the pain of loneliness before. When the border incidents between India and China blew up into an international crisis, with a Chinese invasion seeming imminent, he suddenly pulled himself up. He had stopped drinking and got on with his job. He had never touched anything alcoholic since, not even beer. He disliked wine; where he came from, it was considered a sissy drink, like port.

In the last months in Delhi he had done outstanding Intelligence work. His Ambassador, although a ferocious snob, had recommended him so highly that he was given the top Washington job. From the social side he found it a very dull city, as provincial as only a place can be which is restricted to one section of society, however important. Diplomats mixed with diplomats; if anything bored Loder more than the Foreign Office party circuit, it was the circus which revolved around the White House and the Senate. Also he found the Americans completely alien. He had left his Midlands University with First Class honours, but in spite of this intellectual quality, he was a narrow-minded man, with a streak of suspicious insularity in his nature. He didn't understand Americans and he was not prepared to try. He merely did his job with the flair and efficiency that had always overcome his personal disadvantages.

About this time, Loder detached himself from the company of a dull commercial counsellor from Austria, who was trying desperately hard to discuss the possibility of an Anglo-Viennese trade fair. He moved on abruptly, leaving the Austrian looking red faced, and stared round for someone to talk to; he loathed receptions of all kinds, but he was meticulous in his attendance. He liked to test straws in the wind, and something prickled along the skin round his collar, like a nervous itch. He recognised the sensation. Other men had hunches; Loder's neck irritated when there was something not quite right. A brilliant assembly; he mocked, saying the words to himself, imitating a slightly high pitched upper class English voice. Most distinguished; the ladies of the diplomatic at their most elegant, the French Ambassador his charming self, and Madame, as always, the most outstanding. And so she bloody well ought to be; what her clothes cost he couldn't imagine. He stopped a waiter, and took a glass of fresh orange juice. Then he saw Richard Paterson, and on a mischievous impulse moved towards him. His wife was with him. She was the kind of woman Loder abhorred. Fair, silly, Daddy's an Air Marshal kind of bitch, with one of those dental drill voices, and tiny tits. As soon as she came out she got a bun in the oven and told the whole Embassy about it. He saw Paterson's expression change as he approached, and a very slight grin twitched round his mouth. Loder knew all about the weekly trips to New York. It was his business to keep an eye on everyone.

'Good evening,' he said. 'Crowded, isn't it?'

'Yes, terribly.' Rachel Paterson edged nearer her husband. She had met this rather dreadful man several times. He looked coarse and they way he stared at her made her uncomfortable. She couldn't imagine what such a person was doing in the Foreign Office, but then so many things were different now. People came into jobs from all over the place. That ugly, middle English accent was becoming quite commonplace. She left Richard to talk to him.

'How was Van Ryker?' Loder asked. 'I saw you talking to him.'

'In good form,' Richard Paterson answered.

There was a pause and the Group Captain's chilly attitude was very obvious.

Then Paterson's wife opened her mouth; she had noticed the hiatus and felt she ought to say something. 'He was looking for somebody, wasn't he, darling—some Russian . . .'

'Oh?' Loder waited.

'Sverdlov,' Paterson said. 'He hadn't seen him here. I told him I hadn't either.'

'Oh,' Loder said again. 'Now you mention it, neither have I!' He put a stubby finger under his collar and scratched. His neck was giving him hell. 'Excuse me.' He walked away from them.

The man he was looking for was standing in a small group, talking to a middle-aged Senator's wife. Loder tapped him on the back.

'Commander Buckley?'

The American turned, looked pleased to see Loder, and started introductions. Loder interrupted, speaking quietly. It didn't occur to him that he was being rude. 'I'd like a word with you. Come and get a drink.'

The Commander excused himself with grace; he was a retired Navy man with a reputation for charm. Women of all ages liked him; his staff described him as the most inconsiderate bastard who had ever held the senior CIA post in Washington and hated him to a man.

They drifted out of hearing; Buckley picked up a glass of champagne from a moving waiter.

'What's on your mind, Jack?'

That was another American habit that Loder resented. From the first handshake it was Christian names. He made a point of using the Commander's full title.

'Sverdlov's missing. He was not at the Belgians last Tuesday either. The Dutch are making enquiries about him. What's up? Where the hell is he?'

The Commander looked bland. 'I was going to call you at your office tomorrow,' he said. 'He's left the States. On vacation, we assume.'

'Well.' Loder's face had reddened, it accentuated his ugliness when he was angry. 'Well, if we had a bit of information from you now and again, we might be able to assume something for ourselves. I just picked this up tonight. Sverdlov's their top man. You people keep them all under surveillance—why wasn't I informed before, Commander? This is bloody irregular.'

'I'm sorry.' The American was soothing. He didn't want a row with this prickly little s.o.b. Also Loder was within his rights to complain. When a Soviet of Sverdlov's importance left the United States, all heads of Nato intelligence were entitled to know. The Commander had delayed on purpose; he had the professional's objection to passing on information for nothing, even to allies. 'But it looks like a vacation, nothing more. He's gone to the Caribbean. To Barbados.'

'You're joking!' Loder's surprise was genuine. They never go anywhere except home, for their holidays. He must be up to something.'

'Probably setting up a rocket base,' Buckley made a joke.

'Balls,' Loder said. 'You don't think he's been recalled —the Caribbean could be just a blind. There's that old goat Golitsyn standing round; you don't suppose he's been given the job?'

'Unlikely.' Commander Buckley glanced towards the group of Russians, with the General standing in the middle of it, and then back to Loder. 'Too old. If Sverdlov's pulling out, then his replacement is already here.'

'And we don't know who the hell it is—Christ, that's going to be awkward.'

'Like I said, I think there's nothing major in it. He's gone off on a vacation, maybe to meet someone, we don't know. But the Barbadian Government are keeping tabs on him, they're not happy about him being there at all, but there wasn't much they could do about it. My guess is he'll be back.'

'Let's hope so,' Loder said sourly. 'Better the devil you know. I'd appreciate your keeping me informed, right up to date?'

'Of course,' the Commander prepared to move away. 'Will do, Jack. I'll call you the moment we get anything, and you'll do the same for me?'

'Anything comes to us, I'll let you have it.' Loder didn't wait to be dismissed, he moved first, shouldering his way through the crowd, making towards the door. Sverdlov had left the States and holed up in a Caribbean island. It was so extraordinary, so completely untypical. He had been in America for three years; it had taken the combined Western intelligence services eighteen months to identify him as the head of the KGB in the Soviet Embassy to Washington. He was a brilliant operator; he kept to himself as all the senior officers did; the Martini circuit and the casual pick-up was left to the more junior Embassy officials, masquerading as trade or service attachés. Soviet officers in Sverdlov's position never travelled to places like Barbados and sunned themselves without a purpose. It would keep Loder awake all that night wondering exactly what the hell that purpose might turn out to be.

By the end of the week, Loder attended an Intelligence conference called by Commander Buckley. It was an informal gathering, with the Nato powers represented, and they met in Buckley's office in Georgetown. He worked where he lived, in one of the attractive old houses in the exclusive residential area of the city. He operated under the title of Principal Adviser to the Naval Pensions and Veterans Board. He had in fact a large complex of offices on Pennslyvania Avenue, with any number of resources at his command. He preferred to hold intimate meetings in his own house. The Dutch, represented by Van Ryker, the French, the Belgians, and others bound in uneasy alliance against the Eastern bloc, sat round the Commander's polished table, smoking and helping themselves to drinks and what Loder described contemptuously as cocktail scraps. The object of the meeting was to impart the latest information upon the activities of Colonel Feodor Sverdlov.

There was a hostile glint in the American's eyes when he assembled his documents in front of him, and glanced towards Loder. Loder was aware of the atmosphere. Buckley had got hold of something, and it was not to his British allies' credit. He called him a vulgar anatomical name under his breath.

'Well, gentlemen, I have here a comprehensive report on how our friend Sverdlov has been spending his time in the sunshine. I'd like to say at this point how much we owe the Barbadian Government; they've been extremely co-operative.'

Nobody said anything; Loder lit a cigarette and waited.

'So far,' the Commander had a monotonous voice, 'he's done nothing suspicious. He's behaving just like any ordinary guy having a holiday out of season. He's even got himself a girl friend.' He looked round at them and then stopped at Loder.

'She's British,' he said reproachfully. 'He's been wining and dining her every night; they're in the same hotel.'

'You've got her name?' Loder asked.

'Sure.' The Commander consulted his papers. 'Judith Farrow. Widow. Works for Sam Nielson as his P.A.'

Christ, Loder said to himself. That's nasty. I don't like that at all.

'You think that's why he went over there—to make contact?'

That was the Dutchman, Van Ryker.

'Could be. Nielson's in a very confidential position. This woman must have access to a lot of top level stuff.'

'Seems to me,' Loder said, 'he's a pretty big fish to go all that way to pick up a P.A. One of the glamour boys could have been sent out to do that.'

'I agree with you,' Buckley said mildly. 'It's probably just coincidence but it's unfortunate.

'Not necessarily,' Loder answered agressively. He was out on a limb and that CIA bastard was just about to shake the tree. 'Don't let's act as if she's passing him secrets already.'

'Nobody's suggesting that,' Buckley protested. 'But naturally we have to anticipate.'

'I think that's my job,' Loder said. 'If Sverdlov has made contact with a British subject, then I'll take full responsibility for her. I've got to, as I see it.'

'That's exactly what I hoped.' The Commander was genial again. He had brought the British down, and honour was satisfied. SIS and CIA might work together but there was an acknowledged rivalry. Buckley's organisation had been the butt of sophisticated English jokes because of early failures. The jeers had not been forgotten or paid back in full as yet.

'Otherwise, there's nothing to report on Sverdlov. He's booked to return here in a week, and so far as we can make out, nobody in his Embassy has been promoted lately. So I don't think there's a change in postings. He's just vacationing with Mrs. Farrow.'

Loder could have punched him on the nose. But he said nothing. He had given an undertaking, and though the Commander might think he was scoring points, he had missed out on the most important one of all. Relief at this omission kept Loder quiet for the rest of the meeting. Mrs. Farrow was certainly personal assistant to Sam Nielson, with access to top level information. But she was also the mistress of Group Captain Richard Paterson, senior air attaché at the Washington Embassy. Buckley would really have had himself a ball if he'd discovered that. For a woman with such a valuable double contact at UNO and the Embassy itself, even Feodor Sverdlov might have gone to Barbados. He left the meeting in a mood of depression. There were times when he reviewed the world situation and all he could see was victory for the other side.

In Britain a man like Sverdlov wouldn't have been allowed to advance. He wouldn't have been given a job that did his talent justice; probably shunted into some piddling post in the middle of Africa, or caged up in London doing bugger-all with other people's paperwork. He thought suddenly that maybe it was this frustration that bred traitors in the service. People needed stimulus; if you were good at something, the surest way to break you was to prevent you from ever doing it.

He had his own idea how to deal with Sverdlov and his kind, but that branch had been closed up at the end of the war. Nobody got hit by a passing car, or fell out of a window any more. They went back to being little gentlemen as soon as Stalin declared the Cold War and began holding civilisation to ransom.

It made Loder sick.

He drove back slowly; the weather had settled into a sullen freeze-up. There was no more snow. Everything was ice-bound and when the thaw set in, the streets would be awash. While he was working he was absorbed—people who disliked him said obsessed, but he always had the same reaction of loneliness when he came back to his empty apartment in the evening.

That was when he missed his children most. He hadn't had a letter from either of them for a fortnight. He thought bitterly about his wife; she should have made them write regularly. When he was in Delhi and these moods of desolation hit him, he used to sit down and get drunk. He went into the kitchen and made tea. Another affliction of living in America was the tea bag; Loder drank Lap Sang Su Chow, which would have astonished his old associates. He took a tray into the bedroom, and stood with the cup in one hand, looking at himself in the mirror. He had no personal vanity. He knew that there wasn't one of the Embassy staff with a brain as good as his, with the exception of Fergus Stephenson, the Minister, and the Ambassador himself. But women weren't interested in brain. They liked brawn.

'A real scruffy Civil Servant, that's what you are.'

He grimaced at himself in the glass.

'Much chance of you going to the Caribbean and finding yourself a nice bird . . .' He turned away, to finish his tea and go to bed. He wondered what Feodor Sverdlov was doing at that moment. It was a bitter thought on which to fall asleep.

## CHAPTER THREE

'Will you and Mr. Sverdlov be in to dinner, or are you going out again?'

The manager of the hotel was a pleasant mannered man in his early forties with a neat black beard; he mixed freely with the other guests, and some of the younger women fancied him. In reality he was living with a tall, big-breasted Barbadian Negress. The insipid Canadian wives and the odd English girl on the look-out for a quickie romance on holiday didn't interest him in the least. The rest of the staff were laying bets on whether Mrs. Farrow and the Russian were shacked up together every night. The manager said not; he knew everything that went on in his hotel, he knew exactly who visited between bungalows at night and who slipped in for an hour in the afternoons. Sverdlov and Mrs. Farrow were not among them. They were causing comment, but this was no bad thing. It kept the guests amused. Neither of them mixed with anyone else, they avoided the noisy gatherings at the bar. They dined together and either retired to a table by the edge of the sea to drink coffee, or else went for a walk by the shore. The night watchman reported that both of them came to the pool in the early hours and swam in the moonlight. On the manager's instructions he spied on them, but each went back to their own bungalow and stayed there. Even without the telephone call from the Police Commissioner, the manager would have been intrigued by the situation.

He made a regular report of Sverdlov's activities at the end of every day; he asked no questions of the Commissioner. He was managing the hotel on a work permit. Had he refused to assist the police by watching Sverdlov, he had no doubt that his permit would not have been renewed.

He smiled at Judith, making himself especially friendly. She looked quite different from the tired, unhappy girl who had arrived just over a week earlier. Sun, sea and a man. It was an old formula but it certainly worked. He repeated his question. 'Will you be in to dinner this evening?'

'I think we're going to the Coral Reef,' Judith answered. 'Mr. Sverdlov says there are some fire-eaters in the cabaret.'

'There are indeed,' the manager said. 'They're coming here for our floor show on Friday. I hope you'll stay here for dinner that night—we've got a great steel band.'

'I'm sure we will,' she said. At that moment the Russian came up behind her.

'We should go now,' he said to her, 'before it gets too hot.' He ignored the manager, who started to say good morning. He noticed that Sverdlov took her by the arm.

'Here is the car,' he said. Judith looked round for the Austin Traveller he had used for their last trip to Bridgetown.

'Where?' she said. 'I don't see it.'

'This one—don't you like the pretty roof?' He stood beside her, laughing, delighted with his surprise. He had changed the closed saloon for one of the ridiculous flighty little Minimokes with their striped canvas canopies. They had seen them racing through the crowded road, bumping along like toys, the passengers almost spilling out.

'Oh, Feodor—you got one! You are really crazy—but I'm so glad you got rid of that other car.'

He got in beside her and switched on the engine. 'You said you wanted to ride in one, so I telephoned. Hold on to the rail, or you might fall out.'

Judith looked at him and shook her head. 'Stop ordering me about, I'm not an idiot,' she said. 'Anyone would think I was a child, the way you go on. I can take care of myself, you know.'

'An emancipated woman,' Sverdlov said. 'They all want to be equal and carry their own luggage. Very unattractive; you are not like that. Please keep hold of the rail.'

'I seem to have heard,' Judith said, 'that in Russia the women were equal with the men . . .'

'Capitalist propaganda,' Sverdlov said; he eased the car to a halt as the traffic congealed at a junction. He turned and looked at her solemnly. 'All lies,' he said. 'Some of our women are equal. The rest are normal and happy. You look very pretty today.'

'You're impossible.' She grabbed at the hand-rail as the little car bolted forward. 'And always right. Hadn't I better look up the museum on the street map?'

'I've done that,' Sverdlov said. 'I know where to go.'

'I should have known,' Judith bumped against him as they cornered. He glanced sideways at her and the twisted mouth grinned.

'That was very nice. I like this kind of car.'

He had tried to kiss her the day before. They had driven across the island to see the east coast, where the scenery was said to be very beautiful. Judith had found the savage Atlantic breakers smashing against the rocks a bleak, depressing aspect, and said so. On the isolated road, with a powerful sea wind sweeping round them, Sverdlov had taken a step forward and leaned towards her. She had said 'No', and walked to the car. He had got in after closing her door, and lit a cigarette, which he gave her. He wasn't annoyed, he seemed to find it amusing. Neither of them mentioned the incident on the way back.

He found the Bridgetown Museum and parked in the shade of a group of Queen Palms. The sun was high, and the sky above was a sizzling blue without a cloud in sight.

'I really love this place,' Judith said suddenly. 'I'm having a wonderful time.' She put her hand through his arm. He gripped it against his side. 'Good,' he said. 'Good. I'm glad you are happy. Let us go and get some culture. Then I am going to look at the harbour. I am fond of boats.'

It was cool and dark inside the museum, a long rambling building with massive thick walls, which had been a barracks. Sverdlov stood in the middle of the first room, his hands behind his back, looking round without much interest. A glass case in the centre displayed some china plates from the Governor's mansion. Judith had wandered off to look at the smaller exhibits.

'Look at this,' she called to him. 'This is fascinating.' He seemed to have been thinking deeply: it was doubtful whether the little Barbadian Museum was the object of his preoccupation. 'Ah? Yes, I'm coming.'

He found her bending over a fly-blown glass case. A yellowed poster hung above it, advertising the sale of various male and female slaves, and domestic animals.

He was so close to her that their bodies were touching. 'Look at this,' she said again. ' "A slave on Haywards Plantation, St. Peter, accused of stealing a sheep, was hanged from a tamarind tree; he protested his innocence, saying that the tree would vindicate him. Since then the tamarind tree has borne a seed in the shape of a man's head. The specimen on the left is a normal seed; the one on the right is from the tamarind tree at Haywards . . ." Isn't that extraordinary! Look at that seed—it's exactly like a Negro's head . . .'

'And you believe it?' Sverdlov asked.

'Well there's the seed. You must admit it's very odd.'

'What good did it do the salve? He had been hanged.'

'I wonder what his owners felt like when they saw those seeds appear on the tree,' Judith retorted.

'You think they were worried? You think they had a conscience?'

'Everyone has a conscience,' she said. 'You must know that's true. After all, your whole ideology was based on righting a basic wrong—some people with far too much and the rest with nothing!'

'So you think that Marx had a conscience—the expropriators will be expropriated; is that what you are saying?'

'Yes,' she said. 'In a way it is. You know when you've done something wrong; your conscience knows.'

'I know when I've made a mistake,' Sverdlov corrected. 'That is not the same. I'm interested in your theories. Perhaps I'm converting you to Marxism.' He ran a finger down her bare arm.

'Stop making fun of me,' she said. 'And doing that, Mr. Sverdlov, is a mistake!'

'My apology, Mrs. Farrow. It was the fault of my conscience. It told me it was the right thing to do.'

She let him take her arm and they moved on together through the remaining rooms. There was a collection of beautiful early silver, more china, donated by rich residents on the island, and some ugly, stolid nineteenth-century furniture, including a massive four-poster bed. Then they were outside in the sunshine.

'I'd like to look at that seed again,' Judith said. 'I won't be a minute.' Sverdlov let her go back alone; he waited in the small paved courtyard, eyes half closed against the glare.

He wondered if they had been followed to the museum, and whether any of the half a dozen visitors who wandered round were from the other side. It was being very skilfully done; even he with his experience, couldn't pick out a suspect in the hotel. He lit a cigarette while he waited. Women were erratic creatures; why should she have found the foolish legend of the slave and the tamarind seed so fascinating that she had to go and look at the exhibit a second time? Perhaps she thought it was romantic. He wished she would transfer a little of that romanticism to their relationship. He had been thinking of sex in terms of therapy. In the ten days he had spent with Judith Farrow, he had got no sex and there was very little time left. But the therapy had worked without it. He had begun to see clearly again. He had started to function at his right level of efficiency. There was a schizoid feeling about the life of lazy lotus eating, teasing the girl about the issues which divided one half of the world against the other, giving himself up to erotic fancies as they lay in the sun together. He hadn't wanted to know more than her name and what she was doing in America. She had told him one night she was a widow, and had no children. He hadn't questioned her beyond that. Now he was beginning to find the gaps unsatisfactory. He wanted to know about her past life; about the dead husband and why she was so determined not to be seduced. He smiled as he saw her come out of the museum and hurry towards him. 'I wanted to make sure of the place,' she said. 'Haywards Plantation, St. Peter's.'

'And you are going to look for the tamarind tree—you really believe it exists?'

'I don't know, but anyway, I'm going to look for it. I want one of those seeds—just to prove something to you!'

'I am a Russian,' Sverdlov said. 'We are the people who invented fairy tales.'

'I know, like the existence of God,' Judith said. They

were walking back to the Minimoke. 'You said all that before.'

'We have had a lot of dialectic disagreements,' he remarked. 'And they haven't made a difference to us.' For a fraction of a second he thought of his wife; perhaps his heresy had conjured her ten thousand miles. 'We've proved it's possible to co-exist.'

'Maybe it's because we're on neutral ground,' she answered. Sverdlov put the key in the dashboard socket and turned it.

'Too neutral,' he said. 'But I am optimistic. I put my faith in the fire-eaters tonight.'

'And what difference will they make?'

He switched on the engine and the little car jumped forward. 'They will melt your heart,' he said. 'Now we go to the harbour.'

. . . . .

He drank so much whisky that evening that for the first time he became a little drunk. The dinner was excellent; Judith had bought a culotte dress from an expensive boutique in Bridgetown, and the flaring pink colour suited her; people stared at them as they took their table. The setting was so exotic that they both decided it was funny. Palm trees fringed the floodlit dance floor, candles flickered in the storm glasses on each table, waiters in white monkey jackets and crimson cummerbunds weaved in and out, while a steel band thudded out Western pop music to an African beat. The wind had risen and the sea hammered at the sandy beach behind them. The moon was brighter than the artificial lighting.

It suddenly occurred to Judith, in the middle of the limbo dancing, that she could never have enjoyed such a place with Richard Paterson. He would have made her feel it was ridiculous. At that moment, he was difficult to visualise. She realised with a sense of guilt, that thinking about him didn't bring his face immediately into focus as it used to do. But she knew early on that she would have trouble with Sverdlov. He insisted on dancing in the old-fashioned way which allowed him to press her tight against him.

'Look at them,' he whispered, mouth up to her ear, 'look at these people, dancing with themselves. To us, in Russia, this is degenerate. Don't pull away from me, it's not polite.' And she felt him laughing.

He grabbed her as soon as they started to walk to the car. He pushed her backwards off the ill-lit pathway between the bungalows, till she was up against a tree. He gave her no time to protest or fight him off. He kissed her until he had to stop for breath; his weight was leaning against her.

'Why do you keep your mouth shut?' he said. 'You like me; I can feel it. Are you afraid to make love?'

'Yes.' She didn't move or try to pull his hands away. 'Yes, I am afraid. I've just had one miserable, bloody awful love affair. And I'm not going to start another one with you. Please don't do this. Take me back to the car.'

He didn't answer; he went on holding her, looking down at her face with an expression she couldn't understand. Then he bent his head and kissed her lips; this time he made no attempt to force them open.

'We will go home and you will tell me about it.'

'No,' she said. 'No, I don't want to talk about it.'

'You will,' Sverdlov said. 'I can always make people tell me what I want to know. I want to know about you. Come, the car is over there.'

As they walked back, he put his arm round her.

. . . .

'You understand that the decision is not being made for you. You have a right to refuse our advice. Isn't that so?'

Gregory Tomarov looked at his companion for confirmation. Both men nodded together. The woman standing in front of them said nothing. The interview had begun informally; they had made an appointment to see her on her return from the clinic. She had received them with her usual coolness and composure, offered them a choice of tea or vodka, and passed round a plate of little cakes. Tomarov was an old friend of her father's; he had served under Marshal Timoshenko with him, and when she married Feodor Sverdlov, he had been one of their witnesses at the People's Wedding Palace. He could say, without exaggeration, that he had known her since she was born and regarded her as an adopted daughter. At the time, Sverdlov had been a good match. Tomarov had their wedding photograph on his desk at home. Elena

Maximova in a long skirted dress with a veiled hat and a corsage of flowers pinned high on one shoulder. Sverdlov was in uniform. He was not smiling in the picture and the twisted mouth made him look grim.

'You must believe me,' Tomarov said. 'I loved your father; I wouldn't exaggerate this, or lie to you. I am asking you to do what we suggest.'

'It is for your own good, Dr. Sverdlova,' the second man spoke up. It was like the old days after the war. Tomarov had brought him along as a witness.

'I'm not concerned with what is good for me.' She had a deep voice; it sounded more striking because her appearance was slight and feminine. She had black hair and eyes, with the faint sallowness of Mongolian ancestry. 'I don't think the individual's happiness is the important thing to be considered. What is important is what you've told me about my husband. And that's why I'm hesitating.' She turned to Tomarov. 'I find it so difficult to accept,' she said. 'I can't believe it of him.'

'Nor could I, at first. He was the last man to be corrupted. He had such a good record. He was the best officer we had in Hungary. He never wavered, he never questioned. But now—three years in America, and he has changed. If he came home now, Elena, you wouldn't recognise him. You wouldn't want to live with him.'

'It was my mistake,' she said. 'He wanted me to go to America; I couldn't leave my work, I didn't want to live among Capitalists. He needed someone to support him.'

'If he can't remain true to his ideals without his wife to keep him loyal, he's never to be trusted,' the second man said. His name was Roskovsky; he had worked with Tomarov for thirty years. Together they were among the few originals who had survived into the present political régime. And like all such survivors they were seeing the wheel turn full circle.

'He's marked, Elena,' Tomarov said. 'You must get rid of him or you will be suspected too. That is the truth. File for divorce before he is recalled.'

'Will you have some more tea?' Both shook their heads. Tomarov was pleading with her, out of friendship for her family, regard for her future, and because her rejection of her husband would strengthen the case which was being built up against him. Elena Sverdlova was one of the most eminent pediatric specialists in Moscow.

She was known as the daughter of a man who had been considered great in Stalin's hierarchy; for some years this had not reflected credit on her. Now, with the reversal of the liberal trends and the removal of the moderates Brezhnev and Podgorny from their offices, Party members like Elena Maximova Sverdlova were regaining their prestige. Tomarov had always admired her. She was her father's daughter. Single minded, dedicated, cerebral. A woman who specialised in treating children, but refused to become pregnant because it would limit her work. Women of her calibre had been the inspiration of the Revolution. 'Comrades,' she said, 'I need a little time to think about what you have told me. If you will leave me alone now, I shall make up my mind by tomorrow. Thank you for coming.'

She shook hands with Roskovsky, and kissed Tomarov's cheek. When they had gone, she cleared away the samovar and the crockery, shook out the cushions and emptied the ashtray of their cigarettes. She knew the effects tobacco had on general health, and she had never smoked. In spite of everything she did to discourage him, Sverdlov had persisted in the habit. The last time she had seen him, he had smoked a cigarette in their bed, immediately after they had made love. She remembered it with anger. He had been her husband for ten years; in private he had never conformed in the way that she thought he should. Thinking back, admitting the clarity of hindsight, she could see that Tomarov must be right. As a young man Sverdlov appeared as dedicated to the cause of Soviet Socialism as she was; only when she lived with him did the latent cynicism show itself. It had distressed her; she had argued and rebuked him, albeit gently, using only reason, as befitted rational human beings in a state of disagreement. His reaction had been to laugh at her, and try to take her clothes off.

He had a mind which enquired into everything; he maintained that this quality gave him pre-eminence in his job. What disturbed Elena was the extent to which he questioned things which should have been accepted automatically. His career was spectacular; he was ambitious and without scruple, but his motives lacked the clear, unselfish partisanship which was the rule by which his wife ordered her existence. She practised medicine in one of the most emotional treacherous fields open to a woman.

She worked with children. Sick, incurable, diseased, retarded children; she gave her skill equally without allowing personal preference or maternal instinct to influence her actions. She saved life, and at other times, deliberately, she took it. She had never behaved irrationally; she met her husband's reasonable demands. His desire to have children and for her to accompany him to America and give up the clinic were not reasonable, and she refused them. Now, according to what her old friend Tomarov said, he had gone soft. The man who had gone into Hungary to help quell the uprising had become an advocate of compromise with the West; he was making China the excuse for advocating genuine co-existence with the Capitalist world. Tomarov had explained that for two years General Golitsyn had seen him working to these ends, openly undermining morale in his section in the Embassy and exerting the same pernicious influence in Russian political circles. And only because the insidious liberal attitudes at home had been suppressed and their supporters removed, had the old General dared report back and denounce his superior.

Sverdlov had written to her regularly when he took up his appointment; she had replied with letters full of news about her work, of enquiries for friends in their Embassy, and enthusiastic descriptions of events in Moscow. She had never asked about America; she didn't want to hear anything which might reflect to its credit, and she knew Sverdlov was irresponsible enough to say it, just to irritate her. His work in Washington could not be discussed. She had missed him at first; they had been in love, and in many ways he was a strong man whom she admired. He was also a skilful lover; it was only later on that Elena realised how much she had resented that skill and the degree of dominance he had achieved over her because of it. She had felt degraded. Marriage was a social and sexual partnership which was sensibly dissolved as soon as one or both of the partners were no longer satisfied. His assumption of supremacy in this side of their relationship had surprised and offended her. He had threatened her independence; instinctively she had sensed this and resisted. Nothing would persuade her to give up her clinical work, or to limit her scope by children which she didn't want. He had no right to ask a free and equal partner to submit to the inhibiting consequences of what was done to her in bed. Elena had let him go to Washington, and discovered after a few months of readjustment that she was happier alone. But even so, Tomarov's suggestion of divorce had shocked her. Her husband was marked. There was no mistake about the warning. He was out of favour and under grave suspicion. He would be recalled, and Elena knew exactly what would follow. Sverdlov would be interrogated and put on trial.

She faced that possibility, keeping calm and rational, refusing sentiment a voice in the discussion in her mind. He had turned against his Party and his people. Otherwise he wouldn't be suspected. There were no doubts in Elena's reasoning process. The State was never wrong. If Feodor was not trusted, then he was no longer trustworthy. And she was free of any obligation to support him. To do so would be to compound his treason. Her own motives would become suspect; she could be deprived of her job, cast out into the wilderness inhabited by unreliables, if she was not actually arrested and questioned in conjunction with her husband. Fear did not influence her; in defence of her political ideals, Elena Maximova would have faced prison and even death without hesitating. Sverdlov had gone over to the enemy. That was sufficient reason for dissociating herself as publicly as possible. There was a photograph on the centre table in the sitting room. It was the same as the one Tomarov kept at home; a full-length picture of them on their wedding day. Elena picked it up, removed the print from its painted wooden frame, and tore it up. The following morning Gregory Tomarov presented himself at the office of Major-General Ivanovsky at the Headquarters of the KGB in Dzershinsky Square. The case against Feodor Sverdlov was proceeding satisfactorily and the next step could be taken. There would be no complications with the Maximov family; his wife was applying for an immediate divorce.

. . . . .

'I know Richard Paterson,' Sverdlov said. He lit a cigarette and put it between her lips. 'Why did you choose him? I find that difficult to understand!'

'I fell in love with him.' Judith leaned back, inhaling the cigarette. She felt weary and yet quite calm. But she was deceiving herself. The Russian judged exactly how close she was to throwing the cigarette away and bursting into a flood of tears. When she cried it would be a good sign. Tears were a healing balm; it was a maudlin saying and quite untrue in many cases. But for her it would be of benefit. He reached over and took her hand. 'Tell me what happened. What did he do to you to spoil you for me?'

'I met him about eight, nine months ago. He was the only man I've been involved with since Pat died,' She had told Sverdlov, very briefly, that she had been married and lost her husband in a motor accident. He hadn't seemed interested and the subject dropped. 'I wanted to work hard and get over his death. I kept everyone at a distance; I was quite happy. Then some friends asked me and Nancy Nielson, that's my boss's daughter, to come to Washington for a weekend and I met Richard Paterson. He called me in New York and took me out to lunch.'

'How long did it take him to sleep with you?' Sverdlov asked. 'Did he send you flowers, tell you he loved you?'

'Yes.' Judith sounded unsteady. 'Exactly like that. Lunch, dinner, phone calls. Then the final date when he told me he was getting a divorce from his wife, and I let him come back to the apartment with me. I believed him, Feodor. She wasn't with him, everyone knew she'd refused to come over.'

'And so you became lovers. Was he a good lover, did he please you?'

'I'm not prepared to answer that.' She pulled her hand away. 'You're making this sound revolting, like some sordid roll in the hay. It wasn't like that. I told you, I was in love with him.'

'I see,' Sverdlov said. 'I am sorry. Why is it all over then?'

'Just chance,' she said. 'Pure bloody chance. I was having lunch with some people who knew him, not very well, and they had no idea about him and me—the wife said she'd met *his* wife in Washington. She'd joined him months ago, and he never said a word to me. But the real thing that finished it was when I heard she was having a baby.' Sverdlov said nothing. When she began to cry he didn't move, he went on sitting in the darkness, smoking. Below them the sea rolled up the beach, clawing the stones and sand in its retreat. It was a beautiful clear night.

'I felt so cheap,' Judith said. 'He'd lied and lied to me, letting me think he was serious and that after his divorce we might . . . Oh, all right he never actually said it, but he let me think it! Can't you understand that?'

'Very well,' the Russian said. 'So while he was loving you, he was reconciled to his wife and in her bed as well? And so you can't forgive him for making a fool of you.'

'It's more than that,' Judith said angrily. 'I trusted him. I would never have started an affair if I'd known his wife was going to join him. If he'd told me the truth I'd have broken it off at once.'

'That's why he didn't tell you, because he knew what you would do. He was in a very fortunate position; a charming mistress in New York and a wife in Washington. Aren't you really upset with him because he did it to his wife and gave her a child? Isn't that what hurts, not this great love?'

'It all hurts,' she said. 'You can interpret it how you like—make it squalid and cheap if you want to, because that's exactly how I see it! And especially myself. I feel so sorry for that woman, thinking he was being genuine, staying alone in Washington having his baby while he came up and down twice a week to stay with me! I'm a great judge of character, aren't I?'

'No, I think you are terribly bad,' he remarked. 'He is an ambitious man. Very correct, very interested in himself. I suppose you could say he was good looking, if you like that kind of face. Which you did, of course. I would say he was dull.' He stretched in the chair; below them the night watchman plodded through the sand, his torch flashing round the bungalows. 'Very dull,' he continued. 'I would be much better for you. I make you laugh; did you laugh much with him?'

'No,' Judith answered. 'I suppose I didn't. It wasn't like that. It was too serious, too intense. I'm not a woman who takes these things as a joke, I'm afraid. So you wouldn't be better for me. I'd like to go to my bungalow now.'

'Finish your drink first.' Sverdlov had one hand on her arm. It exerted pressure. 'It will help you sleep. Otherwise you will go to bed and cry again. Even you won't be pretty with a red nose—you see, you smile. So perhaps it is not so very serious, this great love for the Group Captain.'

'How well do you know him?' she asked. 'He never mentioned you.'

'He wouldn't.' Sverdlov grinned crooked mouthed in the darkness. 'I know him to speak a few words when we meet socially. But he doesn't encourage friendship with our people. It might hurt his career. Like divorcing his wife. Couldn't you see it was the most important thing for him?'

'No,' she said. 'Obviously not.'

'That's because you are a sentimentalist. You believe in innocent slaves and miraculous Tamarind seeds. You *are* a very bad judge of people.'

'Anything else?' He was massaging her wrist with his thumb; she was too exhausted and upset to stop him. 'Anything else wrong with me?'

'I didn't say it was wrong,' Sverdlov said. 'In a woman I think it is nice. I have a wife at home. She is a good judge of everything. She knows exactly what is right and what is not right. She draws a line—so.' He gestured with his burning cigarette end in the darkness. 'On this side is the Soviet Union and the Party. They are right. On the other side is the Capitalist world. Wrong.'

'You never said you were married,' Judith couldn't keep her voice steady. She managed to pull her arm away from the circulating thumb.

'That is why I am telling you about it now" he said. 'So you won't say afterwards, "You are married, you never told me".'

'There won't be any afterwards.' Judith started to get up.

Sverdlov didn't move to stop her. 'Probably not now,' he said. 'I have to go back in three days. Tonight I'd like to talk a little, about myself, if you wouldn't mind. Please sit down again.'

'Three days—I thought there was nearly a week.'

'I came before you did.' He reached down and brought up a whisky bottle. He tipped some into her glass. 'For me, not for you.'

Judith sat down. 'You know the night watchman saw us up here. I suppose he'll report it.'

'I'm sure he will.' Sverdlov was smiling again. 'I'm sure we have been watched all the time. You may be asked questions about me when you go back.'

'Who by?' She turned to him in surprise. The hand was reaching out for her again.

'Your Intelligence people. The CIA. What will you tell them?'

'To mind their own business. Stop trying to hold my hand. I don't trust you, Feodor. You said you wanted to talk.'

'You can trust me,' he said. 'Let me hold your hand. I'm afraid of the darkness.'

'You're not afraid of anything.' Judith gave in.

'That is not true.' He was serious, the mockery had gone. He was a man whose mood could change with alarming rapidity. 'Everyone is afraid of something. You came here to run away from your love affair. I came because I have nothing to run away from. Do you understand that?'

'No,' she shook her head. What does it mean?'

'I have a good career,' Sverdlov said. 'Promising. I have a wife who is a famous specialist; she is young and nice looking. I belong to a great country and a great Socialist movement which will one day be accepted by the whole world.'

'God forbid,' she said.

'He can't. He doesn't exist. Don't interrupt me, I am playing at Capitalism and counting my assets. I am healthy, and I can have girls when I want. Except for you. But I don't want girls, I don't want to see my wife, and I don't feel anything about the Socialist Revolution any more. What do I do about this?'

She couldn't think of anything to say to him for a moment. The moon was free of cloud and they could see each other clearly in the white translucent light. He looked harsh, and tense, his mouth pulled to the side. Without any reason, Judith was cold. She realised that the cause, on that sort of tropical night, was a sense of physical fear.

'What are you trying to say to me.' She was whispering, as if the night watchman were still walking near.

'I don't know,' Sverdlov said. 'I'm asking you. What do I do now?'

'You needed a holiday.' It sounded a futile thing to say. 'Perhaps you've been overworking. Don't you feel any different now?'

'Yes.' He was smoking again; he had forgotten to give her one. She had developed a taste of his strong cigarettes.

'Yes. I feel more relaxed. I feel I could stay here indefinitely, with nothing more important to do than spend the time with you. I don't want to go back. I don't want to find a letter from my wife, telling me what a good thing the Czechoslovakians have decided to try all their government officials for treason, and what a mistake we made not to execute Dubjcek right in the beginning . . .'

'Does she really think that.' Judith was horrified.

'That is how she thinks,' Sverdlov said. 'That is how I used to think, but for different reasons. Now I can't accept those reasons either. I'm not even ambitious any more.'

'Can't you apply to go back to the Regular Army?' she asked.

He glanced sideways at her. 'That is the last thing I can do.'

'I can't help you,' she said. 'I'm sorry. I don't know what the answer is. I suppose you'll have to adjust to it. It probably won't last long. As I said, you're overworked and you needed a break. Stay on here till I go home. Can't you do that?'

'Yes.' She felt the strain go out of him. The hand holding her palm had been gripping hard; now the fingers moved, his thumb began its sensual exploration. 'Yes, I can stay if I want to! we can leave on the same day . . . I thought we might go to the harbour again tomorrow. I would like to take a trip across to one of the other islands.'

'It'd take days,' Judith said. 'Grenada's the nearest. You can fly there in an hour.'

'You can fly to Brazil in two,' he said. 'Do you want to swim before you go to bed?'

'Not tonight.' Judith stood up and they moved back inside towards the door. He opened it for her and she stepped outside.

'It's been a long evening. Disappointing for you too,' she said.

'Good for both of us.' Sverdlov held out his hand. When she took it he laid the other on her shoulder. 'I'm surprised by one thing. Why haven't you suggested that I come over to your side? Wouldn't the West want me?'

'Probably.' Judith looked at him. 'But it just wouldn't work for you. I know it wouldn't.'

'I know it too,' he said. He ran his hand up from her

shoulder round the back of her neck, under her hair. I believe you are a neutral. You don't want converts.'

'No. And I don't want to be converted either. I believe in being free to choose. Don't worry about it. You'll get over the feeling; it's just a mood.'

He lowered his voice. 'Do you know something? You have forgotten about the Group Captain—isn't that so?'

'Good night,' Judith said. She stepped across to her own entrance; it was less than five feet away.

'Tomorrow we will go and look for your tamarind tree.'

'And what will you say if we find it?'

'What will you say, if we don't?'

## CHAPTER FOUR

Mrs. Stephenson, the wife of the Minister, had come to the conclusion that she liked Mrs. Paterson better than she did the Group Captain. It was unusual for Margaret Stephenson to prefer women to their husbands; she told her own husband repeatedly that the Embassy wives bored her stiff. They're so common these days.' She said that often too, dwelling on the adjective. Terribly dreary creatures with no conversation.' It was an attitude that annoyed Fergus Stephenson. He had a fanatical sense of loyalty to anyone in the service; he was scrupulous in dealing with the meanest clerk. He never pulled his awesome rank, or took advantage of his equally awesome background to point out a mistake. He was a paragon, as his wife was aware. The staff spoke of him with a mixture of admiration and respect that irritated her beyond endurance. They didn't have to live with him. They saw the impressive façade; she had lived with the occupant of that particular whited sepulchre, and she could swear to its authenticity as a corpse. That evening, as they dressed for dinner, she called her comments through to him from the bathroom.

'She's nice,' she repeated. 'I discovered that her elder brother used to take me out while you were in Ceylon. He was very attractive; great fun. Had a ridiculous Flying Officer Prune moustache.'

Fergus Stephenson moved to the open bathroom door. 'I'm glad she met with your approval. It will help him.'

His wife turned round from the mirror, a lipstick in her right hand. 'Like hell it will,' she said. 'Not unless he gives up that little piece he's been visiting in New York! Oh Fergus, stop pretending you didn't know—that frightful bloodhound Loder had him checked up.'

'Who told you that?' He had moved out of sight. He found it easier when she couldn't see him.

'Never mind. But somebody did. She's having a baby, and she's thrilled. Dresses very badly. That's my only criticism.'

'Good Lord,' Stephenson said. 'She must be remarkable.'

He brushed his hair back, not really looking at the reflection in the mirror. Who had told his wife about the investigation into Paterson? He brushed the hair until his scalp tingled. Who was it this time? . . .

It was a question he should never have asked. They had been married twenty years; they had three children, a nineteen-year-old girl and two boys at school in England. A long time ago, after the last child's birth, Stephenson had decided not to ask that kind of question. He was not absolutely sure of the youngest child's paternity. Sometimes he detected a resemblance to himself, at other times the boy appeared completely alien. His wife had always been publicly discreet. He had reason to be grateful for that; in the early years his career couldn't have survived a major scandal. Attitudes towards that kind of situation had relaxed tremendously. The Foreign Office had been forced to adopt a less rigid code regarding divorce and remarriage; otherwise there would have been a few senior diplomats left in their posts.

He had made a genuine effort to please Margaret. When he asked her to marry him, he believed that she presented an alternative to the preference for his own sex which had culminated in a passionate attachment when he was up at Cambridge. His lover had been all that he admired; brilliant, physically attractive, extroverted and impeccably bred. Fergus Stephenson had fallen in love with him and been seduced. He realised soon afterwards that he had shared this experience with many of his friends. Margaret came into his life when he first joined the Foreign Office. She was the female counterpart of the man at Cambridge. Very physical, with a strong colouring, robust spirits and fearsome energy. She hunted, swam, skii-ed like a professional, was a most stimulating companion on every level. She dazzled; Fergus blinked in the glare of her personality, drawn to its dominance as he had been towards that other, terrifying sexual partnership. He had thought he was in love with her, and that the other episode could be forgotten. Many of his seducer's victims had married and as far as he knew were ordinary heterosexuals. But it had not worked.

Their relationship had faltered, broken down, emerged again in a desperate attempt on both their parts to escape the truth. He had impregnated her often enough to produce two or even three children, but Margaret was not the woman to be deceived for ever. And one night, shamed and frantic for her understanding, Fergus had committed the ultimate mistake and told her about Cambridge. From that moment she was finished with him. They went on together in public; the marriage would last till death for the benefit of the world outside. Inside, their relationship was a charade, played out with cruelty and contempt on her part, with shame and humiliation on his. He didn't find out about her first lover. He would have preferred never to know, but she sensed this, and took perverse delight in telling him. Their son was three months old at the time. She had seen the sudden question present itself in his mind, and burst out laughing. Fergus had never forgotten that laugh. 'How long has it been going on? Is Julian yours or isn't he—well you'll just have to wait and see, won't you? I'm damned if I know.'

He put the brush down and smoothed his hair back with his palm. It was thinning across the top of his head; he could feel the scalp underneath it. Whoever the man was this time, and there must have been hundreds, he had passed on confidential information to her.

This in itself was a serious breach of security.

'Margaret,' he said. 'Whoever told you about Loder's investigation had absolutely no right to do so. You know that, don't you?'

'Of course I know.' She had come out of the bathroom; she was a tall woman, elegantly dressed, her blonde hair bleached to a metallic white because it had begun to go grey. She had piercing blue eyes; they were large, heavy lidded, cleverly made up. At forty-five she was still overpoweringly beautiful. In ten years she would be a formidable matron, perfectly cast in the role of Her Excellency the Ambassadress.

'It was very naughty of him,' she said. 'Pass me my bag, will you?'

'I want to know who it is.' It took courage to say that, and she raised her eyebrows at him, exaggerating her surprise.

'Whatever for? You'd only get him into trouble.'

'I'd make sure he never gave away a confidential report again,' Stephenson said. 'That's all I care about.'

'But it's not important,' Margaret shrugged, looking through her evening bag to check its contents. 'Just a little affair. Men are always having them, darling. After all, it was a woman he was sleeping with. I thought it was buggery that was the big security risk these days?' He didn't wince; she had made that sort of remark too often and it had no more affect upon him.

'I'm not interested in what Paterson does in his private life. My interest is in seeing that the security among our staff is kept to the maximum. Especially at the moment. Something's on with the Russians. Perhaps now you'll realise that I'm not asking for any personal reason.'

'What's on with the Russians? I haven't heard anything.'

'Thank God for that,' he said. 'If you don't tell me, I shall have no alternative but to go to Loder.'

She was on her way to the door; she usually ended an argument by walking out while he was still speaking, but now she stopped and turned.

'If you go to Loder and start stirring up trouble,' she said, 'he'll find out a few things about me you wouldn't like him knowing. I suppose you've thought of that?'

'I am thinking of it,' Stephenson said. He saw the silhoutte of her body outlined against the open door. Arrogant, voracious, merciless. It seemed to have a malignant life independent of the human personality inside it. He had always basically feared the female; there was something secret and alarming about the demands and passions of a woman. He used to think that he hated his wife's body more than he hated his wife. It revolted him at that moment.

She seldom bothered to torment him; she lived her private life, indulged herself in what she chose, and nobody knew. Even he didn't have to know, unless he probed, as he had done that night. Much of her hatred for him had been spent. Also, she wanted him to get to a top Embassy at the end of his career.

'It's exactly seven-thirty,' she said. 'Our guests will be arriving. I'm going down. You can go to that common little bloodhound if you want to; but just think it out first.'

Stephenson stayed behind. He let her go downstairs, to greet their guests, a prominent American economist and his wife, the West German First Secretary, and a sprinkling of his own staff. If he told Loder about the leak, Margaret's connection couldn't be concealed. Stephenson started towards the door. Who was it? Usually somebody younger, but not too young. She didn't go in for boys, thank God. Somebody in a position to know what the principal from S.I.S. was doing, day to day.

Somebody in Loder's section. The more he thought about it the worse it became if he did nothing. He had been brought into a special conference called by Jack Loder to report to the Ambassador.

The information on Sverdlov had been coming through from the Barbadian Police. The Russian had made only one contact on the island, a woman, whom he had picked up at his hotel. Loder had read the details out to them. Information collected on her had been checked and double checked and her identity was established as Mrs. Judith Farrow, domiciled in New York, British citizen, working as personal assistant to Sam Nielson at UNO.

That had started the flap. He found himself using Loder's slang expression. The man was really inexcusable; he sometimes spouted Greek, which annoyed the Americans, or lapsed into the terminology of the wartime NAAFI. Sam Nielson was an international figure. His secretary picking up with Sverdlov was a top security matter. For that reason Buckley and the CIA were scenting blood. Loder's policy, which he had explained to the Ambassador and Stephenson, was to persuade them to accept the story without making a few enquiries of their own. They didn't know, and musn't be told at this stage, that Mrs. Farrow was also the mistress of the British Air Attaché. That would bring the Embassy staff under American suspicion. For this reason alone, the indiscretion dropped to his wife about Richard Paterson's affair with the girl could cause disaster if it was repeated. Stephenson turned back from the door and went into his study. He made a quick note in his diary. See Loder. He locked it in his desk and went on down to join his wife.

. . . . .

The flight back to New York took four hours. Judith had booked on the Saturday morning plane; Sverdlov insisted on driving her to the airport. He had chosen a later flight; Judith suspected that he had done so to avoid travelling with her, but she made no comment. Perhaps he would be met at Kennedy International and saying goodbye to her might be awkward. The last few days had been the best part of the holiday. Sverdlov had not tried to make love to her again, though he kept up a merciless barrage of teasing and innuendo which she described as the Hot War. Far from being sympathetic or offering a shoulder to cry upon, Sverdlov made fun of every aspect of her affair with Richard Paterson, jeering and sniping at what he called her great lost love. Judith was often furious, but frequently driven to laughing at him. Which made her even angrier, because she knew this was his object. The night before leaving they were having dinner at a select but brutally expensive hotel perched on the hills, with a beautiful panoramic view of the sea. They had drinks on the patio under the palm trees, and for several minutes they watched a young Barbadian waiter trying to light the candles which hung in glass storm shields from the trees and bushes. Judith nudged Sverdlov's arm. 'Poor chap, that's the last match! Please, go over and show him how to do it.'

She watched the Russian walk over to him; he moved with a curious lope that reminded her of the cat species. In many ways he was a feline man. Within a few minutes the patio was surrounded by flickering lights, and after watching Sverdlov, the waiter grinned delightedly, thanked him and ambled off.

'Brilliant,' Judith said. 'Wasn't he delighted with you?'

'Of course,' Sverdlov sat down. 'He knew I was a genius, as soon as he saw I used a lighter instead of matches that the wind blew out. As George Orwell said, all men are equal but some are more equal than others.'

'He didn't seem to care,' Judith answered. 'Perhaps that's what matters; making the most of what you have and not worrying about whether someone else has more, or better . . . It's a philosophy we've completely lost sight of—it's all go, that awful expression, whatever it means—get on, make more money, get promoted, get ahead! Anyway, that quotation from Orwell sounds a bit funny, coming from you.'

'Do you talk like this in New York?' Sverdlov asked her.

'I say what I think wherever I am. Why shouldn't I?'

'Because they will think you are a Communist,' he said. 'Especially since you have been seeing me. I should be careful, Judith. You could get into trouble.'

'Don't be silly. What I've said isn't Communism. It's more like Christianity if you only knew it.'

'A philosophy founded upon a superstition is not a philosophy,' Sverdlov said. 'It is as valid as your tamarind tree, which didn't exist.'

'You'll never let me forget that, will you? But I believe it did exist. I believe it was cut down.'

He smiled in his crooked way; it had been a triumph for him, and he hadn't been chivalrous and refrained from reminding her. He had driven her to Haywards Plantation and spoken to the owner who listened courteously but with obvious disbelief to the story of the slave and the miraculous tree, even accompanying them on a tour in search of any tree old enough to qualify. They had found nothing. Sverdlov had hung on to her arm, and squeezed it every time they picked a pod of seeds and found them the normal shape.

'A legend,' he repeated, smiling at her. 'Like the political agitator who rose from the dead.' He laughed out loud. 'How can an intelligent woman like you even think of such nonsense! Shall I tell you the truth—there was no tamarind tree, there was no innocent slave—there is no force outside this world which gives justice to the weak. There is nothing but man, and his standards of justice are not consistent. One year you are right to do a certain thing, then the next year it has become a crime. There are no standards, only expediencies.'

'That is the most cynical statement I've ever heard.' Judith stared at him. She disliked his attacks upon religion; it was the only time when there was real discord between them. But this was different. This was an attack upon his own political ideology.

'You talk about me getting into trouble in America,'

she said. ' Just what would happen to you if you talked like that at home?'

'It would depend,' Sverdlov said. 'Two years ago, eighteen months, it would have caused no comment. But now—now it would be thought of as a crime. That's what I meant. The wind changes, the weathercock turns. That is what ideology is, a weathercock which is subject to the wind of expediency. Or of whim. There was an Empress of Russia who made it high treason to wear pink, did you know that? It was her favourite colour.' He began to laugh. 'There are people in your Western world who feel the same way about someone with a red tie. High treason . . . none of it makes sense. In a way that is the glory of materialism. It teaches you in the end to despise all things which are material.'

'And leaves you nothing of value?' Judith asked him.

'Survival,' Sverdlov said. 'That is the only end worth any effort. To live; because afterwards there is nothing.' He reached over and held her hand, he shook his head. 'There is no reward for the good and no punishment for the evil. There is just darkness; nothing. A man has to live for himself. To be alive is the important thing.'

'I don't believe that. If you simplify it, it's just absolute selfishness; I don't think that makes anyone happy. And most of all, I don't believe *you*. Why did you help that idiot of a waiter? Why should you do anything for him?'

'I did it to please you,' he said.

'All right, why bother to do something for me?'

'Ah,' Sverdlov said. 'Because I hope to get something out of it for myself. And you know what *that* is.'

'I see; thanks.'

'You believe me,' he said. 'You are very gullible. No wonder the Group Captain made such a fool of you. He told you he loved you, and you believed him. I tell you I do something to please you because I want to go to bed with you and you believe me. We are both liars. How are you going to survive, if you can't tell the difference between one lie and another—I am really worried for you.'

'Stop making fun of me. And I've asked you not to keep on mentioning Richard. I shouldn't have told you. It was very stupid of me.'

'You don't know how charming it is to find an intelligent woman who does stupid things,' Sverdlov said solemnly. 'Now tell me something. Are you as sad about your lover as you were when I first met you? Is your heart still broken—we have a clinic in Moscow where they do wonderful operations for the heart—does it really hurt so much when I talk about him?'

'No,' Judith admitted. 'No, it doesn't. It seems less real out here. But I'm not looking forward to going back.'

'It will be easier than you expect. You will think of me, instead of him. We can meet perhaps, in New York. If we are very discreet about it.'

'It mightn't be a good idea for you,' Judith said. 'I'm sure it wouldn't be popular with your Ambassador.'

'I said discreet,' Sverdlov reminded her. 'Leave the arrangements to me. Now, if you are hungry, we will have dinner.'

It was their last evening, and as they drove back to the hotel Judith noticed that he was silent. Normally he talked most of the time they were together. He came to her door with her and waited. His face was in shadow and she couldn't see its expression.

'Will you meet me in New York?'

'I don't know,' Judith answered truthfully. 'Here is different. There'd be so many complications there. Wait till we're both back at work. You may feel it would be better not.' She put the key in the lock; it was stiff and he had to turn it for her.

'You've been very nice to me,' she said suddenly. 'And you've helped me a lot over that other business . . . to get it in proportion. I hope you feel happier too, about going back.'

'I feel the same,' he said. 'This is not just a broken love affair for me. It is a way of life. But it is the only one I know. I told you tonight, survival is what matters. I will be ready to drive you tomorrow morning.'

She let him kiss her; there was no gaiety between them now; she felt torn and sad by saying goodbye to him outside the door. But nothing would have made her ask him in. She'd had enough of that with Richard Paterson. Enough of the impermanence of sex, the sense of crushing anti-climax watching him dress and whistle happily as he prepared to walk away. She got free of the Russian with some effort. He had bruised her mouth; she could feel his arms trembling. 'Good night.' She said it very quickly and went inside her bungalow.

When he drove her to the airport he was his usual self;

he joked and talked through the short twenty-minute drive. Everything seemed brighter that last morning, even the blood-coloured poinsettias appeared richer in colour, the graceful bougainvillaeas more royally purple.

If I never see it again, Judith thought suddenly, I'll remember this place all my life. At the reception lounge she said goodbye to Sverdlov; the flight was called, there was no point in delaying. She had a sense of unreality, as if the man and the island were part of the same suspension from life. 'Here,' he said. 'I kept this for you. And I have one; a souvenir of our holiday.'

He gave her an envelope. She opened it as she walked to the plane. Inside was a tamarind seed.

. . . . .

'Tell me about your holiday, Mrs. Farrow. Did you have a good time in Barbados?'

'I'm not answering any questions.' Judith was standing: the man with ginger hair was sprawling back in one of her armchairs. He had met her with a car at the airport; another man, who was also in the apartment but out of sight, picked her up as she came out of Customs. He had established himself as a member of the Embassy staff, and Judith, supposing that there must be some link-up with Nielson and the work in hand for the Security Council Meeting, accepted and followed him. Inside the big blue Chevrolet she found the second man, who walked into her apartment with her. There was nothing she could do.

They didn't lock the doors or adopt a sinister attitude. The senior man with the ugly freckled face and regional accent told the younger one to go and rustle up some tea. Then he just sat down, lit a cigarette and asked her if she would give him an hour of her time and answer a few questions. 'You may be asked questions when you get back.' Sverdlov had warned her what might happen. She felt angry as well as frightened. How dare they behave as if they were in some third rate espionage movie. Loder saw the look on her face and guessed what her reaction was going to be.

'What is this all about?' She stood in front of him, hoping it gave her an advantage. 'You collect me in a car and you come up here without any invitation from me, and have the damned nerve to start asking me questions.

Who and what are you, Mr. Loder?' He had introduced himself in the car, holding out his stubby hand to shake hers.

'I told you. I'm the Liaison Officer with Plans,' he said. 'Tell me about Barbados. I've never been to any of the islands. You've got a nice tan; weather must have been good.'

'The weather was marvellous; you didn't come all the way from Washington to ask me about that.'

'No,' Loder agreed. 'I didn't. But I do want to hear about your holiday. Meet anyone interesting?'

Standing looking down at him didn't give her an advantage; it made her feel as if she were on trial in some way. At that moment the younger man put his head round the door. 'No tea,' he said, speaking to Loder. 'Coffee do?'

'Coffee's all right. You'll have some, won't you, Mrs. Farrow?'

If she hadn't been so scared of him, Judith would have told him to go to hell. She should have done so, and she was furious with herself for not taking the initiative away from him. He had no right to sit there, no right to send his driver out to her kitchen. No right to look at her like that and offer her a cup of her own coffee.

He wasn't a big man, he didn't look like a detective or a strong-arm investigator; he looked like a middle-aged official in a government office. He wore an R.A.F. tie. She should not have been afraid of him, but she was.

'You haven't told me,' he said. 'Did you meet anyone interesting while you were abroad? Make any friends?'

'You know very well I did,' she surprised herself by answering with a confidence she didn't feel. 'That's why you're here, isn't it? He said you people would come round.'

'Well he should know,' Loder remarked. 'I'd be glad if you'd tell me exactly what happened. What was this man's name anyway—you said "he", didn't you, Mrs. Farrow?'

'His name was Feodor Sverdlov. He's a military attaché at the Soviet Embassy. That's all there is to tell you, unless you want a day by day account of how many times we went swimming, where we went to dinner, what we ate. I can't remember every little detail, I'm afraid.'

'You won't be asked to,' Loder answered. 'I wonder what our boy Joseph's doing with the coffee—I hate the bloody stuff myself. But it's better than nothing. Did he make friends with anyone else, besides you?'

'No,' Judith gave up and sat down herself. She found some of Nancy Nielson's cigarettes in a box and lit one. It tasted thin and insipid after Sverdlov's brand. He had given her a box to take home.

'We spent the time together. As far as I know he never spoke to anyone else.'

'Did he go out alone at all—take trips round the island; did he start off with you in the car and then leave you on a beach while he went somewhere on his own? Anything like that?'

'No,' Judith said. 'We spent all day together. He never went anywhere without me.'

'Sounds as if you got on very well.'

'If you're going to speak to me like that . . .' She half got out of the chair; he held up his hand, palm outwards like a schoolmaster admonishing a difficult pupil.

'Don't take it personally, Mrs. Farrow. I'm just doing my job. Here's Joseph. Where the hell have you been? Cooking a three-course dinner?'

'Sorry,' the driver said. 'Couldn't find the gear.'

'You're not domesticated,' Loder said. 'How do you like it, Mrs. Farrow—milk and sugar?'

'I don't want any, thank you.' She looked up and caught the man he called Joseph watching her. There was a curious relationship between the two. Both had completely dropped the Foreign Office pose of official and chauffeur. They seemed to be playing a private game for her benefit. Or perhaps to amuse themselves.

'Don't be like that, Mrs. Farrow. You can't expect to pick up a senior Soviet official like Colonel Sverdlov and not set a cat among the pigeons. Especially here. You know how the Yanks feel about getting chummy with them. You must have known we'd be calling on you.'

'I don't see any reason why you should.' Judith found it more difficult to keep up with him because of the second man's presence in the room. She couldn't understand why, but it was so. 'I've done nothing wrong. I met a man staying in the same hotel, we went around together. I liked his company and he liked mine, apparently. I don't see how that concerns anyone else. I'm sorry.'

'That's a point of view,' Loder admitted. 'But not a very valid one. You work for a man in a very important position, don't you, Mrs. Farrow? Sam Nielson deals with a lot of confidential stuff.

'You're a very attractive woman. Don't misunderstand me, but don't you think it's a bit odd this man choosing you, out of the whole island? It couldn't be he had another motive, besides being friendly on a holiday?'

'No,' Judith said. 'You're absolutely wrong. I know what you're getting at, and it's not true.'

Loder turned to Joseph. 'Go and see you switched off all the gadgets, will you? We don't want anything burning.'

When the other man had gone out, Loder suddenly stood up. His expression was unpleasant.

'You got very friendly, didn't you? You got well past the chummy stage. You spent every minute together. But he hadn't any ulterior motive. He just liked you, is that it? He didn't know who you worked for, you never discussed your job . . . he's going to try and contact you again, isn't he? Here in New York?'

'Yes,' Judith said, 'but not to recruit me; that's what you're trying to infer, isn't it?'

'It's what I expect,' Loder answered. 'It follows the pattern. That's why he went out there, to get hold of you.'

'You're wrong.' She saw his mistake and she found the nerve to strike back at him. 'He didn't go there to meet me. He was already there when I arrived, and I only arranged the trip at the last moment; forty-eight hours before. He couldn't possibly have gone to Barbados because of me. I didn't know I was going myself.'

'All right, all right.' Loder agreed with her. 'But they don't miss a trick, these boys. He met you, he found out who you were and he latched on. Did you sleep with him?'

'How dare you ask me that!'

'I'll ask you what I bloody well like.' Loder's voice was pitched low. 'And it's not just Sam Nielson, is it? You work for one man in a confidential post and you're having it off with another. We know all about Group Captain Paterson. Did you tell your Russian boy friend about him too? For Christ's sake, you're a gift to them.'

He had come closer to her until he was standing directly in front of her and over her. Then he walked away and went back to his chair.

'He'll get in touch with you again,' he said. 'I'll make a bet on that. And when he does, Mrs. Farrow, you won't try and fuck about, you'll come direct to me and tell me.

Do you understand that? Immediately. They've baited a big hook to catch you. That means there's something they want which must be within your capacity to give them.

'I'm not saying you'd do it. I'm not suggesting anything like that. But they don't play according to the rules. It's surprising what you can make a woman do when you've got a hold on her. Like blackmail.'

'Get out of here.' Judith got up. 'Get out of this apartment. I'm going to Washington and complain to the Minister. You won't get away with this.'

'The CIA will be the next,' Loder said. 'If I can't persuade them that you're co-operating fully with us, they'll get their boys on your back. You'll lose your job with Nielson, that's for sure. And if you don't like me, believe me, Mrs. Farrow, you won't like the way the Yanks'll handle you. They've had enough of our people farting around with the Russians. And I don't blame them.'

He used the language deliberately; it was part of the technique. He wanted to insult her and frighten her, to show that he could say and do whatever he liked. Then he waited. She looked very upset, likely to cry if he pressed her too far. She was a pretty woman. He remembered his envious thoughts about Sverdlov. He *had* been having a nice time. Setting up a useful operative the pleasant way. He could see that the threat of the CIA had really worried her.

'You should co-operate with us without all this being necessary,' he said. 'You know how important security is; you've been here for two years, you're not a newcomer, all pink and white from England. One thing you must undertake. Cut out the liaison with Group Captain Paterson. We've kept that quiet from the Americans or they would be on to you like a ton of bricks. Drop him flat.'

'I've already done so.' Judith had another cigarette and was trying to light it in spite of shaking hands. 'That's over anyway, so you don't have to threaten me. That's why I went to Barbados if you want to know. I wish to God I'd stayed right here!'

'Oh I don't know,' Loder sounded quite genial. 'Things have a way of turning out for the best. Let's suppose I'm right, and Sverdlov thinks he'll set you up as an agent. We could pass him a whole lot of dud information through you. It could be very useful.'

'I've told you,' Judith said wearily, 'you're wrong.

You're so wrong it's ridiculous. He'll never try to do that. I know him.'

'Do you?' Loder looked at her, his mouth pursed up. 'I doubt that, Mrs. Farrow. I doubt that very much. Now just forget I've been to see you, understand? Go to your work, see your friends, do everything you usually do, and don't get worried if your phone's tapped. It'll be the Yanks. If Sverdlov doesn't contact you, then I'll apologise. But I don't think I'll have to—the moment you hear from him, you call me at this number. You'll do that, won't you?' He put a card with a Washington exchange and number printed on it, propped against the cigarette box on the table beside her. 'Won't you? You won't do anything silly and try playing with fire, like seeing Sverdlov and not telling us?'

'No,' Judith said. 'I promise I won't do that. But I'm going to tell you something else. If he gets in touch with me I'll let you know. If you're right and he tries to involve me in anything, I'll tell you. At once. But I won't be used to spy on him. And you can tell that to the CIA. Nothing you can say will make me do anything like that.'

'Fair enough.' Loder went to the door and opened it. 'Goodbye, Mrs. Farrow. Thank you for talking to me. And not a word to your friend Miss Nielson. Nor Mr. Nielson. Just keep this in the family. Goodbye again.'

He went out. Joseph was waiting a few feet from the doorway. They left the apartment together, slamming the door so Judith could hear.

'Well, Joe—did you hear all that?'

He was Loder's immediate junior, a bright, coldly intelligent man with a love for his work.

'Yes,' he said. 'I heard. Put up quite an argument, didn't she?'

'Yes.' Loder stepped out of the elevator and walked rapidly across the lobby to the entrance. 'I think we're too late. I think that bastard's got to her already. I wouldn't trust a bloody word she said.'

. . . . .

As soon as he returned, Sverdlov was immersed in his work. He had a first floor office in the Soviet Embassy with large windows overlooking the trees and lawns of the extensive garden. The Ambassador's office was two doors away. Golitsyn and three junior officers worked in a row on the same floor, but only Sverdlov had the view over the gardens. He was glad of the volume of work he found waiting for him; he had never regarded Sunday as a holiday, and after a restless sleep on the Saturday of his return from Barbados, he had gone into his office the next morning. He was tired; it would have been untrue to say he slept as badly as before his holiday, but it was spasmodic and shallow, alternating with periods when he found himself awake for an hour or more before he drifted back into an uneasy limbo. His head ached, and he felt a distaste for food. He shut his office door and took refuge in the files and letters which were laid out neatly on his desk. He had an excellent secretary. Kalinin had been with him since his appointment. Sverdlov had chosen him in preference to a woman. He was too shrewd to take on an attractive girl, because experience showed that it was difficult to maintain an impersonal relationship when working in close contact every day, and he refused to look at some efficient harpy with a face like a battleship's rear for hours on end. Kalinin suited him perfectly. He was twenty-seven, very intelligent, efficient, and he had a sense of humour, which Sverdlov appreciated. He was not on duty that Sunday. When Sverdlov rang through to Kalinin's office to call him in, a young woman came in carrying a dictation pad.

'Who are you?'

'Anna Skriabine, Comrade Sverdlov.' She looked away quickly, as if he made her nervous. She remembered General Golitsyn's instructions and tried to retrieve her mistake by smiling at him.

'Where is Kalinin? Why are you in his office?'

'He is sick,' the girl said. 'I am a temporary replacement. I hope you'll find me satisfactory, Comrade Sverdlov. I'll do my best.'

She carried it off quite well. Sverdlov gave her credit for the shy smile, the diffident look. He felt his headache progress from a tired ache to an angry pounding.

'What is wrong with Kalinin? Where is he?'

'I don't know, Comrade Sverdlov,' the girl said. She had blue eyes, outlined with dark shadow. She opened them wide. 'I was just told to report to you.'

'All right,' he said. 'I see there was a meeting between the Ambassador and the Czechoslovakian chargé, on the

11th. I can't find a full report in my papers. Do you know where it is?'

'It should be there,' the girl said. She came to the desk. Her timidity was not all pretence. Sverdlov watched her sort through the thick file of papers. She took several sheets clipped together and handed them to him. 'This is the report, Comrade. I'm sorry it was not in its proper place.'

'It's not good policy to make a mistake on your first morning,' he said. 'But as you are only temporary, I will overlook it. Don't make another one. I'll ring through when I want some dictation. And bring me some tea.'

When she had gone, he read through the report. Everything which was conducted at Ambassadorial level had to be reported to him. The Czechs had asked for an interview because they had been approached by *Time* with a very delicate enquiry. How would the present government in Prague view any attempt to interview the deposed Prime Minister Dubjeck? As Dubjeck was living in retirement in the country, the editor was extremely anxious not to do anything which might put him in a false position with his own Party. The Embassy had been approached and asked to send a tentative request to Prague. Since the government in Prague was even less anxious to give their Moscow colleagues any cause for complaint than the Americans were on behalf of the former Prime Minister, they had promptly referred to the Soviet Ambassador and asked for his advice.

Sverdlov read through the transcript of the meeting. The Ambassador had advised against any interview being granted. Dubjeck was only permitted to remain under house arrest because he had promised to disappear from the public scene completely, and to say nothing to anyone.

On the other hand—the Ambassador was a cautious man, and with moderate leanings—it must not be refused in such a way as to make America suspicious that Dubjeck was not in good health and was subject to restrictions. There was a lot of talk, occupying several pages.

The Czech chargé didn't want to grant *Time's* team of reporter and photographer visas. It would be difficult to prevent them speaking to others when they were at liberty in the country, but playing into the hands of Capitalist propagandists by having them escorted on the trip. The

Soviet Ambassador had suggested a solution. Make no objection to Dubjeck being interviewed. But reject the choice of team to be sent out. And do the same with the replacement. In this way the project could be postponed until the magazine lost interest. Sverdlov initialled each paper as a sign of his approval. At one moment the girl came in with his tea; he didn't look up or speak. He worked through a lengthy correspondence on the question of an American proposal to invite the Israeli Premier to send a representative outside the United Nations to meet an accredited Egyptian agent. This was of major importance to Russia. Sverdlov began to concentrate. The correspondence was a copy taken from the originals which had been through the State Department, the Israeli Embassy and the British, with copious comments from the British Foreign Secretary. Reading and digesting this occupied Sverdlov for the rest of the morning. He had seen at least half a dozen similar folios of stolen papers, all covered in the same hessian file, marked Very Confidential, Grade I. Each had contained information of major political significance, and they all came from the same source. 'Blue'. He had often wondered whether, hidden within the ranks of Soviet officialdom, there existed an agent who betrayed to the West the kind of explosive secrets which their spy passed on to them. There had been Penkovsky; he had caused a lot of damage. Sverdlov had met him several times in Moscow. He had been a spectator at his trial, seated out of sight in the body of the court with the picked audience. It had been a contemptible charade. The judges condemned a man who had been induced to convict himself. Sverdlov appreciated the point about propaganda, but he despised the hypocrisy. He would have taken Penkovsky out of his cell and had him shot without the gruesome play in court.

No one in the Embassy knew the identity of 'Blue'. This alone indicated his importance. That secret was kept in Moscow, known to General Alexander Panyushkin the head of the K.G.B.

Sverdlov rang the bell and the girl came back. She smiled and without speaking sat down, her knees together under a respectable length of skirt, and waited to take his dictation.

Sverdlov referred to the file by the code name for their source of intelligence. He dictated a long cable which was to be coded and relayed to Moscow. Its content was to authenticate the information sent by 'Blue', and to suggest that in view of the Cambodian escalation it might be prudent to encourage a temporary peace move between Israel and the Arab states.

Why had Kalinin so conveniently fallen sick? He kept asking that question while he gave the girl his dictation. Why had Golitsyn replaced him with such an untypical member of the secretarial staff? . . . Was Anna Skriabine one of the 'doves'? Doves were used for several purposes. Often for meeting and entrapping men from outside. They were all trained in professions; some were manicurists who operated in the luxury hotels, others, like this girl, were excellent secretaries who could be attached to someone who was under surveillance. Someone in allied Embassies; even in their own Chancery. Sverdlov took a cigarette and lit it. What was she doing in Kalinin's place?

'Where is Comrade Kalinin?' he asked her again.

'I don't know,' she gave the same answer. 'Shall I put a call through and see if he's in his quarters?'

Sverdlov let her do it. One of Kalinin's colleagues answered. The girl turned towards him, holding the telephone covered with one hand.

'That is Comrade Tretchin. He says Igor Kalinin has been flown home on sick leave. He says he was very ill while you were away.'

'I'm sorry to hear that.' Sverdlov blew smoke into the air. 'But it's very inconvenient. That's all, you can ring off. You wouldn't know what was the matter with Kalinin, would you?'

'No, Comrade. He just said he had been very ill.' She wet her lips with her tongue; they were full and painted with the fashionable translucent lip colour. All the 'doves' were trained in every kind of sexual deviation. He smiled at the girl, his mouth twisted sharply to the side.

'Perhaps I shall keep you permanently,' he said. He looked at her, deliberately taking stock. She lowered her arms so that he could see the shape of her breasts; she wore a dark sweater and skirt, her hair was blonde and drawn back simply. A big freshwater pearl gleamed in each small ear. Very nice. Very appetising, like a little fondant cake, with soft pink icing on the top. The type that melted in a man's mouth. If he had had any doubt, that calculated movement to expose her bosom, silenced it. Golitsyn had planted a 'dove' on him, hoping to catch him off guard after his holiday and trap him into keeping her. Sverdlov had long mastered the art of appearing to be the victim of someone else's cleverness. He would certainly keep her. Because as they had got rid of Kalinin, who would never have been turned against him, she would only be replaced by another kind of spy.

'Would you like that?' he enquired. 'Would you like this job with me?'

'Oh, yes.'

'You'll have to work very hard. No mistakes.'

'I will do my best to please you, Comrade Sverdlov.'

'Yes,' he said. He was still smiling at her. 'I am sure you will.'

## CHAPTER FIVE

'Sit down, Richard. Sorry I had to ask you to come up this morning but I have to go to New York this afternoon.'

Fergus Stephenson opened the big crested box and pushed is across his desk. Richard Paterson took a cigarette and lit it. That's quite all right, sir. Lovely morning, isn't it?'

'Yes,' Fergus said. 'Beautiful. Let's hope we have a nice spring. Last year was very disappointing. But you weren't here, of course.'

'No,' Paterson answered. He went on smoking, waiting for the Minister to come to the point. The technique was different to that used in the services. He passed the few moments in speculating on the origins of the word 'diplomatic' and its connotations; tact, social sensitivity. It had passed into common use outside its original limitations. It was used to describe someone with a knack for saying the unpleasant in a painless way. Which was exactly what Fergus Stephenson was about to do. It was so English, so typical to talk about the weather, as if the sudden burst of sunshine made the slightest difference to either of them. He watched Stephenson, and noticed with surprise that a film of sweat showed through his hairline at the forehead.

He was going through agonies, as if he, and not Paterson, were on the wrong side of his imposing desk.

'Have you been happy here? I expect you missed your wife when you first arrived. It's not easy being a grass widower.'

'I'm very happy, thank you,' Richard said. 'And as you say, I'm really settled now that Rachel is here too. She loves Washington; everyone's been very kind to her. Especially your wife. Rachel adores her.'

'She's very fond of Rachel,' Fergus said. It was coming along in the right direction; it was almost as if Paterson knew where he wanted to go and was giving him the cues he needed.

'I had a couple of postings myself when Margaret couldn't join me; I remember I got very lonely and rather bored, especially in the evenings. I expect you did too, when you first arrived.'

Paterson saw at once where he was leading. He had finished his cigarette, and he rubbed it out carefully in the ashtray on the corner of the desk.

'Yes,' he said. If he balled it up now, Stephenson could put a serious mark down against him. It could affect his next job. He made a quick decision, based on his judgement of the man in front of him. The very worst thing would be to lie. He looked at Stephenson.

'I was hellish lonely,' he said abruptly. 'Also, to be honest, things were very uncertain between Rachel and me at that time. She didn't want to be uprooted from England, and I cared about this posting too much to give it up.

'I'm afraid I made rather a fool of myself as a result of all this. Is that what you want to discuss with me, sir?'

'I don't want to discuss it with you at all,' Fergus said. 'The last thing I wish to do is pry into your private affairs, Richard. I have never believed that anyone has that right. Unfortunately, it's out of my hands. You became very friendly with a girl in New York, I understand?'

'Yes,' Paterson admitted. 'I did. I used to fly up and see her regularly, every week. May I ask how you know about this?'

'I'm afraid not,' Fergus shook his head.

'I can probably guess.' Paterson took out his own case, offered it to Stephenson, and the smell of his distinctive Turkish cigarettes drifted through the room. 'A security check was run on me. I suppose I should have expected it.'

'I find it just as nauseating as you do,' Fergus said. 'Absolutely nauseating, the whole idea of spying and playing Peeping Tom on our own staff. But none of us are exempt from it, if that's any consolation to you. What I've got to tell you, Richard, is simply this. Firstly, we don't want any scandal from the Embassy point of view; I mean, your wife is expecting a baby, I hear, and the Ambassador is very sticky about this sort of thing. But apart from that, and what is really important, is that this girl you've been going about with is now considered a security risk. You have got to sever all connection with her. At once.'

He saw the shock and astonishment on the younger man's face; it was a good-looking face, sharp featured and clean cut, rather the type his wife admired. It was changing colour, turning a dull red, the mouth had actually slipped a little open.

'Security? But that's impossible, sir! I don't believe it!'

'I'm afraid that's not relevant,' Fergus remarked. 'I don't believe half the things security tells me either, but I've got to accept their word and act accordingly. Mrs. Farrow is under suspicion. Justified or otherwise, she's been classified as unreliable. If you have anything more to do with her, you will be recalled. Our security will see to that.'

'My God,' Paterson said. He was obviously shaken, and Fergus left him a moment or two to get over it. He wondered whether he had been in love with the girl. His own instincts, sharpened to these things by years of observation in his own home, doubted that the emotional entanglement had been very complex. Men like Paterson were more in love with themselves than with women. He knew the type.

'I'll have to ask you for your assurance. Nothing in writing, just your word.'

'Of course,' Paterson said. He was beginning to feel angry. Unreliable. What in God's name could that mean? What could it have meant in relation to their sleeping together, to his trusting her and talking . . .?

'You can have my word of honour, sir. I'll never see or communicate with her again. We had in fact, broken off,' he added. 'About three weeks ago. My God,' he said again. 'I can't believe it.'

Suddenly his head came up. 'She works for Sam Nielson at UNO,' he said. 'Do our security people know that? That's a very confidential job!'

No, Fergus decided, not a very deep relationship on Paterson's part. Definitely not in love with her. 'I'm sure they know everything necessary about her,' he said.

'Nielson should be told,' Richard was going ahead, angrily pursuing her. At the same time he was trying to remember if Judith had ever asked him questions or shown any interest in his work. She could have ruined him by the association.

'I should leave all that to the bloodhounds,' Fergus said. He was beginning to dislike Paterson.

'She never got anything out of me, I needn't tell you that,' Richard said. 'And to be fair, I'm sure she never tried.'

'She's not a spy,' Fergus interrupted. 'Don't get this out of proportion. She's regarded as a risk, but that has many implications. I should forget all about this, if I were you. I should certainly forget all about Mrs. Farrow.'

'Oh don't worry, I intend to do just that.'

'Thank you, Richard. I hope it hasn't been too unpleasant for you. It's not exactly the sort of interview I enjoy myself.'

'You let me down extremely easily, sir.' Paterson got up. He held out his hand. Fergus shook it. 'Thank you very much for the warning. Have a good day in New York.'

'I shall have a very bad day,' Fergus answered. 'Very dull, sitting as an observer through the frightful opening session of the equally frightful Security Council. I've been invited by our UNO Embassy and I couldn't refuse.

Loder had spent the previous evening with him. He had invited Loder himself, and Margaret Stephenson refused to come down and observe the civilities by having a drink before dinner with him.

'Vulgar little beast—he ought to be out directing the traffic somewhere instead of working in an Embassy with decent people. If you have him in the house, that's your affair. Not mine!' She had said that before she walked out, banging the door after her as usual. Fergus had forborn to remark that it was in fact *her* affair which had brought Loder into their circle in the first place. And Loder's tact, so unusual in a man of his type, had placed Fergus deeply in his debt. It had been one of the worst experiences Fergus could remember, that half an hour with Loder in his office, trying to find the words to tell him that his wife, Margaret, had been informed of confidential information, and had refused to say who gave it to her. All the questions and answers were there, trumpeting themselves in the silences between the two men. Loder had never asked them. There had been a leak. Naturally Mrs. Stephenson didn't want to get the person into trouble. But it wouldn't be difficult to find out who the culprit was. The Minister could leave that side of it to him. Neither he nor Mrs. Stephenson would be troubled over it again. It was so gently done that Fergus over-compensated for his previous dislike of the man. He asked him to dinner. Loder tried to refuse, sensing that this was a way to thanking him for all that he had left unsaid. But Fergus had insisted, and so they had dined together, alone, the night before his interview with Richard Paterson.

To his surprise, Fergus Stephenson had enjoyed it. He gave Loder time to get over being shy, a little on the defensive; he went out of his way to make him feel that he was being a success, and the man began to display himself, cautiously at first, and then with greater confidence. He had a remarkable brain; he had a genuine love for the classics which was so unexpected that Fergus encouraged him to go into a long dissertation about the merits of Tacitus as a social as well as a military historian. It was a curious exposition, pedantry alternating with a vulgarity of expression which somehow gave everything he said originality. Fergus forgot the time; Loder never even thought about it. Both discovered that they shared more than a devotion to classicism; for a time Loder had introduced a course in medieval music during his term at university. Stephenson possessed a fine collection of early Gregorian church music. They ended by listening to some of his records. As he left, Loder had turned and held out his hand. His face was flushed, making an ugly contrast of his reddish hair, his eyes were pinker than usual. He had drunk nothing but water, otherwise Fergus might have thought he had been affected by alcohol.

'I've had a most enjoyable evening,' Loder said. 'The

best evening since I came to Washington. It's quite taken me back to my time after the war. Thank you very much, sir. It's been a real pleasure.'

'And for me too,' Stephenson said. He had meant it. 'You must come again.' He had gone upstairs to his own room; his wife's door was ajar and her reading light was on. Her voice came through, angry and dictatorial.

'Fergus! Don't go to bed yet. Come in!'

He had gone inside, just inside the door, no further. She was sitting up in bed, her face bare and handsome without make-up, the eyes with the eternally contemptuous look in them. 'And how did the evening go?' She mimicked Loder's accent. 'Did he tell you who it was, this time?'

'No,' her husband answered. 'He never mentioned your friend. And I am sure he'll do his best to protect you in every way. So you don't need to worry.'

'I'm not worrying,' she said. 'You're the one who ought to worry, you're the one who'll look the fool, not me.' But she was uneasy; he could tell that by the way she spoke. She was too aggressive to be confident.

'Loder won't ever involve us in a dirty scandal,' Fergus said. 'He's a decent man. I got to know him a little to-night. I like him.'

'Oh?' The eyebrows arched over the bright, hostile blue eyes. 'Oh, really? Don't tell me, darling—he's not one of those?'

He closed the door without answering her. It was the best way. He had never won a verbal battle, because by nature he was peaceful and the ability to wound with words was not a talent he possessed. Or had ever tried to acquire.

When his wife made those kinds of remarks he thought of her simply as an obscene person, and retreated as far from her as he could. He changed his mind about going to bed. He went back downstairs; switched on the lights in his study, and sat down to listen to the last recording he had played for Loder.

It was the Kyrie Eleison, sung by the choir of St. Peter's. It soothed him to think that eight hundred years ago, the armies of the Crusades had chanted that music before battle with the infidel.

• • • • •

The telephone in Judith's office was ringing.

The switchboard operator answered. 'Mrs. Farrow, there's a personal call for you, a Mr. Sverdlov is on the line. Shall I put him through?'

Her pulse bounded; she found herself with one hand pressed against her left breast in a ridiculous gesture, like an actress in an old melodrama.

When the phone rang at the apartment over the weekend she had been prepared to hear his voice. When it didn't, she had begun to think he would never contact her. She had never expected him to call her office.

'Mrs. Farrow? Shall I put the caller through?'

'Yes,' Judith said. 'Thank you.'

Over the telephone his accent was more pronounced.

'Hello,' he said. 'How are you?'

'I'm very well,' she said. 'How are you?'

'I am very well too. We could go on saying this for the rest of the telephone call. I want to see you. Will you have dinner with me tonight?'

She didn't answer. 'He'll contact you,' Loder had said. 'Just promise you'll let me know as soon as he does.'

'No,' she said. 'I don't think we should.' She hadn't even thought of making an excuse.

'Oh. Have you had visitors?'

'Yes. Just as you said.'

'And you are frightened to come?' The tone of voice made her see him as clearly as if he were in the room with her.

'Not at all. Why should I be?'

She thought of Loder again. She heard Sverdlov laugh. 'Then I shall meet you after your work is finished. What time is that?'

'Six—six-thirty. But are you sure it's wise—for you, I mean?'

'Very wise,' he said. 'Very necessary. I have missed teasing you. From Saturday my weekend was very dull.'

'So was mine.' She had begun to smile. 'Where will you be?'

'In a car, round the corner from 98th. At six-thirty exactly.'

'All right. Six-thirty.'

He didn't say goodbye; the line went dead. He had just rung off. She held the receiver for a moment. Her door was open, Nielson must have heard everything she said.

None of it could make any sense to him. She went back into his office, and took the afternoon dictation.

* * * * *

Pavlov Ilyievitch Golitsyn was seventy years old. He had been born in the Ukraine in the sixth year of the last Tsar's reign. His great-grandparents had both been serfs; his grandfather was freed by decree of the liberal autocrat Alexander II whom the revolutionaries had rewarded by blowing him in halves with a bomb. The house where Golitsyn was born was a hovel in a village on the estate of a Muscovite prince whom nobody had ever seen. The enormous palace in a hundred acres of park and gardens had never been occupied within the memory of Golitsyn's father. The Prince owned the land, his father before him had owned the human beings who cultivated it; there was a school which Pavlov attended; unlike most of the children he made an effort to learn. When he left to begin work apprenticed to one of the estate carpenters, he could read and write. There had been eight children, all of them tow-headed, square little Ukrainians, cheerful and independent, barefoot and with stomachs that never knew meat except twice a year. Three girls and five boys; a sister and twin brothers died one winter when Pavlov was twelve. There was no medicine for them, not even extra blankets to keep the dying girl warm. His mother crouched on her knees before a crudely painted ikon of St. Nicholas the Miracle Worker, praying in a trembling monotone for the recovery of her children.

Her son had watched her; often when the whole family knelt with her, he had stayed silent, watching and thinking, wondering whether the lump of wood with its stylised portrait of a dead saint would really be able to save their lives. When they died, within two days of each other, Pavlov Golitsyn became an atheist. He said nothing; it was better to keep quiet about thoughts which touched on the forbidden, like the total submission of the people to the decrees of the Tsar being insupportable tyranny, and the possibility that the after life promised by Orthodox Christianity was a myth.

He learned his trade of carpentry and in his spare time he borrowed books from the school teacher. He read everything, making a determined effort to improve himself. He was fourteen when one summer afternoon the local police arrived and took the teacher and his wife away. A store of revolutionary books and pamphlets was discovered at their house and publicly burned. Nobody found the literature which the teacher had entrusted to Golitsyn. He had buried them in a canvas bag in a ditch behind his home; they remained there for a year. The new teacher was an old man so ignorant that he could hardly read his own text books. Loud mouthed and slovenly, he was unlikely to inspire independent thought or revolutionary activity in the youth of the district. It was Pavlov Golitsyn who performed that office, in the name of the teacher who had been sentenced to twelve years' hard labour in the Siberian mines. His wife had died of the flogging given to both of them after their arrest. But through those early years Golitsyn conducted himself with extreme caution. He had never possessed that reckless ardour that brought so many of his contempararies into the brutal hands of the Tsarist Okhrana. Golitsyn took no risks; he saw no virtue in martyrdom when there was so much work to be done and so few with the education to do it. He was a revolutionary in the mould of his hero, Lenin, one of whose great achievements was to spend only four years in jail during that turbulent political period. At the outbreak of war between Russia and Germany the revolutionary fever abated. The natural patriotism of the people supported the war and endured crippling losses, criminal bungling and inefficiency at the highest level for the first year. By 1917 the Russian soldiers' morale collapsed as a result of rumours that the government was in the control of the German-born Empress, their casualties had assumed horrific proportions, and in many cases, there were no bullets to fire at the enemy. The Army dethroned the Tsar and marched back from the front. One of the leaders of the Volinsky Regiment, which garrisoned St. Petersburg at the time, was Pavlov Golitsyn; the regiment shot its officers, raised the Red flag and joined the revolutionary crowd in the street.

Forty-five years later he was a General, one of the last survivors of early Bolshevism, a man whose caution had kept him safe during the terror reign of Stalin; unswerving, dedicated, immovable in his belief that the ideological war could only be won by total victory, never through peaceful compromise. He had changed very little in mentality from the youth of seventeen who had tied the Red flag to his rifle and led the mob through the streets of St. Petersburg to change the course of the world's history. He thought and felt much the same as an old man as he had done all those years ago. His absolute obedience to the authority of his Party was identical with the submission of his great-grandfather the serf, to the Prince who owned him.

He hated Feodor Sverdlov; he regarded him as one of the most dangerous men in the Intelligence Service, someone whose attitudes had become contaminated through contact with the Capitalist enemy, an advocate of compromise and co-existence. Golitsyn himself had joined the Cheka in 1919, and set about suppressing the counter-revolution with bloody fervour and utter lack of mercy. He regarded his career as a vocation; he had accepted and adopted the methods of Beria without question. The idea that he was supporting a rule of terror as inhuman as the original tyranny he had rejected, could never have occurred to him.

And yet he retained the one quality which had left him in his job after the fall of Beria. He was a follower, rather than a man whose ambitions made him suspect. He was content to serve under Feodor Sverdlov, who had a brilliant reputation and an impressive record during the Hungarian uprising. Personal gain would not have influenced Golitsyn against his chief; political deviation inspired him to the depths of cunning and disloyalty to Sverdlov which previously he had not dared expose to their chief in Moscow. He had the peasant's suspicion of intellectuals; he disliked Sverdlov as a man and a member of a generation with which he felt little sympathy; too young to have known either war, the edges of their belief blunted by liberalism, the old man watched and grumbled silently, but for Sverdlov he waited with infinite patience and implacable hate. He was betraying the Party with the subtelty of the politically corrupt. Now, because of the change in Russian policy, Golitsyn could denounce him with safety. The General was on his way to Sverdlov's office that morning; he walked slowly down the corridor; everyone knew his ponderous foot, thudding along the ground.

This was his last post. He was long past retiring age, but at his plea he had been allowed to stay on in the

States for the full term of his appointment. He was a widower with grown children leading lives independent of him; without work he had nothing to live for, no destination beyond the armchair in transit for the grave. Anna Skriabine had made her report to him after working for Sverdlov for three days. He had studied the copies of Sverdlov's reply to the information passed on to them by 'Blue' and written his comments in the margin. The copies, along with Sverdlov's original report, would go to Dzershinsky Square. The soft line again; cleverly advocated, with the Cambodian venture as a covering excuse. Only a traitor would advise that the relentless Soviet pressure in the Middle East should be lifted. The idea of encouraging Egypt to receive an emissary from Tel Aviv was only further confirmation of Sverdlov's conversion to the Capitalist world. He had said this in his marginal comments.

Sverdlov's decision to take a holiday had given Golitsyn the opportunity to do something which was a vital part of the plan to remove and ultimately indict him. In his absence Golitsyn had been able to get his hands on the secretary Kalinin. Kalinin's loyalty immediately made him suspect; it was easy for Golitsyn to arrange for the young man's return home, where he had been arrested and taken for interrogation. Whatever could be got out of him would be produced at Sverdlov's trial. Golitsyn was not a coward, but he had been anxious about Sverdlov's reaction to losing his secretary and finding him replaced. He had trusted in the attractiveness and charm of the replacement to divert Sverdlov's attention from the true significance of Kalinin's 'illness'.

He had covered himself very carefully, by getting the secretary examined by the Embassy doctor, who obediently pronounced him in danger of a nervous breakdown and prescribed that he be sent home for a long rest. Kalinin had protested angrily against the examination and then the verdict. In the end he had been forcibly sedated and confined to his bed till a car removed him, with male nurses in attendance, to Kennedy International Airport. The doctor's report had been given to Sverdlov on Monday morning, with an explanatory note from Golitsyn. He had waited till the report was read, and then decided to present himself.

Anna Skriabine was one of his best girls; he had chosen

her, rather than another member of the Embassy secretarial staff, because she had been trained to spy on her employers, and also because he knew that she was the type that Sverdlov admired. Sverdlov had a weakness for women; it was well known that there had always been competition among the girls on the staff of his attentions. The attentions were always businesslike and brief. Anna Skriabine needn't survive for long; just long enough to keep him quiet while the experts got at Kalinin in the Lubiyanka.

One of the other items which Golitsyn had collected during Sverdlov's absence was his association with an English woman at the Barbadian hotel. It had been easy to arrange surveillance; they had a permanent man on the island, mainly because political unrest was making the Caribbean an important zone, and Barbados might be expected to follow Trinidad and Guiana on the bloody path of Black Power. So an insignificant little man had been recruited as a 'pick-up'—establishing the nucleus for a proper network on the island when the need arose. He had passed money to the hotel waiter who served Sverdlov, and in turn he bribed the chambermaid. Nothing was found in his room, no visitors from outside were recorded; however every detail of his friendship with Judith Farrow was also on the file Golitsyn had compiled for his superiors in Moscow.

He reached the outer office and walked in. Anna Skriabine was at her desk, filing a thick sheaf of documents. She looked up and got quickly out of her chair.

'Tell Comrade Sverdlov I am here.'

She knocked on the inner door and opened it. He saw Sverdlov behind his desk look at her and smile.

There was a brief exchange between them, and then she held the door open and Golitsyn went in.

They shook hands, he accepted a cigarette and sat down; they faced each other across Sverdlov's desk. He looked extremely well; he had put on some weight, and his expression was humorous. Golitsyn disliked the twisted mouth. It was difficult to decide sometimes whether he smiled or sneered.

'You look very well, Comrade,' he said. 'Your holiday was a success?'

'In more ways than one, but I'll come to that later.

Tell me,' Sverdlov's eyes flickered against a plume of cigarette smoke, 'tell me about Kalinin.'

Golitsyn was ready. 'I made a full report.'

'I've read it. But tell me the details.'

'He was showing signs of strain,' Golitsyn said. 'It was reported by several people that he didn't sleep at night, and he was drinking. Did you know about that, Comrade? No? Well, his room was searched and there were empty bottles under the bed and hidden in his drawers. I became alarmed; in your absence, and knowing he had access to a lot of very confidential information, I asked him not to leave the Embassy until you returned. He refused to give the undertaking. I decided he should be medically examined. The rest you have already read in my report. It's most unfortunate.'

'An understatement,' Sverdlov said. 'He was invaluable to me. I feel responsible for his illness. Perhaps I worked him too hard.'

'Yes,' Golitsyn's grizzled head nodded. 'That was the doctor's opinion. If you are not satisfied with Skriabine—I can replace her with a man if you prefer.'

'She does very well,' Sverdlov said. 'Her standards are high. It may be that I shall keep her permanently. Maybe not. A man in this position is more reliable. Women tend to get too involved.' He watched Golitsyn through his half closed eyes. He was like a rock. He had placed his spy, a specially manufactured arsenic pellet coated in sugar. It wouldn't do to pretend to swallow it too quickly.

'I have seen the reports you compiled during the two weeks,' Sverdlov said. 'Including that very interesting contribution from "Blue". I have made my recommendations.'

'I saw them,' Golitsyn said.

'You disagree?' The question was asked quietly. Two years ago the old General would not have dared to tell the truth. Two years ago Sverdlov held the power of life and death over him and everybody in the Embassy, the Ambassador included. But no longer. He didn't know it, but now the executioner's pistol was pointing at *his* neck. Golitsyn answered with confidence.

'I don't think we should encourage any peace moves in the Middle East, Comrade. I think we should carry the war against Capitalism into every corner where Imperialist influence survives.'

'You don't consider that if Cambodia becomes a full-scale American intervention, we are inviting the participation of China . . . I don't believe we can afford to tie ourselves to an Arab-Israel war any longer. We have to keep the Far Eastern sphere independent of Chinese influence. That is my point, Comrade. Whether the Jews murder the Arabs or the Arabs kill the Jews is not as important to us as the maintenance of Soviet power against the aggression of Maoism. Nothing will alter my conviction on that. I'm surprised you don't share it.'

'I don't believe we can't solve our differences with Socialist China,' Golitsyn answered. He was being put to the test, and he felt sure enough to respond truthfully. 'Our general aims are the same; the misunderstandings which arose were due to leadership errors in the past. Too soft an attitude towards our true enemies. The Capitalist world has to be destroyed, Comrade Sverdlov. Our way of life and theirs cannot co-exist. The phrase itself is treachery to Revolutionary Socialism. We must overcome their system if our own is to survive. We should ally more closely with China in this common aim.'

'I don't believe that the aim is common,' Sverdlov said. He too was putting his case; if the old enemy opposite him has any sense of global reality, he just might see what Sverdlov saw. He might, but it was doubtful. That type had never seen beyond the precepts of their Bolshevik upbringing. For that reason it has been necessary to kill so many of them after the Revolution was established.

'I believe that China is what she has always been—a nationalistic power with Imperialist traditions that have not been fundamentally changed by Marxism. I believe that if you look at the position historically, China has not progressed so much as turned backwards. She has rejected her immediate past, ceased being a federation of disunited provinces, ruled by gangsters like Chiang Kai-shek, and become what she was eight centuries ago. A huge, hungry land mass, with the largest population on earth, ruled by Mao Tse-tung, Emperor of China. They will certainly destroy the Capitalist world and rule over what is left. If anything is . . . But equally, they will turn upon us, as their only surviving contender for absolute power. I love my country, General; I don't believe it's possible to ride the Chinese tiger; I don't believe it's possible to get close enough to try, without being eaten alive.'

Golitsyn shook his head. He had been listening carefully, without hearing the sense of what was said. He had only noticed that Sverdlov had attacked China without referring once to the iniquities of Western Capitalism.

'You see it this way,' Golitsyn said. 'But I do not.'

'Then we agree to disagree,' Sverdlov said. 'But that will not prevent us continuing the morning's work. Among ourselves at least, we know how to co-exist.'

He pressed his buzzer. Anna Skriabine appeared in the doorway.

'Bring some tea for the General,' he said. 'And get the Scotch whisky and a glass out of that cupboard over there.'

Golitsyn watched in silence while his tea was brought, teaming in a glass with a silver holder. He sipped it, while the girl poured out a measure of whisky for Sverdlov. He reached up and took the bottle from her. He poured on until the neat alcohol was within two inches of the top. He swallowed some as if it was water. The girl went out, she moved with grace and without making noise. Sverdlov thought it was more like a glide, as if she operated on ball bearings. After three days he was beginning to hate her.

'I wonder who recruited "Blue",' he said suddenly.

'I've heard it said that it was you, Comrade Sverdlov,' Golitsyn answered. He had always believed this. It was also believed among Sverdlov's subordinates that his extraordinary promotion was due to his acquisition of a brilliant Western traitor.

'I don't even know "Blue's" identity, Sverdlov said. 'Nobody knows that, except Panyushkin. That's the measure of his importance. Nobody else who worked for us has been so well protected.'

'It's a wise precaution,' Golitsyn said. He was watching the whisky level fall in Sverdlov's glass. That was another degenerate sign; he wouldn't have criticised him for drinking vodka. 'It makes certain that nobody on our side can betray him. We had defectors who knew about Fuchs and Nunn May; that was a terrible mistake.'

' "Blue" is our best source of information on so many subjects,' Sverdlov said. 'And everything he passes on is of the highest priority. He knows what is important. I've seen a dozen of these "Blue" files in six months, and all have been extremely well compiled. Not an unnecessary word and the quality of his opinions is so high.'

'And the nationality?' Golitsyn probed. He would have liked to know whether Sverdlov was telling the truth; whether he in fact did not know who the mysterious 'Blue' really was.

'I don't know. Nobody knows. Now, to change the subject but not the object, I have had some good luck on my trip to Barbados. I have made a useful contact.'

Golitsyn waited. He had an instinct of imminent disappointment.

'I met a woman on the island,' Sverdlov said. 'She has a very confidential job, and several contacts with the British Embassy in Washington. We became friends.' He smiled his crooked smile, and finished the whisky.

'I shall resume the friendship here, I believe I will be able to recruit her.'

'That will be very useful,' Golitsyn said glumly. Mrs. Farrow would have to be expunged from his report on Sverdlov. She would be a credit, instead of a minus. At the end of an hour Sverdlov dismissed him. He put a call through to Judith's office in the UNO building. He could sense that Anna Skriabine was listening in the outer room. He caught the four o'clock plane to New York.

When Judith came out it was six-thirty-five; she turned left and walked the half block down to the corner where Sverdlov had said he would wait. There was a dark green Mercedes parked at the sidewalk. As she came near the window slid down and he put his head out.

'Hello,' he said. The door opened and she got inside. He held out his hand and she gave hers to be shaken. He held it, and then kissed it, palm upwards, smiling triumphantly at her afterwards.

She ignored him, and drew her hand away. The game was beginning between them as if there had not been more than an hour's interruption.

'Have you been waiting long?'

'Twenty minutes. I enjoyed myself showing my Soviet passport to the traffic policemen. They wanted to arrest me for parking so badly, and they couldn't. You look very pretty this evening. Would you like a drink?'

'Yes, I would,' Judith said. 'I've been working very hard all day. Take your arm away, Mr. Sverdlov, necking on the public streets isn't allowed.'

'Anything is allowed in this degenerate country.' He

started the car and the Mercedes slipped into the traffic stream.

'You are not trying to tell me that when they permit copulation on the stage, they object to an honest Soviet citizen kissing a pretty girl in a car?'

'No,' Judith said. 'But it stopped you trying, didn't it?'

'I will remember that,' Sverdlov promised. 'I will pay you back.'

They went to a downtown bar on 67th Street; it was a dim, intimate place with tiny tables and phoney Hawaiian decor, full of plastic palms and piped hula music. He insisted on ordering an alcoholic atrocity in a coconut shell for her, and laughing unkindly at her attempts to get through the fruit and foliage to drink it. She looked very pretty, very elegant. It was a different person to the casual, bare-legged girl in Barbados. She was chic and uncluttered by jewellery or the status symbol fur coat. She looked a little older; he didn't mind that at all.

'What are you looking at?' Judith asked him. He too was different; the same thoughts were passing through her mind. She had never seen him in a suit before. It was dark, and his shirt was plain white with an unpatterned tie. In spite of his intimacy he seemed somehow on edge.

'At you,' he said. 'You look different to when we were on the island. Very competent, very efficient. Have another coconut.'

'No thanks, one was enough. I take it you are making a criticism, is that it?'

'No, no! If I said I prefer you in a bikini, is that criticism? You look very pretty. I told you that in the car. Don't you like me in my working suit?'

'I'm not sure,' Judith said. 'Give me a little time to get used to it. I'm surprised by one thing. You're not wearing a red tie.'

He laughed. 'I'm in disguise. I'm a Russian spy, didn't you realise that?'

'Well, if I don't by now, I never will,' she said. 'You were quite right about my visitors. I was met at the airport—would you believe that?'

'I'm sorry.' Sverdlov reached over and held her hand. She didn't try to move away. 'Tell me what happened. But first, another drink. Whisky for me, and the same for you. No more coconuts. I only did it to tease you.'

'I know.' Judith looked at him. 'That's why I was determined to drink it!'

'At the airport,' Sverdlov murmured, almost to himself. 'That was very quick of them. What happened?'

'I had an interview; there were two men, they drove me back to my flat and came in with me. I was furious.' The memory of Loder made her angry again. He went on holding her hand, watching her and saying nothing. 'They told me we'd been seen together. Why do you smile, Feodor? It wasn't funny, I can tell you!'

'I'm sure,' he said quietly. 'I didn't mean to smile. I'm sure we were "seen" together by half a dozen British and American observers. Please, go on.'

'The man who did the interviewing—it was more like interrogating—he said that you would get in touch with me again and I was to let him know immediately you did.'

'I see,' he said. 'And have you done that? Have you let him know we are together?'

'No.' Judith opened her bag, searching for a cigarette; it gave her an excuse to get away from him, and to look down, avoiding the light eyes with their peculiar, penetrating glance. 'No, I didn't do anything.'

'Did he say anything else,' Sverdlov asked. He saw her hesitate.

'Not really; just the usual about not mixing with Russians, my job being confidential, you can imagine the sort of thing.'

'Only too well.' He sounded relaxed, almost amused.

'And now I will fill in all that you have decided not to tell me,' he went on. 'He said I was a dangerous Soviet agent, and that I was only interested in you because I hoped to recruit you as a spy. You know it's charming to see a woman blush like that. Never try and lie to me.' He shook his head. 'I can see straight through you. Like glass. Is that what you think? Do you believe him?'

'I wouldn't be here if I did,' Judith defended herself. Then she faced him, suddenly she wanted to be reassured, to have something more than her own instinct to rebut Loder and what he had insinuated.

'It isn't true, is it?'

'No!' Sverdlov met her look. 'Ah, what a bad interrogator you would be—you stare into my face to see if I am lying. People can lie with their eyes. But I am telling you the truth. I'm not going to seduce you and then persuade you, or blackmail you into telling me what Mr. Nielson says to U Thant, even though I have told my own people that I am going to do this.'

She turned to him in horror. 'You told your own people . . .'

'Yes. I said I hoped to recruit you to work for us. That way I can meet you whenever I want, without suspicion.'

'I don't know what to do,' she said. The whole thing is getting completely out of proportion.'

'The first thing you must do,' he said, 'is to inform your Intelligence man that we have been together. Otherwise, you could be in great trouble. I am serious. Give me your hand to hold. Let me teach you the first lesson in these little games. Always tell the truth as long as possible. Then when the times change and you have to lie, there's a chance you will be believed.'

'You said yourself I'm a bad liar,' she reminded him.

'Never mind, I will teach you. I am an expert!'

'You say the most extraordinary things about yourself. Why should I believe a word you say, after you've admitted—no, sorry, *boasted*, that you can lie like a trooper?'

'Like a what—what does that mean? Trooper?'

'It's just an expression, it doesn't mean anything really. Besides, I'm not going to lie to anyone. If I see you, that's my business. I'm not doing anything disloyal and I never would. All right, I'll say we've met, and that I was right and they were wrong.'

'They won't believe you,' Sverdlov said. 'You'll be followed, watched. Do as I tell you. Play their game for them and we can have our evenings together. Maybe a weekend?' The eyes glanced sideways at her, slyly.

'No weekends,' Judith said.

He pulled a face. 'Another whisky for me, and one for you. Then we will go to a nice dark place for some dinner. You like to dance with me?'

'No dancing,' Judith said. She leaned back in her seat and smiled at him; she felt relaxed and warm. 'You behave too badly; it's not safe.'

'I don't behave badly,' he protested. 'You won't let me! You look happier now.'

'I need food,' she said. 'What was in that filthy coconut thing? It's gone to my head.' He put his head back and laughed out loud. A couple sitting near turned round to stare at them. It suddenly occurred to Judith that very few people found life amusing enough to laugh like that in a public place.

'What's the matter—what's so funny?'

'Vodka.' He banged his knee in delight. 'It was vodka! Russia's secret weapon!'

When they left the bar it was dark and a cold wind blew. He put his arm round her in the car. 'I am glad to see you.' She couldn't see his face, but she sensed a change of mood. He was no longer joking.

'I'm glad to see you too,' she said. To her surprise he didn't try to kiss or hug her, making fun of her resistance. He started the engine and drove uptown towards 57th.

The restaurant was a smart, dimly lit sequel to the bar; Sverdlov had a table booked at the back of the room. There was a blaring discotheque which made conversation impossible except where they were sitting. Judith brushed her hair in the powder room, and examined her lipstick. When she came back he took her arm and they went to their table. He was a very proprietary man; he was always establishing physical contact as if it gave him some kind of ownership. Judith had noticed it before. It seemed natural to him. It was his way; if she tried to disengage and be independent he would have made her feel ridiculous. Richard Paterson had never taken her arm in a restaurant, or run her across a windy street, hugging her round the shoulders. He had never liked intimacy outside of sex. They had never met in a place like 21, or La Popotte, where Sverdlov had chosen, because Richard was afraid they would be seen. Mostly they hid out in chichi little restaurants downtown, or risked a nightclub on a Monday night, always a dead day in the social calendar. If she looked back on the six months she had lived with him, she had spent most of their time together in her flat, letting him make love to her. She lit a cigarette and watched the dancers; Sverdlov was looking at the wine list.

If it had been Richard and not him beside her, she wouldn't have been sitting so, relaxed and able to leave the silence. He had always demanded full attention, subtly suggesting that it would never do if he were allowed to get bored.

She would have been watching him, going over the wine list, anxious and subservient, because she was only his mistress and probably more in love with him than he with her. There was no danger of that situation with the Russian. He had no hold over her, because she had been wise enough to see the risk involved.

She would never give way to him, and begin the inevitable downward swing in their relationship. She had no idea, at that moment, where the relationship would lead, or how it could be defined. It was more than friendship. He wasn't a man with whom a woman could be friends.

'Stop thinking about that dull Englishman.'

She glanced up at him. He was watching her, unsmiling.

'How did you know?'

'When I first saw you,' Sverdlov said, 'you had a look on your face. It was very unhappy. You have the same look now. That's how I know. Come and dance with me.'

He was not a good dancer; he rejected the selfish concept of modern exhibitionism; he neither gyrated, nor bucked in imitation of the sex act. He caught hold of Judith, squeezed her tight against him, and hardly moved at all.

At one moment, after they had been on the tiny floor for about ten minutes, she heard him speak to someone. A couple were just behind them. She couldn't understand what Sverdlov said; it was a murmur, and not in English.

'A man from our Embassy,' he explained. 'With his friend, she is American. I've asked them to come to our table for a drink. In about half an hour, when we are tired.'

'Half an hour? Feodor, stop blowing in my ear.'

'Red would be a good colour for you,' he said. 'You are always staying stop. Madame Molotov. No. *No*. NO. Why don't you become a Communist, and come to Russia with me?'

'No thank you.' Judith twisted her head backwards, away from him. 'Red doesn't suit me; politically I'm true Blue.'

'True Blue,' Sverdlov repeated it. 'What is that? Is it a political joke?'

'No, it's quite serious to some people. True Blue means an ultra Conservative. It used to describe the heroes in Victorian novels; all loyal to the Queen and the Empire.'

'That's funny,' he said. 'Blue. True Blue. I must remember that.'

When they were sitting down, Judith was able to find

the other Soviet diplomat and his girl friend. They were at a less exclusive table, half way to the edge of the dance floor. She thought the man looked over at Sverdlov as if he was waiting for a signal. He got up so quickly that it must have been given, though she didn't see it. The girl with him followed more slowly, picking her way towards them. He was a short, dark man, younger than Sverdlov, with spectacles. His companion was also young, and blonde, with heavily made up eyes and a mouth painted livid pink. Sverdlov introduced them; she heard the name Memenov, and the American girl was Miss Something or other; the discotheque was giving their eardrums hell at that time. The couple sat down; the younger man seemed awkward. He pulled out a chair and perched, rather than sat. He watched Sverdlov with unnatural concentration, giving one quick glance at Judith and a brief smile.

'His English is not very good,' Sverdlov explained.

'Excuse me,' the Russian said to her and lifted himself slightly from his seat. 'I speak only little.'

Judith wondered how he managed with the blonde; so far she had said nothing beyond hello, and she was looking round the room, paying no attention to any of them. 'You will excuse us if we speak Russian?' Sverdlov asked Judith.

'Of course.'

He leaned close to her and said under his breath, 'Only a few minutes; he won't stay long.'

A drink was brought for them, and Judith copied the American girl and relaxed, letting the two men get on with their conversation. As Sverdlov said, they didn't linger for long. He talked, and the younger man listened; there seemed to be little in the way of exchange. And she was interested to see how Sverdlov changed during the ten minutes the other man was with him. He leaned forward, talking quietly, but there was no smile, no easy gestures; he did not offer him a cigarette. In the pink light his face looked hard and the twisted mouth was grim. It was a different man to the one she knew. There must have been a second signal, a dismissal as discreet, but decisive, as the summons. The younger man swallowed his drink in one, and was on his feet, drawing out his girl friend's chair. She took her glass away with her.

'I am sorry,' Sverdlov said. 'That was very dull for you.

I thought the girl might have talked to you, but she had no conversation.'

'As he doesn't speak English, it wouldn't matter if she had or not.'

'He doesn't want her for talking,' Sverdlov said. 'She is good at other things. And harmless. We know all about her; she likes presents, not money. She likes a fur jacket, expensive handbags, a gold cigarette case. These she can show her friends, to prove how good she is with men.'

'And how does a good Soviet Socialist get the money to buy fur coats and gold cigarette cases? It sounds a lot like Capitalism to me,' Judith said.

'I give him the money,' Sverdlov explained. He was himself again; the mocking look and cynical grin were reassuring to see. Judith hadn't liked that other aspect of him. 'I pay his expenses, because he is a good man, and loyal to me. He does what I tell him. I have told him to do something now, and I know he will do it.' He leaned back, his arm slid along the banquette; without Judith knowing he twisted a strand of her hair in his fingers. 'Here is our food. It should be good; he recommended this place, because of the food.'

'What did you tell him to do?'

Sverdlov was eating. He didn't answer immediately, and Judith put down her own fork and said: 'Now I know what you're thinking. I just wondered, I'm not asking for anybody else. You don't have to tell me.'

'I can always lie,' he said. 'You don't speak Russian, you wouldn't know. He is going back to Russia on Wednesday. I asked him to find out something for me; about my secretary, who was sick while I was in Barbados. He was sent home. I have a new one who is not so good.'

' "He"—you have male secretaries? No girls?'

'I prefer men. They're more efficient; but now I have a girl. Very very pretty.'

'Lucky you.' Judith pushed her plate aside.

'So pretty,' he went on, 'with golden hair and blue eyes, like a doll. Are you jealous?'

'No; she's probably fifty, wears bifocals and has a huge bottom.'

'You are jealous,' Sverdlov said. 'But I tell you, I don't like her as much as you. I don't like blondes.'

He smiled at Judith and patted her knee. He had arranged to meet Alexis Memenov in the restaurant, that was why he had brought her there. It would look natural, to see a fellow staff member and invite him for a drink. He had lied when he said Memenov didn't speak English. But he had told the truth when he said he had entrusted the enquiry about Kalinin to him. Memenov was one of the young coterie in the Embassy, whose views on future Soviet policy agreed with Sverdlov's own opinions. He was an adherent, although the word was too strong to describe anything so tenuous as an instinctive sympathy of view. Memenov had spent two years in New York and eighteen months in London before that; he knew Western life and could see it without the violent prejudice of the older men, nurtured on the hate and blind suspicion prevalent in Cold War diplomatic service. He had gone out among the enemy, and remained a perfectly convinced and loyal Communist Party member, as well as an extremely patriotic Russian. He had learned to sleep with an American girl and enjoy the experience, without a sensation of national betrayal because he preferred her techniques to the inhibitions of his wife. He had learned that it was possible to co-exist, and like Sverdlov he believed sincerely that the victory of Soviet Socialism was a matter of course, provided that the process was not accelerated by means of a global war. He was not officially on Sverdlov's staff; but he had undertaken several delicate, though minor missions for him, when he had not wanted to use his own subordinates. The arranged meeting, and the few instructions passed across the table, were the safest means of investigating Kalinin's illness and the truth of what Golitsyn and the doctor had told him.

The loss of his secretary worried Sverdlov like a toothache. He knew Golitsyn hated him, he knew the old man watched and waited, even attempted a little private spying, in the hope that one day he could find a serious fault. But to replace Kalinin with a 'dove', showed an alarming degree of confidence. He had never dared show his disapproval of Sverdlov before, even though Sverdlov was aware of it, as he was aware of everything which concerned his organisation and the working of the Embassy. Only Golitsyn's position, not unlike that of a national monument to the old Revolutionary Secret Police and the early fight against international Capitalist attacks on the Soviet, only his reputation and imminent retirement from Washington, prevented Sverdlov from ordering his recall.

He was a young man, tough and confident in his ability to carry an old relic of the past, and survive his antiquated hatred. But now, suddenly the past had overtaken the present and was threatening to assume the aspect of the future. At home the leadership had changed, the moderates had lost temporary control; Russia was in a private ferment to determine the ultimate direction of her policy, both domestic and cosmic. Sverdlov's advice remained consistent; his power and his position could not be challenged on any legitimate count.

He would not serve, nor appear to connive at, the ideological form to which his wife adhered so passionately. Elena was of the very stuff of martyrs; it was this almost mystical obstinacy which had attracted him when they first met. He had seen it as a challenge, and believed that no woman could truly maintain it, without some leavening of humour or of female weakness. Equally he was prepared to be strong, ready to exercise the authority his State had given him to suppress a counter-revolution with the tank and the execution squad.

He had done this in Hungary, and it had thrust him upwards on the ladder of promotion and political influence. He had not minded shedding blood; he was Russian and the tradition was old, far older than the principles learned at the Intelligence School in Leningrad. The satellites of the Soviet Union could not be permitted to reject her or to seek independence. Sverdlov had done what his ancestors did in Poland in the service of the Tsars. He had put down the revolt of a subject people. In his way, he had reverted to his historical type as truly as the blindly obedient Golitsyn. For a year, after the Hungarian uprising, he and Elena had been truly happy.

It was an indication of the change which had taken place in him, that if she had been transported to the seat beside him, in place of Judith Farrow, he wouldn't have been capable of making conversation with her.

Memenov was lucky. He would go home with his girl. Sverdlov looked down at Judith and smiled. She had courage; silly courage, which could only get her into trouble. He couldn't imagine anyone at home refusing to do what one of his men suggested, like reporting on a Western diplomat they had picked up. But the circumstances were different. Trouble for Judith Farrow wouldn't mean imprisonment and a sentence of ten to fifteen years' hard labour. It was not a pleasant comparison, and he discarded it. She had a pretty chin, and a narrow neck, which he wanted to stroke with his fingers. He had seen her near enough naked on the Barbadian beach to know that without her clothes she would be smooth and beautiful to the hands. He wished that he could have taken her home somewhere.

He felt so disinclined to go back to the UNO Embassy alone, that he dragged out the meal with a dessert he didn't want, and urged more coffee and liquers upon her.

They danced, and he forgot his tension and uneasiness in taking little liberties with her, retreating only, as he whispered in her ear, like all good Russians, to advance another step. By the end of the evening he was happy, as if nothing had changed before he went to Barbados, and everything was the same when he came back.

'Good night.' He had come to the entrance of the apartment with her. She had refused to kiss him in the car, and he hadn't persisted in case she became angry. 'When will you see me again?'

'Feodor, listen to me for a minute.' Judith paused at the door, one hand on his arm. A yellow light burned above their heads. It made them look garish and unreal.

'There's no good your going on with me. I'm not having an affair with you. It's just a waste of your time. And think of all the complications; your people watching you, mine going after me. I feel I'm leading you on, and I don't think it's fair. We ought to say goodbye. Properly.'

Under the ugly light his face changed.

'You don't want to see me again? What have I done?'

'I've tried to tell you . . .' She shrugged at him helplessly. 'You haven't done anything. But I'm just not—not prepared to see you and let you think I'm going to give in and go to bed with you. I'm not. Never.'

'Because of the Englishman?'

'Yes. I've had enough. I've been married, I've lost my husband, I've had a man living with me for six months who was just having fun at my expense. And now there's you. No, Feodor. I'm not coming out with you again.'

He did something she had never imagined he might do. He stepped back from her, turned round and walked quickly down the steps. Shaken, Judith put the key in the door. His car drove away, and he had not even looked back.

When she got into the apartment, Nancy's door was open, the bed not slept in. She often stayed with a man for the night if she felt inclined. Lucky, hard-headed Nancy. She wouldn't have sent him away and come back to an empty flat and cried herself to sleep. She was still crying when the telephone rang beside her bed. She was so startled that she picked it up, and said hello, her voice thick with tears.

'I don't want to sleep with you,' he said into her ear. 'You can stop crying. I'll be outside your office at lunch-time tomorrow.'

Judith was saying no, when she realised he had rung off. She got up and heated some hot milk to drink, made a grimace at herself in the mirror as she got back to bed, and fell asleep determined not to leave the UNO building in the lunch hour.

## CHAPTER SIX

'I find it quite revolting,' Margaret Stephenson said. 'You and that dreadful little man, lunching together. What has come over you?'

He had called in on her before leaving his office in the Chancery, to say that he would not be at home for lunch. For someone who professed such contempt for him, his wife showed an inconsistent degree of curiosity about his movements. He had been forced to admit that he was meeting Loder in a restaurant in the centre of the city.

'I could have invited him here,' he said. 'But I didn't think you'd approve of the idea.'

'Approve! I've got one of those dreary wives' luncheons—I don't want you here either, let alone that creature. What have you got in common with him?'

'Nothing in particular,' Fergus said. 'I feel he's rather a lonely person. Nobody pays much attention to him here. and he's got a good brain. Which is rather rare these days.'

'Oh my God, hearts and flowers again.' She turned away from him. 'He's just a policeman in plain clothes. I must remember to look at his feet next time I see him; I'm sure they're enormous.'

Fergus said nothing; he understood his wife's dislike of Loder. He had offended her initially because she was a snob, and he refused to crawl. Now he was in a position to look down upon her because of her private activities, and worst of all, he had obviously deprived her of the services of her lover. Fergus knew this because she was irritable and more bitchy than normal. It was always a sign that she was in between men.

He opened the door and paused before leaving. In a way he was sorry for her. She had spent twenty years trying to punish him for his failure as a man, and only succeeded in destroying herself. He was conscious that the whole thing was ultimately his fault.

'Have a good lunch,' he said. 'Who's coming?'

'Cyphers, Personnel, Military, Navy and Air. All ghastly, except Rachel Paterson. Thank God it's only once a year.'

'You're very good with them,' he said, hoping to please her.

'I should be, I've had enough practice in the last twenty years. I keep to simple things like the Sports Day, the nursery school . . . what will everybody do on their next leave. Christ, it's unbelievable how dull they all are.' She heard the door close as he went out and stopped pretending to open letters.

One was from a friend, hoping to glean an invitation to stay during a coming trip to the States that summer; another was a very short note from her second son saying he had run out of money. Damn Fergus. Damn him for trying to play the diplomat with her, of all people. 'You're very good with them.' As if she was a bloody Third Secretary's wife, spreading her wings for the first time as hostess. Of course she was good with the subordinate wives. She had made it her business to be; she knew how to be pleasant, condescending and formidable all at the same time. She was not liked or disliked, but she was held in awe, and that was what she wanted. She thought of Loder, and the blood rushed up, staining her neck a patchy red. He must have found out that she had been sleeping with his own assistant, Joe MacLeod. MacLeod had not kept an appointment with her for three weeks. His excuses were polite but unshakable. He was on duty, he had a previous engagement. He had not turned up twice, and she had spent over an hour in the room they rented at a motel ten miles out by the Potomac, waiting for him. He was much younger than she was, and he was a strenuous lover, devoid of sentiment or emotional after-thought. It had been an excellent arrangement; when it came to bed she was prepared to waive her class attitudes. MacLeod was no more of a gentleman than Loder, but he was six feet two inches tall, pleasant looking and very fit. He was the first very young man she had got involved with, and now that he had backed away, she felt the full humiliation of what she had done in selecting him. It was a bad sign, to go for youth like that. It was a real indication of age in a woman when she started lusting after her sons' generation.

But he was discreet; she could be sure that there wouldn't be any gossip, any vulgar hints among his colleagues. She had always chosen men who had more to lose by opening their mouths than to gain by a masculine boast. Men who were ambitious, and anxious not to make an enemy, after they had been dismissed.

Now, it was her turn. And all because of her husband talking to that scruffy little brute, taking a high-minded attitude about security. She ripped open her letters one by one, read them through without pleasure, and clipped them together to be answered. She took a cigarette from her box and searched unsuccessfully for matches. Her desk lighter didn't work; she knew this but she tried instinctively. It gave no spark. It was one of the old-fashioned variety, a large presentation piece from the staff at some other Embassy, given to her and Fergus years ago. She swore, and began opening all the desk drawers. No matches. It would have been easier to replace the cigarette, but suddenly smoking it had become important. She must be able to find a light. It was too ridiculous not to be able to have a cigarette when she wanted one so badly.

She got up and went downstairs. Fergus's study was next door to hers. It was a meticulously arranged and maintained working room. There were no concessions to his taste, and he had rejected her attempt to decorate it when they first arrived. There was a huge, business-like desk, a hideous green angle-poise lamp, bookcases from the floor to the ceiling, and a small filing cabinet. A photograph of her and their children was the only touch which she privately described, with nausea, as 'homely'. There were cigarettes in a small shagreen box, another present, but no desk lighter and no matches. She opened two drawers before she found anything. The lighter was right at the back, packed neatly in a box, and inside a chamois leather sleeve. She took it out and looked at it; she had never seen Fergus use it before. It looked new, and it had the special sheen of high carat gold. How the hell had he come by it—he never bought expensive nicknacks for himself. She pressed the tiny catch and it burst into flame. She lit the cigarette, turning the lighter over in both hands. It was gold; she could see the hallmark on the bottom. Beautifully chased, long and elegantly shaped. She examined the box. Tiffany. Very expensive indeed. Certainly, Fergus had not bought it for himself. When the idea formulated, she literally swallowed smoke, and coughed. He had somebody. Not a woman—she was sure of that. By Christ, it had better not be a woman, after denying her, if he had been able to do it with somebody else . . . That couldn't have been borne. She rejected it instantly; that just couldn't even be considered. There was a limit to what she could take in a marriage to a homosexual. Normality with another woman went beyond that limit. It must be a man. Fergus must have a man, a lover. A rich lover. She stood there in the study, the cigarette hanging in the corner of her mouth, holding the lighter like a talisman. Her hands were shaking. After all these years, cheating and humiliating him, believing that he lived a eunuch's life; *she* had been deceived, at the end. He could afford to be browbeaten and insulted by her when she felt like it, because he had a refuge of his own.

She took the lighter back to her own room. She hesitated, wondering where to put it. He would miss it, and start searching. He would never look in her handbag. She put it in a zipped compartment and closed the fastener. When he couldn't find it, he might have to mention it to her. And that would be her moment.

She looked at her watch; she was still shaking slightly. It was eleven-thirty. She went downstairs to see that the flowers had been arranged and to see the housekeeper about the menu for dinner. They had eighteen guests that evening.

. . . . .

'It's an interesting situation,' Loder said. 'Very interesting; how long will the bastard string this girl along before he tries to pull her in?'

'That must surely depend upon the girl.' Fergus Stephenson sipped his wine. It was a fine, light Riesling, which he considered paid a delicate compliment to the fish. Loder appeared to enjoy his; he was eating steadily and talking at the same time. The subject had come up because Fergus had mentioned his interview with Richard Paterson. Loder had conveyed his impression of the Group Captain without saying much. The discussion about Judith Farrow followed naturally.

'I know,' he said, 'that you don't like this business much. I know you think it's dirty work, poking around other people's private lives. But it has to be done, Mr. Stephenson, and somebody has to do it.'

'Of course it's necessary,' Fergus said. 'It's just distasteful. I feel sorry for this girl, Mrs. Farrow. If she's telling the truth this relationship is perfectly innocent.'

'Oh she's certainly doing that,' Loder admitted. 'I wasn't sure, but I am now. She's not up to anything, but it's inevitable that before long she'll get the squeeze put on. I've told her, but she won't accept it. She can be an awkward piece, too.' The word made Fergus smile; it should have made him wince. He liked Loder more and more. How did the French describe such a relationship—*nostalgie de la bou.* It was an intranslatable description of the impulse to frequent an environment and cultivate friends of baser degree than oneself. A wish to roll in the mud. A poor, inadequate attempt to turn the succinct French phrase into clumsy English. However, true of him or not, he found Loder a refreshing experience.

'You're sure this man Sverdlov is going to try and blackmail her, or exert some pressure?' he asked. 'It couldn't be just—well, a friendship?'

'Not with him,' Loder said. 'We know all about him, Mr. Stephenson. He's the unfriendly kind. You know, it took some time to put him in the right slot. He was here about eighteen months before we connected him with the Sverdlov who was their trigger man in Hungary.'

'How did you find out?'

'Just a check; one of those things we ought to do more often and don't, because we've got so much unimportant bumf to deal with. I looked up his record. He'd been promoted from Lieutenant to Colonel inside two years, round about the time of the uprising. Then a rotten posting to Copenhagen. The jump was in the wrong direction, the promotion spelled him out as a big fish, Copenhagen was a backwater. Copenhagen wasn't a serious posting, just a blind, a rest period to let the heat cool off him after Budapest. He was four years there, with a stint in East Berlin and a gap which must have meant he was in Moscow. Then he comes here. Assistant to that old Army mule Golitsyn. I tracked back on him, and I found that he and the Sverdlov who cleaned up in Budapest were one and the same man. That made him K.G.B. and in my opinion, the General's boss, not his subordinate. So it's not likely he's wining and dining Mrs. Farrow because he likes blue eyes, is it?'

'No,' Stephenson said. 'If he's that sort of man, it obviously isn't.' Loder lit a cigarette. 'He's a bloody butcher,' he said. 'He murdered the Hungarians; treason trials, executions, the lot. I haven't told her yet, but when the crunch comes, I'm going to. Then we'll see how she takes it. She may just be shocked enough to work for us against him.'

'But wouldn't that be very dangerous?' Fergus looked at him with surprise.

'Yes, very. But that's part of the price for getting mixed up with these people. I'm going to try and see she pays it.'

'If you don't mind my saying so,' Fergus said, 'it *is* a dirty business. And I do feel sorry for her.'

'Anyway I've kept the Americans happy,' Loder said. 'They're leaving this one to us. I send regular reports, and keep Farrow under watch. From what you say, Group Captain Paterson won't be seeing her again, so that's the main problem out of the way.'

'He practically offered to inform against her,' Fergus said. 'But he couldn't think of anything to say. I really don't admire him for it. My wife doesn't think much of him either.' He mentioned Margaret from time to time, just to keep up the appearance of normality.

'She's a good judge,' Loder said. 'But he's no security risk. In my judgement, he'd turn in his own mother if it threatened his career.'

Coffee was brought to them, and Stephenson ordered a small glass of William; the sharp scent of pears drifted into Loder's nostrils. He noticed how moderate the Minister was; he drank very little, but always the best; he smoked lightly and never between courses. He had chosen a liqueur that Loder had never even heard of; he rather liked the smell. A curious man; gentle, but by no means without cynical appreciation. A scholar, but lacking in arrogance and self esteem. Conversely when Loder was with him, he was stimulated to give his best. He would never have believed it possible to like someone in Stephenson's position. Now he enjoyed a friendship which was increasing in value. He thought of that randy cow, with her bleached silver hair and her imperious attitude, getting a subordinate like Joe MacLeod to knock her up. His mental vocabulary sank to its lowest level when it was describing Margaret Stephenson. The Honourable Mrs. Stephenson. The daughter of a bloody peer, with a string of politicians and a Scottish duke in the background. Screwing a man young enough to be her son, in a scruffy motel room, twice a week. He thought of her with loathing. He had said a few well chosen words to MacLeod, which he hoped had impressed him with the inadvisability of sleeping with Ministers' wives, or *any* wife, come to that, of *any* member of the Embassy staff, and the even greater folly of opening his bleeding mouth about his work. He had verbally killed MacLeod, and then resuscitated him, because he was a very good man at his job and he was entitled to make one mistake without losing his career. But only one. Loder felt confident that he wasn't likely to make another.

Besides, he himself had decided to bend the rules a little. He should have made a private report on Mrs. Fergus Stephenson's moral activities to his own chief in London. But he had not done so. And he never would, for the sake of her husband. There was no harm she could do, except get involved in a scandal, and from what he gleaned from MacLeod, she was experienced enough to keep clean in public. Besides, Fergus knew. He felt so sorry for him; poor bastard, putting up with a wife who did that sort of thing, going through the motions, year after year. Loder would have liked to knock her head off. A man like Stephenson didn't deserve to be treated like that.

'Have a cigarette?' He offered his case to Stephenson, who took one. He had noticed that the Minister smoked Benson and Hedges, and he had bought some specially.

'Thank you.' Stephenson felt in his pocket. 'I'm afraid I have no lighter. I must have left it behind.' He accepted Loder's match. He had left the lighter in his desk drawer in its usual place.

He finished his coffee and paid the bill. Loder thanked him for a very pleasant lunch, and suggested, somewhat diffidently, that perhaps he might lunch one day later that month with him.

Provided his engagements permitted, Stephenson said, he'd be delighted.

. . . . .

'Comrade Sverdlov?'

He looked up at Anna Skriabine; she had put his mail down on his desk, neatly sorted into piles, and instead of going away she hesitated.

'Yes?'

She glanced downwards and then back at him, her hands were locked in front of her, and they twisted nervously. 'I opened a letter, Comrade Sverdlov. I just want to say there was nothing to indicate it was so private. I'm very sorry.'

'If it wasn't marked, then it's not your fault,' Sverdlov said. Her attitude irritated him; she cringed and she simpered, until he could have taken her by the seat of her skirt and run her out of the office door. She must have sensed that her attempts to ingratiate herself were not succeeding. Consequently she made the mistake of exaggerating, instead of altering, her technique. Like a lot of women who had been highly trained to operate in a certain way, she was incapable of using her initiative.

'Which is the letter?'

'This one, Comrade.' She leaned across and touched one of the pile with her finger. She wore an expensive French scent, which Sverdlov had also grown to dislike. He let her go out of the room before he picked it up and read it.

It had come through the diplomatic bag; it was a personal letter from Gregory Tomarov, who had known him since his marriage, and been a witness at his wedding. It enclosed the official document notifying him that his wife, Elena, had applied to the courts for a divorce. Tomarov's letter was handwritten, and ran to four pages. Sverdlov read it quietly; he had pushed the court notification to one side. Elena was unhappy. She had complained of loneliness and of infrequent communication from him. The writer became almost apologetic, as if a wife were not entitled, after three years' absence, to such feelings.

Even more apologetically, he hinted that she feared Sverdlov had found another woman, though this was obviously a figment of her imagination.

A divorce was not only unnecessary, Tomarov wrote, but it was a serious political mistake. He urged Sverdlov to return to Russia for a short visit, and to effect a reconciliation with his wife. He insisted that she still loved him, and would be only too glad to abandon the divorce.

The advice he gave was prompted by his affection for her, and for Sverdlov, and an old man's distress at seeing two young people making a needless mistake. He ended by suggesting that Sverdlov fly back for a short leave, and urged him to come as quickly as possible, before the divorce could be granted.

Sverdlov put the letter down, on top of the document. He lit a cigarette. So Elena was lonely, and suspected him of being unfaithful. She was unhappy because of their separation. It sounded very reasonable. It indicated that his wife had become like any other woman. Dependent, insecure, feminine. A year ago he would have been delighted by that letter of Tomarov's. He could win back Elena as soon as he got near enough to drag her into bed. He knew this; he had always known it. But he had always known that it was a victory she resented. She lost, only to despise herself and retreat from him again. If he went back home, and persuaded her to drop the petition, would she agree to leave the clinic and come to Washington—would she consent to have a child and behave like a wife? He picked up Tomarov's letter and let it drop again. If he returned home, would he want her to do any of these things? What about his feelings—how had three years absence affected him? He knew the answer to that question. He had known it for a long time. He had formulated it very clearly to Judith Farrow, when he said that along with his political beliefs, his wife meant nothing to him either.

He could fly home for a week. If, as he suspected, his position was under attack from Golitsyn and others in the Service with retrograde views, then it would harm him to lose the heroic Yuri Maximov's daughter, to be divorced by her for reasons which his enemies could easily turn into political capital behind his back.

He rubbed out his cigarette and swore. He had work piled in front of him; even though he lacked enthusiasm for most of it, he was infuriated by this intrusion of a domestic matter. He was also infuriated by Tomarov's letter, speaking of them as if they were a pair of teenagers, instead of a mature couple who had spent a large part of their married life apart. Elena was no housebound partner, pining away in her empty flat. She was a dedicated careerist with a life of her own which she insisted upon leading to the exclusion of her husband. If they divorced, it might be a political mistake, but certainly not an emotional disaster. He thought of Golitsyn's spy reading that letter. She had destroyed the envelope, so there was no way of proving that it had no confidential mark. Now Golitsyn would know about the divorce; Sverdlov could imagine his satisfaction. Elena Maximova was his kind of woman; in theory at least. His own choice had been a plump and homely girl from his home province, dull and compliant, to whom equality was a word she couldn't spell.

Golitsyn would make the most of the divorce. He locked the notification and Tomarov's letter in his desk drawer, and cursed his wife for not giving him some warning. Before the change of government in Moscow, he could have let her petition go through and ignored it. Now he knew it was unwise. Perhaps even unsafe.

He would have to go back home and see her.

He sent for Anna Skriabine and dictated a cable to Tomarov and one to his wife. He instructed her to book him on a flight to Moscow at the end of the week.

. . . . .

'You don't know,' Judith said. 'You may feel quite differently when you see her again.'

They were lunching together, and she had chosen the place. It was a small Trattoria in downtown Manhattan, where the food was simple, superb, Italian cooking, and nobody from the diplomatic circle would be likely to go there. They had been spending two or three evenings a week together for the past month, and often he persuaded her to lunch with him. Sverdlov had the inevitable whisky on the table; he had promised her to try some Chianti, but without enthusiasm.

'Why should I? Absence does not make the heart grow fonder. It just makes the memory unreliable.'

'You don't want to make up with her, do you?'

'No,' Sverdlov said. 'As the time comes nearer for me to go back and try, so I don't want to do anything about it. Don't look at me like that, trying to be a good Christian and persuade me to love my wife. Just because she is my wife. There was no church service, you know.'

'You needn't tell me that,' Judith said. 'And I'm not trying to be a good Christian and persuade you to do anything.'

'Then you're trying to persuade yourself that you don't mind,' he suggested. 'That you would be happy if I could love her, and that you're not jealous at all. I understand. I won't make fun of you; I'm sorry.' He lifted her hand and kissed it. She dug her nails into him.

'That wasn't very religious of you,' he observed. 'You should be meek, and obedient. Look, there is a mark!'

'No more than you deserve,' she said. 'Can't you be serious for a minute?'

'If you insist on it, I will be serious. But I don't feel serious when I am with you. I feel happy. Now I don't feel happy with my wife. Does that answer your questions?'

'No, it just brings up another one. If you don't love her and you'd like her to divorce you, why are you going back to try and stop her?'

'Ah.' He leaned his head back and his eyes half closed. 'Ah, now that is difficult to answer. And it has nothing to do with me and Elena. It has to do with politics.'

'I don't see it,' Judith said. 'What's political about your marriage? It's your private life.'

'Then a man's career isn't affected by divorce or scandal in the West? Come, come, you don't know very much about your own society.'

'I'm talking about your society, not ours. I thought you got a divorce like an abortion. On demand.'

'That depends on who you are,' he said. 'It shouldn't do, but it does. Don't smile, I haven't conceded anything to you. My wife is an important woman, from an important family. If she divorces me, it can affect my career. She will be given the divorce, but it will not please my superiors. That is what I am thinking about now.'

'I didn't realise you were so ambitious,' Judith said.

'I like to stay alive.'

'You're joking!'

'A little; but not completely. Why don't you eat—it will be cold.'

'Feodor, stop talking like this. You're a professional soldier, in a diplomatic post—how could a divorce put you in that kind of danger? For God's sake, you're not married to Stalin's daughter!'

'Her father knew him well. Hasn't your Embassy man told you anything about me?'

'No,' Judith said. 'Nothing. I ring him up every time we see each other, and then I ring off. I told you that.'

'You like me, don't you?'

'Yes. You know I do.'

'Very much?'

'Quite a lot.' She began making patterns on the red checked table cover with her knife. 'How long will you be away?'

'I don't know. It depends how long it takes to make her change her mind. Stop cutting the table cloth and look at me. When I come back we'll see each other?'

'You may not want to—you never know, you may fall in love with your wife when you get home. If I don't hear from you, I'll understand. I won't mind.'

He laughed out loud. 'If you don't mind, why do you look so miserable? Listen to me; I'm not a boy, going home to a lost love. I've been away three years and nothing but care for my own skin is making me go back to her at all. She doesn't mean anything to me; I wish her well, I would always be glad to see her, but as a woman—nothing! Finished!' He banged on the table. 'As for you, we haven't even begun anything. All you ever say to me is no. Are you a secret Maoist?'

'How did you guess?' Judith had to smile. 'I can't start the day without reading his "Thoughts".'

'I couldn't start the day if I did,' Sverdlov said. 'The monotonous ravings of a Chinese megalomaniac. Do you know it has sold more copies than the Christian Bible?'

'So what does that prove?' Judith had recovered herself. Hearing that he intended going back to Russia had been a shock.

He bent down and kissed her on the side of the neck. 'That there are too many Chinese.'

'Feodor? You wouldn't really be in trouble, would you? That was just a joke?'

'No,' he said; he was quite serious. 'It was not a joke at

all. Don't you understand, politically, I could be suspect if I made no attempt to be reconciled? A lot of her father's disciples are in power now. Things have changed backwards, instead of forwards. The West doesn't realise it yet.'

'And you still feel as you did—you've lost faith in it all?'

'I've lost interest,' Sverdlov said. They were drinking coffee, and he had spooned in a third of the sugar in the little bowl. 'You can call it faith if you like. Once I believed that our way of life was the only reasonable answer to the problems of the world. I was never a fanatic, not like Elena. I always asked questions.

'But after Stalin, people stopped talking about annihilating one half of the world as a way of spreading Communism. There was more freedom, more moderation.

'I worked for that, and I believed in it. I still do. But it's gone.' She looked into his face; she had never seen it so grave. 'It's gone, and we have reversed, thirty years back. So now, I am like the majority. I want to survive if I can. That's what I meant when we talked on the island that day. There is no justice, no ideal, only expediency and the pleasures to be had like going out to lunch with you. Have a Russian cigarette.'

'Why don't you get out, if it's as bad as that? Why don't you just get off the plane in Europe and disappear?'

'Because I am a Russian and I don't want to be exiled from my country. I will go on with my work, and maybe there will be another change. I hope you are not trying to persuade me to defect?'

'You know I'm not,' Judith said. 'You'd be selling out on your own people if you came over to us. I meant what I said. Just vanish. Disappear. But it was silly, it wouldn't be possible.'

'No,' he agreed, and for a moment the twisted smile appeared. 'It would be very difficult for me to hide anywhere without help. So there is nothing to do, but get the bill, and take you back to the United Nations to work for wicked Western Capitalism. I am going on Friday; I hope to be back in ten days, or less if I can get my wife to agree. And then I will telephone you.'

They drove back in his car. He pulled in to the kerb outside the entrance to the tall black glass building, and put his arms round her.

'Goodbye,' he said and kissed her. '*Dushinka.*'

Later that day Judith caught one of the interpreters on his way past Nielson's office. She asked him what the word meant. He grinned at her.

'It means darling, in Russian. Who's been chatting you up?'

She said 'Thanks' and closed the door on him. She couldn't bring herself to report to Loder that day.

. . . . .

Loder was in bed when his telephone began to ring.

It was the chief coding officer on night duty at the Embassy.

'I've been trying to find you, sir.'

Loder had been to the cinema and eaten a Chinese dinner afterwards. Alone, as usual.

'All right, what is it? It's bloody nearly one o'clock in the morning.'

'An open cable for you; marked extremely urgent. Shall I read it to you, sir, or will you come down?'

'Is it suitable to read?'

Loder was now wide awake. As far as he knew his telephone was clear, but the devices improved all the time. God forbid he should suspect that apart from the Eastern bloc, anyone among Britain's stalwart American supporters at CIA would think of plugging in.

'It's personal. Shall I read it?'

'Go ahead,' Loder said. He had a pencil and not pad by his telephone.

'Daphne ill. Please return immediately. Condition very serious. Signed Vinney.'

Loder had copied it down. 'Thanks,' he said. 'Cable back, will you? "Taking first available flight, Thursday 27th. Jack." Okay—get it off tonight, urgent rate.'

He put the telephone down and got out of bed. He found a cigarette in the packet he had taken out of his jacket pocket; he had never gone in for cases, since he lost the one his wife gave him as a Christmas present the first year they were married. Daphne was his wife's name. But Vinney was the code name used by his chief in Queen Anne's gate in London. The bogus personal message and the method of sending it as an open cable showed that something very important indeed had occurred. So important and so confidential that no one in the Embassy, not even the Minister or the Ambassador himself, must know that Loder had been called back to England on official business. He went back to bed and began dialling B.O.A.C.'s number.

. . . . .

'Could I speak with Mrs. Farrow please? Is she at home?'

Nancy Nielson opened the apartment door and the blonde woman stepped into the hall. 'She's not here right now but I'm expecting her any minute. Come inside and wait, won't you?' Nancy led the way into the living room; she saw the visitor glance round it quickly, taking stock of the decor and the pictures. In the hallway she had been partially in shadow; in the brightly lit room, her hair showed a brassy colour, and she wore a long silver-blue mink stole over an expensive but inelegant red suit. 'You didn't say your name,' she suggested.

'Sandy,' she said, and smiled. 'Sandy Mitchel. Hi.'

'Hi,' Nancy replied. 'Nancy Nielson. Have a drink while you're waiting.'

'No thanks,' the girl said. She slipped the fur back off one shoulder and sat down; she perched on the edge of the chair with her knees together. She had beautiful legs and she was extremely pretty. She could have been a singer or a small-time actress. Nancy couldn't make out how she connected with Judith Farrow. She watched the girl, her blue eyes narrowed like her father's, wondering whether letting her inside had been a mistake.

'You know Judy well?' she asked.

'No. No, I'm not really acquainted with her. We just met once.'

'I see,' Nancy said. 'She's not expecting you then?'

'No.' The beautiful smile flashed at her, but it was nervous.

'I'm just calling for a friend. Say, is that her now?'

The front door had opened and shut. Nancy got up. 'I imagine so. I'll tell her you're here.'

She shut the door firmly after her. In the outer hall, Judith shook her head. 'I don't know anyone called Sandy Mitchel . . . I'd better see what she wants.'

As soon as she walked in, the blonde got up, and Judith recognised her. It was the American girl who had come to Sverdlov's table with the young Russian. She remembered his name suddenly. Memenov.

'Hello,' she said.

'Sandy Mitchel,' the girl said. 'Do you remember me? We met at the Popotte, it was quite a while ago . . .' She seemed uncertain what to say next; she looked beyond Judith to where Nancy was standing.

'Mrs. Farrow, could I see you privately for a minute?'

'Yes, of course.' Judith turned, but Nancy was already on her way out. When they were alone she sat down. 'What is it you want to see me about, Miss Mitchel?'

'I'm Peter Memenov's girl friend,' she said quickly. 'You probably don't remember me, but we had a drink at your table that night. Look, I had a call from Peter, he's in Paris right now, on a two weeks' trip. He asked me to get hold of you, because he has a message for your friend, Colonel Sverdlov.'

'Oh? Why couldn't he give it direct?'

'I don't know,' the girl shrugged. 'And I don't want to know, Mrs. Farrow. I wouldn't have looked you up and come here, only I like Peter—we got along fine together, and he really asked me, just as a favour. He said it was terribly important I find you and get this message to your friend.'

'What is the message?'

'I wrote it down.' She began searching in her handbag and brought out a piece of paper with a large untidy scrawl pencilled across it. Judith held out her hand, but Sandy Mitchel shook her head. She looked embarrassed.

'He said I could write it down but I mustn't give the paper to anyone. After I've told you, I have to burn it. Believe me, Mrs. Farrow, it all sounds crazy to me, but like I said, he's an old friend and I'm just doing it for a favour.'

'All right then, read it to me, please.' Judith had lowered her voice; it was a subconscious defence against Nancy, who might just have been able to hear through the door.

' "Kalinin is in the Lubiyanka. They are waiting for you. On no account let them persuade you to return to Russia." That's all.'

'Oh my God,' Judith whispered.

'I don't understand it,' the girl said. 'But it sounds like

trouble for your friend.' She looked at the English girl; she was as white as a sheet.

'I'd better go now. Peter said to tell him as soon as you can.'

'It's Thursday evening,' Judith said. 'I've got to tell him tonight!' She walked out of the room and into the hallway with Memenov's girl. She held out her hand, and Sandy Mitchel shook it.

'Thank you,' Judith said. 'Thank you for finding me and telling me this. Now go home and burn that message and forget the whole thing.'

'I will,' the girl said. 'I don't know what it's all about, but I smell trouble. I hope you find your friend tonight.'

'God help him if I don't,' she said. 'He's flying home tomorrow morning.'

. . . . .

Loder's chief in London was a retired industrialist, who had picked up a title for services to industry after the war, and a D.S.O. plus bar for services of a very distinguished kind during it. He was not an imposing man, not tall or distinguished looking. He had thinning hair and thick spectacles; the only relic of his Army career was a small, neatly trimmed moustache.

He had been a Regular soldier, with peace-time experience of intelligence in the Middle East and India; he had a reputation for flair and personal courage. During the war, when Military Intelligence distinguished itself early on by some disastrous blunders, and the amateurs at S.O.E. were forming into a body, he was then a Brigadier who became incorporated into the larger S.I.S. which fell under Naval direction. He proved to be that rarity in the espionage field, a man of immense courage, who was too intrinsically clever to get caught and die heroically. He was a superb organiser, and with his experience in active operations, not, alas, shared by some of the other Intelligence heads of sections, he knew how much to ask of his agents and how best to use them. He had gone into industry when the war ended, where he applied his talents to various public companies with distinction, and was knighted at what seemed the end of his public life. At that point he became the head of the entire Secret Intelligence Service and moved into the hallowed premises in Queen Anne's Gate. He gave Loder an appointment late on Friday afternoon. His predecessor would never have graced the office after lunchtime. He had considered the weekend a sacred institution, which nothing short of war should be allowed to interrupt.

'Sit down, Loder. You look well. Washington agreeing with you?'

'Yes sir. I get along all right.'

'Sorry to drag you back at such short notice. We've had a No. 1 memo from the Foreign Sec.' He had a habit, which offended Loder, of shortening words. 'There's a real row brewing up. But we've got to keep it very much in the family. That's why I had your wife's name used on the cable.'

'I understood that, sir. I let the Embassy know she was ill and I had to come back. It was all covered my end. What's the trouble?'

'Middle East. Bloody plague spot it is, too; never anythings but crisis with those people—Jews, Arabs, they're all the bloody same. Anyway, briefly, there was a move, initiated by the State Department, to get a mediator from Israel to meet one of Egypt's boys; all completely unofficial, nobody supposed to know, you get the idea? Right. Nothing ventured nothing gained, etc. The Israeli Government was willing, so long as nobody could say they were climbing down; they had a special man lined up to do it; the Arabs had let it be known that an Egyptian might just happen to be on neutral ground at the same time, and provided nothing official was known about it either, the two of them could talk. This would have been a start, at least. In fact, Loder, as you realise, it was even more important from the Western point of view because it showed some sign that Egpyt might be ready to shake off the Russians in the future.'

'Why should they? You don't mind me asking, but just out of interest,' Loder said.

'Very good question. Self preservation, as usual. The Arab guerilla movement is beginning to get out of hand. It's not just El Fatah now, there's a whole young movement growing up, a kind of Che Guevara revolutionary crusade, which doesn't think it can get Palestine back without destroying everything connected with the West, and that includes the oil sheikdoms, who are paying Egypt a bloody fat subsidy on the quiet to keep the Canal closed—they're beginning to find the guerillas are too Left for their liking. If the Jews retaliate and there's another Six Day clean-up—and I can't see them taking much more from the United Arab Republics without giving them a proper poke in the nose—the Egyptian Government will lose, Russian MIGs notwithstanding, and their own young fanatics will cut their throats. Which would suit the Russians very well, depending on the circumstances. I think the Egyptians are about ready to look in our direction. But the whole thing has blown right back in our faces, Not so much us, but certainly the State Department.'

He paused and pulled at the end of his nose between the nostrils; it gave his ordinary English face a bizarre disproportion for a moment. Loder took out his cigarettes and offered one. It was accepted; the chief's habit of smoking other people's cigarettes and keeping the big box on his desk unopened, was rather a wry joke among his staff.

'The Russians got the tip-off,' he said. 'And not just a hint, but documentary proof. Letters, memos, recommendations from the F.O., support from the President—the whole bloody lot. They faced the Egyptians with it and that was the end of the meeting. The Jews are furious, because it was leaked, but in a way that made it look as if they were in a weak position. Now *their* hotheads are screaming for action.'

'How did they get their hands on the papers?' Loder said. 'How do we know they had them?'

'We have a friend in Cairo,' his chief said. 'He saw the photocopies; he told us. He's not very happy either. His name wasn't mentioned but it might have been. I think we've lost him as a result of it, but that can't be helped.'

'If they had photocopies,' Loder said it slowly, 'that means somebody on our side gave it to them. Somebody passed the whole scheme on to them.'

'Yes.' The eyes behind the spectacles were angry. That's exactly what it does mean, Loder. 'We've got a snake loose.'

'The Americans must be doing their nuts.' Loder was sufficiently shaken to forget himself and his accent came out straight Midlands.

'They're starting an immediate security investigation into everyone who had anything to do with the idea, or could possibly have had access to the correspondence. As you say, they're not very happy about it. Naturally they're saying it's somebody on our side.'

'Naturally,' Loder said unpleasantly. 'It was their baby, why should we wet the nappy?—whoever it is, is in their own back yard.'

'I hope so,' the chief said. 'But I see their point. We've got rather a bad record for that kind of thing. I wasn't sitting here when MacLean was in Washington, or I rather think he might have been recalled, but you must remember he gave our entire plans for the NATO defence system to the Russians.

'I hope to God it isn't one of our people, but I'm not prepared to say it isn't. That's why I send for you, Loder. Washington is going to get pretty hot from now on. I want every member of our Embassy there gone over with a fine-tooth comb. Everyone.'

He saw Loder's face and repeated it. 'And I mean everyone, from the Ambassador down. I propose sending you a couple of good men some time next week. Both Naval, both classified as Plans.'

Loder hesitated; he had been thinking very quickly. 'You'd better make that three, sir. I think I'll send MacLeod back.'

'Why?'

'He's got himself involved with a girl in Personnel.' He had already decided not to involve Fergus Stephenson and his wife, and he had the lie ready. 'He just might let her know there was something up. He's a good man, sir, don't misunderstand me, and it wouldn't matter a damn in the ordinary way, but as we've got to be so tight on security over this . . . I'd rather have a replacement.'

'Fine. Shall be done. Incidentally, we're going to be pretty busy over here, too. I'm going to Downers on Monday to report.' For a moment Loder didn't understand Then he realised it was one of the chief's abbreviations.

'You mean you're seeing the Prime Minister, at Downing Street?'

'Yes. He's busy or I'd have gone to Chequers tomorrow. That's how serious this is, Loder. This whole Middle East thing was the top-most priority. Whoever gave it to the Russians knew exactly how important it was. And that means that American or English, we've got more than just a leak, or a single instance of some colossal bloody blunder. This is a deadly menace to our whole Western security. A double agent that could make Mr. Philby look like a filing clerk.'

'Christ,' Loder muttered. 'I just hope it isn't one of ours.'

'I hope so too,' his chief said. He pulled at his nose again. 'But I have a nasty little instinct that in spite of everything, it is.' He stood up and shook Loder's hand. 'It's your party now. You might as well stay over for a few days, see your children if you like—then get back Wednesday.'

'Thanks, sir,' Loder hadn't liked to ask for that particular concession. It was part of the man's ability to manage people that he should think of it at all. Thanks. I can see the kids and get a plane on Tuesday night. I'd like to get on with it. Goodbye sir.'

He went out and down into the bright spring morning to find himself a taxi back to his hotel.

. . . . .

Sverdlov was not at the Washington Embassy. Judith telephoned three times within the hour; the first time she asked to speak to him and after a five-minute wait, the line went dead. Frantically she dialled again; this time there was the same pause, but the operator cut in to apologise for keeping her and Judith hung on. A man's voice answered, speaking slow, careful English. He said that Colonel Sverdlov was not in Washington. No, he could give her no further information, but if she would give her name and call back within half an hour?

He had cleared the telephone call with General Golitsyn by the time she rang again. The name decided Golitsyn not to suppress the fact that Sverdlov was in New York. Farrow was his contact; she might have something important which she wouldn't pass on to anyone else. She had sounded urgent, according to the night clerk who had spoken to her.

She was in her bedroom with the door closed; she had managed to avoid Nancy, who wanted to know who Sandy Mitchel was, and what she wanted. Judith made up an excuse about finding an address of a mutual friend. It didn't fool Nancy for a moment, but it brushed aside the questions, and accounted for the spate of private telephone calls.

When she phoned the Washington Embassy a third time, she was frantic as the same maddening hiatus lengthened from two minutes into five and then eight, with the operator's mechanical voice asking her to keep on holding. She felt like bursting into tears and screaming down the telephone.

Finally the same man who had spoken before came on the line. Colonel Sverdlov was in New York, and could be reached at this number. There was a moment when she panicked; he was repeating the number, slowly and distinctly, but she had no pencil and in her anxiety she feared she might easily get them the wrong way round. 'Wait a minute, wait a minute,' she shouted down the phone, as if he were too far away to hear properly. 'I haven't a pencil. No, for Christ's sake I said *pencil*, I want to write the number down! Hold on, don't ring off . . .'

Then she was back, with a dress bill and an eye-liner, which was all she could find to write with. But it was enough, and ten minutes later she had got through and Sverdlov's voice was answering.

'I have to see you,' she stumbled over the words. 'It's terribly important.' There was a silence, and she thought they had been cut off. Then he spoke.

'It's difficult,' he said. 'I am very busy. I leave early tomorrow.'

She sensed that he was not alone; he sounded impersonal, almost curt.

'Feodor, I've got something to tell you. For God's sake cut your business short and meet me tonight. Whatever happens you mustn't go home tomorrow!'

'All right, if it's really urgent. I will go to the place we met last time. In about an hour.' He hung up without even saying goodbye.

He was already in the trattoria where they had lunched that week; he was sitting at the same corner table with a glass of whisky in front of him. He looked up as she came through the door. The place was quite full; the atmosphere was hot and steamy with Italian smells; a large party at a long banquette table were toasting each other and making a lot of noise.

He pulled out her chair, and for a moment his hand rested on her shoulder and squeezed. The first thing she said was so irritable and petty that immediately afterwards she was ashamed.

'You were very offhand on the telephone. I wouldn't have asked you to come if it wasn't important.'

'I'm sorry,' Sverdlov said. 'I was in a room full of people. Also I was surprised. How did you find me?'

'Your Washington Embassy gave me the number. Listen, I've been nearly frantic trying to find you. You mustn't go back tomorrow!'

'So you said.' Sverdlov picked up his glass. 'Take some of this, you look very white. Then tell me what this is about.'

'Someone came to see me this evening, when I got back from the office she was waiting in the flat. It was the American girl that was living with your friend we met at La Popotte—Memenov. That's what she said, Peter Memenov. He'd given her a message to get through to you and she'd found out where I lived.'

'What was the message?' He sounded calm to the point of being unconcerned.

'She had it written down, but she wouldn't give me the paper. I memorised it. "Kalinin is in the Lubiyanka. They are waiting for you. On no account go back to Russia"—no, it was "on no account let them persuade you to go back to Russia".'

'Kalinin is my secretary,' Sverdlov said slowly. 'You are sure about this—you are sure it was Lubiyanka?'

'Absolutely,' Judith answered. 'I've even heard of the place. It's a prison, isn't it?'

'Yes,' he said. 'It's in Moscow. It is an interrogation centre for the K.G.B.'

'"They are waiting for you," what does that mean?' She had reached out and gripped his hand. He caught and held it, locking her fingers in his. He held them so tightly that it hurt.

'It means that my secretary has been arrested,' Sverdlov said. 'And questioned. It could mean that when I go home, I will be sent to join him in the Lubiyanka.'

'Oh my God,' Judith whispered. 'Just because of the divorce . . .'

'No,' he shook his head. 'No, the divorce has nothing to do with it. That was just a trick to get me home.' He thought of Tomarov's letter, full of paternal sentiment and good advice to come immediately. His eyes went to slits and he said something in his own language which Judith didn't understand.

'This is something much more serious.' He smiled, and the twisted mouth made it a bitter grimace. They took Kalinin back to manufacture evidence against me. By now they must have got it. So my old friend writes to persuade me to come back; my own wife agrees to divorce me . . .'

'But what have you done?' Judith exclaimed. 'Why should they "manufacture" something? I don't understand it . . .'

'No, I don't expect you do,' he said quietly. 'You wouldn't understand it, because in your world these things do not happen except in books. Spy novels, where the hero bites through the electrified wire with his teeth and escapes into the night. Nobody escapes from the Lubiyanka. I am sorry it was Kalinin. I hope he didn't try to hold out.' He gave her a cigarette and lit one for himself. 'So the policy has been decided,' he said. 'We have gone back to Stalinism. And now the purge begins. I have been very blind and foolish; I should have seen it coming.'

'But why you?' Judith asked him. 'Why all this trouble about you?'

'I belong to the so-called moderates,' Sverdlov said. 'I believe we can conquer the Capitalist world by a peaceful infiltration, by political manœuvre, by the sheer progress of history. But not by war. Not by the old Marxist theory of a world revolutionary movement sweeping all into the sea and building a new paradise on the ruins. You see I have become corrupted; I like Scotch whisky. Didn't you realise when we first met, that alone proves I've lost my Marxist soul?'

'You have lost it,' Judith said suddenly. 'You told me that yourself, the night you made me tell you everything about Richard. You said you had lost faith in all of it. You said you only cared about surviving. You must have shown this to your superiors. Oh Feodor, why didn't you keep quiet?'

To her surprise he laughed. 'Not my superiors,' he said. 'My underlings. One in particular.' The same look was in his eyes as when he thought of Tomarov. 'Never underestimate an old dog; he can still bite with one tooth. It's a good proverb. All our Russian proverbs are good.'

'If you don't stop trying to make this into a joke and talking about proverbs I shall scream,' Judith said suddenly. 'You're in terrible danger. 'You're going to be arrested if you go home; what will happen to you if you don't go? They could just put you on a plane, couldn't they?'

'Not without authority,' Sverdlov said. 'But that would come. That would come when they suspected that I knew what was going to happen and so I made excuses not to go. You know, you have given me a chance. Because of you I can cancel my trip tomorrow and re-book for later. I can say I have succeeded in recruiting you, and you have a tremendous secret for me. You are going to blow up Nielson's safe and give me all his correspondence.'

'I don't know how you could laugh,' she said. She was so frightened for him that she was becoming angry.

'It's better than to cry,' Sverdlov answered. 'It helps me think. You must be hungry; let's order something for us both to eat. And drink,' he added, as if that were the most important aspect of the evening. 'My glass is empty.'

'I couldn't touch food,' she said. 'And you shouldn't drink, you need to think clearly, not fuddled up with alcohol!'

'*Dushinka*,' he said, 'stop looking sad. I told you, I believe the only thing that matters is to survive. They won't get me! I promise you.'

'But you can't cancel again,' she pointed out, 'what are you going to say then?'

'That will depend,' he said. 'That will depend on what I have decided I must do.'

Judith did her best to eat, but found it impossible. She sat smoking and drinking wine, not talking to him or breaking the silence. The divorce had been a trick; that must mean that his own wife had been persuaded to turn against him. He had talked of an old friend. Slowly, as she watched him, Judith realised that the humour was grim, and the man was concealing his real feelings behind a façade of cynicism.

She appreciated then how little she actually knew him, how lightly she had touched on his real character. That he had another, less attractive side she knew already; she had glimpsed it briefly in the restaurant, when the young man Memenov had sat down with them, deferent and ill-at-ease. It had exposed itself for a few moments when she first gave him the message. If he was afraid, he knew how to hide it, but he had been unable to conceal his anger. *Dunshinka.* He had called her that again. Darling. Oh God, she said to herself, what are you getting into . . . He doesn't mean anything to you, just because he's taken your mind off Richard. She almost caught a breath at that. He hadn't taken her mind off Richard Paterson, he had driven him out of it altogether. She hadn't thought of him for weeks. She hadn't thought of anyone but Sverdlov, and until now she hadn't realised it. When he made fun of his own danger she could have slapped his face to make him take it seriously. And she knew almost nothing about him; he had come into her life like an alien from Mars. He had moved his chair close to hers; their knees were touching.

'Can I go back with you tonight—to your apartment?'

'My friend is there,' Judith said. She had used Nancy as the excuse for keeping Sverdlov out so many times that he had said he didn't believe she existed at all. But she was home that evening, and she couldn't risk bringing him back without Nancy knowing. It never occurred to Judith for a moment that his suggestion had its usual motive. Even in the pink trattoria light, designed to flatter women, his face was grey.

'I have got to think this out,' he said. 'I can't decide in a moment.'

'I'll go and call up,' Judith said. 'Sometimes she stays away for the night or comes in very late.'

He watched her leave the table; several men glanced up at her as she passed. She was an attractive woman, at times she could look beautiful, as she had done the first time he saw her clearly under the light by the swimming pool in Barbados, drying her wet body with a towel.

Sverdlov lit a cigarette. His wife had asked for the divorce; was it genuine, or had she agreed to bait the trap being set for him? Tomarov he could understand, because the type was incapable of change, incapable of a true personal relationship independent of political attitudes. But he had loved Elena, spent hours with her in his arms, wanted to have children by her . . . Had this counted for nothing too? Had she no sentiment, no weakness which could be described as human, that she could agree to turn her husband over to his enemies? Would she have sat in the body of the court as he had done when Penkovsky was tried, and listened to the death sentence?

And suddenly he had seen it in perspective. His wife was not devious, neither was she capable of personal cruelty. But in the service of her ideal she was without compassion for herself or anyone else; she would divorce him because she believed him to be a traitor. The suggestion of such a crime was enough to annul their ten years of marriage, to make an association with him something unclean, to be cut off as if it were a gangrenous limb capable of infecting and destroying the rest of the body.

'She's at home tonight. I'm sorry, but I couldn't do anything about it.'

He looked up into Judith's anxious face, and smiled.

'It doesn't matter,' he said 'We can sit on here. And I will not drink a lot of whisky. I promise you.'

'I wish I knew what you could do,' she said. 'It seems like some kind of nightmare. Is there nobody you could go to—your Ambassador? Couldn't he help?'

'No,' Sverdlov shook his head. The Ambassador would know nothing about it and he wouldn't want to know. The decision to arrest someone like Sverdlov was quite out of his province. When you are at the top there is no one to whom you can go for protection against an attack coming from below. He had thought of Panyushkin, the dour, aloof head of the K.G.B. itself; he knew him personally, and had received marks of signal favour, like an invitation to spend a weekend with him at his Black Sea villa. He and Elena had gone together. It had been as stiff and formal as if they were visiting royalty.

It would be useless to approach Panyushkin direct. He must have given permission for the interrogation of Kalinin; he had already doomed Sverdlov by agreeing, because he knew that the findings could not possibly be negative. As he had said to Judith in the first moment of shock, the purge was beginning. No doubt Panyushkin remembered the most feared and infamous of all the K.G.B. directors, Beria, who failed to detect the change in policy in time, and fell before the firing squad of Krushchev and the moderates. Panyushkin would order him home, assure him he had nothing to fear, and then sit behind a screened window in the Lubiyanka while he was being assisted to confess.

'Feodor, what are you going to do? Couldn't you just disappear? I know I suggested this before but it wasn't really serious then—you could just walk out of here and vanish. I could give you some money . . .'

'Thank you,' he said. 'But it is not possible. Believe me, it could never be done. I have two choices, and not so much time to decide which one I should take. I can go home and try to defend myself, which will be useless and I will be shot, or I can do what others have done, and ask for political asylum.'

Judith didn't speak when he said that. It was the obvious conclusion but he had to arrive there without any suggestion from her.

'If I had a chance,' Sverdlov said slowly, 'I would go home. But I might as well go back to my Embassy and put a bullet in my head. Perhaps that would be the easiest.'

'Please,' she said calmly. 'Please don't say things like that. It makes me feel quite ill.'

'There is always a moment when you think of death as a way easier than life,' Sverdlov said. He leaned over and took her hand and kissed it. He found it icy cold. 'But I don't believe in it. It's the solution of our century, have you noticed? To all the problems of the world, we have only one good answer—death. Too many children being born—abortion. Too many people living too long, being a burden on the state and a nuisance to their families. Euthanasia. You have political opponents—you kill them. It used to be war, but now it is spreading, this civilised solution. And always it is said to be better for the people who have to die. Better for the bastards, the children who will grow up poor and deprived, better for the old sick, who won't have to suffer. Better for the misguided who don't see your point of view, because they can't go around spreading wrong ideas among the rest. It would be better for me to do what I said: go and shoot myself quietly, and make it easy for them. Like an officer and a gentleman. But I am not one of those, so you needn't look at me like that. I am not going to kill myself or let anyone kill me for a reason I don't agree with. I am going to need your help. Will you do what I ask?'

She looked away from him. 'You know I will. I'll do anything I can.' The restaurant was almost empty; the big party of Italians, who were in fact celebrating a birthday, were paying their bill, laughing and singing in snatches, making jokes with the manager who seemed to know them well. Sverdlov kissed her hand again.

'They will think we are lovers,' he said. 'They won't mind if we stay longer. They are such sentimentalists, the Italians. Can you make another telephone call for me?'

'Yes. But it's late, it's midnight. Who do you want me to ring?'

'Your friend from the Embassy,' Sverdlov said. 'Mr. Loder. Say that I would like to see him.'

'But it's so late, Judith said. 'There won't be anyone there.'

'He will be contacted,' Sverdlov interrupted. 'Please, make the call.'

This was his one safe chance to make contact with British Intelligence; nobody could trace Judith's telephone calls, and even if he had been followed to the trattoria on Golitsyn's orders, he was only meeting a prospective recruitee who was more likely going to the powder room than the telephone booth which was round the back of the room, near the kitchens.

He clicked his finger and the manager himself came up. He was red faced and extra genial. His guests had invited him to share their celebration and he was in an expansive mood.

'Signore—where is the beautiful lady?'

'Putting some powder on her nose,' Sverdlov said. 'Would it be possible to have some more coffee, and something to drink? It is not too late . . .'

'No, no. You can have what you like. We are not closing yet.' He leaned towards the Russian and beamed, his black eyes glittering with too much wine. 'I will bring a Strega for the lady. It has certain properties, you know?' He went off, calling in Italian. His accent was thick, and he spoke without Americanisms; he had only arrived in the country five years ago, and already his trattoria was well known and making a huge profit.

Sverdlov got up as Judith came back to the table.

'He's not there,' she said. 'I got through to somebody, and he's away. They don't know when he'll be back.' She looked up at him. 'I did my best—I said it was terribly important. They couldn't tell me anything except his wife was ill and he went home. I asked for the other one, his assistant, but he's not there either. Oh God, Feodor, what are we going to do?'

'Think again,' he said. 'They don't know when he will be back? Or where the other man is, the assistant?'

'No,' she said. 'He was very cagey over the phone, it must have been someone on the night staff. He said MacLeod had left Washington, that's all he could tell me.'

'Drink your Strega,' Sverdlov said. 'It is an aphrodisiac. You will let me make love to you tonight and then we will think of something.'

'Don't joke,' she said. 'This is terrible—I don't know anyone to go to now. Feodor—what about the Americans? Don't you know anybody?'

'I know several—by sight and by name,' the twisted mouth grinned at her. 'But I am not going over to the CIA. I will go to the British, but not to the Americans. Your people are more neutral; the Americans are the worst enemies of my country, and I won't give them information to use against us. It is Mr. Loder or nobody.'

'We can't sit here indefinitely,' Judith said. 'Everyone's gone—we'll have to go too. Oh why couldn't Nancy have gone off with one of her damned boy friends tonight, instead of staying at home!'

'What did she do when you were with Richard Paterson,' he asked. 'Go to a hotel?'

'I used to tell her in advance,' Judith said. 'Anyway he often came at tea time—she's usually working till around seven.'

'Judith?' He was watching her intently, but the look was guarded.

'What is it? Why are you looking like that . . . ? Oh, no, not him! Not Richard!'

He shrugged lightly. 'All right. I understand it would be difficult.'

'I can't get in touch with him,' she said miserably. 'Please, isn't there anyone else?'

'I expect so,' Sverdlov answered. 'We will think of something.' He called for the bill, and they sat in silence while it was brought and he paid. Outside on the pavement, he took her arm. 'I'll take you home,' he said. 'Then I'll go back to our Embassy. Don't worry.' He squeezed her arm. 'By tomorrow morning I will have thought of another way. Maybe we can try to find Loder's assistant.'

'Oh don't be such an idiot,' Judith burst into tears. 'I'll get through to Richard first thing tomorrow morning.'

. . . . .

Rachel Paterson had indigestion. It was not the ordinary discomfort she associated with eating heavy food; it was the result of her enlarged womb with its fluttering little foetus pushing her stomach out of place. As a result acid regurgitated into her throat and pain accompanied every meal. The nights were the worst; she found herself unable to sleep through, and Richard had simply moved into the guest room, being unable, as he said when she protested, to do a full day's work on four or five hours' broken sleep. She had tried getting out of bed as quietly as possible, but she was naturally noisy. The bedsprings creaked, inadvertently she pulled the sheet which he had wrapped round him, and he was struggling up, awake and furious. Now she slept as best she could, poured herself medicine in the night, and comforted herself feeling the tiny movements of the baby under her hand. Towards dawn on the Saturday morning she fell into a deep sleep. She enjoyed the weekends; Richard played golf most mornings, which allowed her to be lazy, and they went to a movie or had friends in to dinner and to play bridge, which was a hobby she had taken up to please him. For someone who considered herself a fool, she showed a surprising aptitude for the game. She played so well he hadn't known whether to be pleased or irritated. He was attentive to her, apart from refusing to sleep in her bed; he was kind and affectionate within well defined limits which did not include giving up what he liked doing or refusing an amusing party if she felt too tired to go with him.

Rachel had never been happier; the Embassy doctor said she was in excellent health, and her mother was planning to come over for the baby's birth. Everyone had been friendly and kind among the staff, and Mrs. Fergus Stephenson, of whom Rachel was a fervent admirer, had been particularly amiable. At eight o'clock she woke suddenly, a bell was ringing through a muddled dream, becoming the dominant part of it until she realised in the dark bedroom that the bell was a reality. Her telephone was ringing.

She groped for the light and found the receiver instead.

'Hello. Is that Washington 275680?'

'Yes,' Rachel croaked back, her throat full of sleep.

'Could I speak to Group Captain Paterson please?' It was a woman's voice, and Rachel hadn't answered when there was a click, and she heard her husband's voice on the extension. 'Hello?'

'Richard? It's me—Judy.' She held the received against

her ear; the voices sounded very loud. Judy. At eight o'clock in the morning.

She was going to put it down; she told herself that later. She was just going to hang up and go back to sleep when the woman said 'Richard' again, right against her ear. 'Richard, I have to see you.'

Her husband had tried to refuse; she couldn't deny that. He had been curt and angry. At one point he told the unknown woman that it was all over and he had no intention of seeing her again. Rachel had listened to the desperate pleading on the other end, and finally the last, unbelievable threat that unless he saw her, the speaker would come down to Washington. That was when she dropped the phone back on its cradle, not caring whether her husband heard the extension click or not. Five minutes later he came into the room which was still dark, and he heard her sobbing.

He was doubly shaken, first by hearing Judith on the line and then by the realisation that his wife had been listening in. What Judith had said seemed so incredible that he couldn't believe it was not some trick to embroil him. He remembered Stephenson's warning to cut loose, that she was classified as unreliable. In the end, when he refused either to believe her, or to come up to Washington that day, Judith had told him to be at her apartment by four o'clock, or she would go down to Washington and call at his house. He had never expected her to make such a threat. It was so completely out of character that he was forced to believe her when she said it was a life or death business, and nothing to do with their past relationship.

But before he made up his mind, he had to go in and face his wife. His first impulse was to lose his temper and tell her not to be such a hysterical bloody fool. But he suppressed it; he had decided to make the marriage work, the course was set, a child was on the way, and besides the Minister's wife had taken Rachel as a protégé. If he upset that bloody woman, she'd make sure his career would suffer. He knew the type and it was far too determined and tough for his liking. Stephenson must have felt he was lying under a steam-roller at times.

'Darling, you've got it all wrong. Listen for God's sake—I'll tell you exactly what that call was about, if you'll stop crying!'

'I heard her,' Rachel cried on, 'I heard her begging to

see you, saying she'd come down here if you didn't go. That was a girl friend, and I know it! I'm going home—you never wanted me to come out anyway! You'd taken up with someone else, that's why! I'm going to go straight home on the first plane tomorrow . . .'

He had a moment of insanity when he nearly reminded her that there was a perfectly good flight to London she could catch that afternoon. A year ago he would have done so, but not now. Things had changed between them. If he wanted his career unspoilt, he was in thrall to this silly woman, at least until they left Washington.

'I used to take her out,' he said. 'I was damned lonely over here and she was English. For Christ's sake, Rachel, I never slept with her—I can't help it if she fell for me, you know how it is with these girls who come over here—all they want is to get their hooks on some man! As soon as I saw she was getting serious I dropped her—flat.

'This is a diplomatic thing, that's why she called me. Darling, please listen to me. Why the hell didn't you listen to the end, then you'd know I'm telling the truth.'

'She wants you to go to Washington. She threatened you,' Rachel said. 'I heard that much!'

'She's got herself mixed up in something,' Richard said, trying to be patient, choosing his words. He even felt a momentary regret at the sight of his wife's wet, distorted face. This sort of thing couldn't be good for a pregnant woman.

'There's a Russian from the Embassy here; she says he wants to defect. He wants to see somebody from our Embassy. Now, darling, do you understand why she phoned me? If only you hadn't hung up . . .'

Rachel lay back and closed her eyes. The outburst had exhausted her completely. Nothing he said was making sense, not compared with the sense those remarks on the telephone had made. Then he had put his arms round her, and she gave in temporarily, because the alternative presented so much pain and the wreck of her new happiness. She opened her eyes and looked at him.

'You never slept with her? You promise me. Richard?'

'I promise,' he said. 'I had dinner with her a few times. I never even kissed the girl good night. Now listen, darling, you're going to take a sleeping pill and get a good rest this morning. You musn't upset yourself, it might be bad for the baby. And I'm going to New York this afternoon and see what this is all about.' He paused for a moment, half forgetting about Rachel. There were two sharp frown lines between his eyes.

'If this is a defector, it could be pretty serious if I refused to go. On the other hand if I helped to bring him over . . .'

He patted his wife, and kissed her cheek. His mind was already far away, exploring possibilities. A Russian from the Washington Embassy. Who the hell could it be? . . He should get in touch with Loder right away, but he had already decided not to do that. He wasn't going to give the credit to 'C' when it could well be claimed by him. He would bring in Loder later on, after he'd established his own part in it in official records. He could ask to see the Ambassador that night if this was a serious proposition. He got his wife a sleeping pill and a glass of water, and made her swallow it. That would keep her quiet for a while.

## CHAPTER SEVEN

The lighter was not in his desk drawer. He took everything out and searched; he did the same with all the drawers. He looked under the chair, even moving the bookcase in case it had wedged underneath. He looked in every corner of the room, and then he began hunting for it in his bedroom. He could not find it. He spent ten minutes going through the pockets of his suits, even including his dressing gown, which he knew was a waste of time. Then he rang for the maid who cleaned his suite of rooms. She had not seen the lighter. She denied ever having seen it, and he knew that this was true. He never left it lying around; he always put it away in its cover in the Tiffany box and buried it at the back of a drawer. When he first got it, he used to keep the drawer locked, but after three years he had become careless and omitted that precaution. He stood in the middle of his study, and tried to think back to the last time he had used it. The occasion was only too clear. He had replaced it in the desk. He looked round once more, as if it might suddenly appear in the middle of the floor. Someone had gone to his desk and taken it. If it was stolen . . . He touched his forehead and his fingertips were damp with sweat. He grimaced with fastidious dislike and wiped his face and hands with his handkerchief. Nobody ever went into his study except the maid, and of course his wife. The maid had certainly not taken it; he was convinced that her denials were the truth.

That left his wife. And he needed the lighter that morning. Even if he hadn't needed it, he dared not leave the mystery unsolved. His mind reeled with panic for a moment, and then steadied. He was a sensitive man, but his earliest upbringing had taught him to despise and conquer fear. He went upstairs to his wife's bedroom and knocked.

She was dressed, standing in front of her dressing table, drawing on one glove. He noticed with senses sharpened by his predicament, that she was wearing a striking shade of violet with a wide brimmed hat like a sombrero.

'Margaret,' he said. 'I'm sorry to disturb you, but I've lost something. It's a lighter—you haven't seen it, have you?'

When she looked at him there was an expression on her face which he had never seen before. He had seen a variety of emotions there and he knew them all. Contempt and dislike were the most constant, with the occasional distortions of rage that transformed his wife from a beautiful woman into an ugly one. She didn't answer him; she waited, staring at him with that odd expression. She seemed to be holding herself together for some powerful physical effort. He was forced by her silence into repeating himself.

'I've lost my lighter. I don't suppose you found it?'

She undid her handbag; she held out her closed hand and then opened it.

'I found this,' she said. 'It looks like a lighter, doesn't it? I was quite taken in. I've been using it, as a matter of fact. Till I tried to refill it with petrol and I pressed the wrong knob.'

With the lighter lying in the palm of her hand he could see what had happened. The shutter concealing the tiny camera eye was up; it appeared to be jammed at an angle.

'I didn't realise what it was at first,' Margaret Stephenson said. 'I tried unscrewing it. It's probably broken. So you won't be able to take photographs will you?'

'No,' Fergus said. Had their relationship been different, he would have bluffed. The hidden camera could have been explained away; another woman would have accepted a variety of lies without connecting its possession with the truth. But twenty years on the defensive had removed the capacity to deceive with any confidence. She had always been the dominant partner, able to destroy him with a word or a glance, armed with the mortal weapon of knowledge which he himself had put into her hands. Whatever he said, she would know if it was a lie; she had the gift of ripping through defences, tearing the truth out like entrails. He might have satisfied her; with any other opponent his courage and intelligence would have supplied a feasable answer. But with Margaret he didn't even try. It was his role to be discovered by her and despised.

'I should have kept that damned drawer locked,' he said. 'I never thought you'd go to my study. It's my own fault.'

Margaret had kept control throughout. She was gripping the lighter so hard that the edges were cutting into her skin, but the same hectoring, contemptuous tone was in her voice as she asked the inevitable question.

'What are you doing with a thing like this? What are you photographing secretly? What filth are you mixed up in this time?'

He didn't see the direction she was taking; his guilt was too obvious to him for him to understand that his wife was referring to sexual, rather than political, deviation.

'It isn't filth,' he said. 'But I don't expect you to understand. You've never had an ideal in your life.'

'Ideal?' She was losing colour fast; against the harsh violet of her clothes, her face was ghastly.

'Ideal,' Fergus repeated. 'An abstract idea for the betterment of humanity. I've believed in it for a long time. You would call it filth, treason, anything you like, but I don't accept that it is. I think what I've been doing is right.'

While he spoke she had been standing; suddenly she felt as if her legs were broken. She dropped on to the dressing stool, and clutched at the table edge; the bottles ranged like soldiers across the glass surface rattled with the impact.

'Treason,' had he whispered it. 'Treason . . . Jesus Christ! *That's* what you're doing!' Her mouth had half opened; there was an expression of such horror in her eyes that Fergus was shocked.

'Who's paying you?'

He shook his head. 'Nobody's paying me, Margaret.' She didn't seem to have heard.

'The Russians . . . is that who it is? I suppose it was being a bugger—that's what they had over you!'

'No,' he answered. 'You still don't understand; it's not blackmail. I'm not being forced to do anything. I'm doing it because I want to. I've believed in it since I was up at Cambridge.'

'Believed in *what*?' She almost spat the last word at him; gradually she was recovering, shock was changing to a loathing so intense that he felt an impulse to recoil from her, as if she might spring from the seat and attack him with her long nails and her white teeth.

'Communism,' he said, 'I became a Communist. Long before I met you.' He made a gesture, which was almost sad. 'I'm sorry,' he said. 'This is yet another dreadful shock for you. I only wish you could understand how I feel. I wish we'd ever been able to talk to each other about the things that mattered.'

He turned away from her; he felt weak and slightly sick. In spite of what she had inflicted on him, Fergus disliked hurting his wife. To his astonishment she burst into tears. It was years since he had seen her cry. The sight made him feel frightened, insecure. He came towards her, with his handkerchief. She lashed out, knocking it out of his hand.

'Don't you come near me, don't you dare come near me! You bloody, dirty traitor! Traitor! A Communist—you stand there and say you were a Communist, and you ask me to try and understand?'

'Don't shout,' he said. 'Someone may hear you.'

'Yes,' Margaret blazed at him. 'Yes, someone might! Here, take the filthy thing!' She threw the little gold lighter at him. It missed and crashed against the wall behind. She turned back to the dressing table, and began to repair her make-up, savagely wrenching the drawers open, rubbing her wet cheeks with powder. Then she stood up. 'Get out of my room,' she said. 'I have an appointment with the Marches and I'm late already. Get out of my sight.'

He picked up the lighter; it was superbly made. The

impact against the wall had not broken it open. A gold lighter, with a forged Tiffany mark. It was his own refinement, adopted by his superiors. He slipped it into his pocket and went out, closing the door quietly behind him. He never made noise if he could help it. His grandmother, a formidable Edwardian figure, once remarked of a grown man in his hearing, 'No gentleman bangs doors'. With this the offender was dismissed forever. Fergus had never forgotten it. He went back to his study and sat down at the desk. He remembered his childhood very clearly. His mother and father were shadowy figures, encountered at set times between five and five-thirty; they seemed very tall and their attempts to introduce themselves outside the nursery embarrassed him. His nurse loomed large, the substitute mother to whom his parents had given him. Unlike the monster nannies of popular biographies, whose inhumanities were blamed for the subsequent failings of their children, Fergus had no such excuse for the direction he had taken in adult life. He had been well cared for, loved within limits which depended upon his being good, and suffered no traumas in the process. In the years of his young manhood, when he had discovered his own nature, he had tried to analyse the motives which had driven him to a conviction so completely opposite to everything he was supposed to represent. The key to it was not his genuine humanism, or the atheism which he had adopted while he was still at school. With his temperament, he could just as easily have gone into the Church, where his career would have been comparably brilliant to the height it had reached in the Foreign Office. But there was nothing positive enough to attract him in the placid Christianity of the Anglican Church in the 1930s. A different environment and the opportunity could have converted him to that bastion of dogmatic strength, the Roman Catholic Church. But in Fergus's background Catholics were to be found in the same sphere as Non-Conformists, below stairs. He had often described himself as weak; this was not a just assessment. As a character, he needed a direction that satisfied both his intellect and his emotions; the system of class privilege and public service which was the framework of his early life was insufficient on both counts. Having found this authority and accepted it as a basis for living, Fergus Stephenson was capable of great courage, tenacity, and self sacrifice. But the need was still there, unfulfilled by the time he went up to university and discovered that besides this inner craving, he was also a homosexual.

Again, the pattern did not run. His seducer had no Left Wing leanings. He had no political opinions at all, and no convictions beyond the hedonistic. He would have laughed at Fergus's emotional gropings towards truth, had he known they existed. Fergus's conversion happened suddenly; it coincided with the wretched turmoil of his love affair, from which he was struggling to free himself. He met a well known Communist author at a party. It was during the time when half the aristocratic undergraduates were enthusiastic followers of Marx, and the Internationale was sung with passionate vigour at the end of debates. The author was one of many distinguished exponents of the wilder forms of Socialism who was fêted by the new enthusiasts. He was a revelation to Fergus Stephenson. He was an ugly man, but he had a fiery conviction about him which was extraordinarily attractive. He personified strength, and unquestionably, like the fanatically religious, it came from within. He invited Fergus out to dinner, and that was when his search for the meaning of life came to an end. He found faith. He also found a weapon with which to fight his own unhappiness and self disgust. He discovered a common bond with men and women of all classes and ages. Most important to him at this time, he had a place among them. In his own world, he felt an outcast, living a lie; the alternative was to abandon it completely and retire to the squalid twilight in which confessing homosexuals lived, subject to blackmail and public derision. The mincing extremists were utterly repulsive to him. He couldn't have lived among them without going mad. Now he could accept his role in the conventional world because he had a refuge, friends, and a goal in view. Also the secrecy appealed to him; it gave him that sensation he had always lacked in depth, a sense of belonging to a group. He left university with First Class honours, and within a year he was in the Army. He fought in North Africa and then in the Italian campaign. His brother officers remarked that for such a quiet man, Stephenson pursued the Nazi enemy as if it were a personal fight between them. He had entered the Foreign Office when he met and married Margaret. That tragic failure drove him deeper still into the catacombs of his political affiliations. So far the war had prevented conflict arising between his country's interests and his beliefs. But if the war gave them a common aim, the peace was a very short-lived truce, in which time Fergus sensed that the decision must soon be asked of him.

The Americans' attempt to revive the corpse of Nazi Germany was the end for him. Western society had outlawed itself by that action, using the same argument which had allowed the dreadful monster to emerge and try to devour the world—a strong Germany was the bulwark against Soviet Communism. Fergus didn't bother with his party contacts. He offered himself directly to the Russians.

His introduction was effected by a member of the Soviet Embassy in London; he had been recalled to Moscow soon afterwards, and as far as Fergus knew, he had not followed the usual practice and appeared at another Embassy under a different name. Fergus had been given a controller and he had chosen his own code name. Blue. True Conservative blue. The colour of his class politics, and his pedigree blood. He sat on in his study, at the age of fifty-four, brilliant, distinguished, marked for the top in his career, and wondered what his wife would do.

He had disappointed her and she hated him. The hate had subsided into a mixture of irritation and contempt, but it was still there as a base. He had deceived her grossly when they married. He had failed her as a husband and committed the worst possible mistake with a woman of her type by trying to enlist her sympathy. In revenge she had goaded him for twenty years, humbled him with lovers, even with the suggestion that the last of their children wasn't his. But nothing had satisfied that burning female desire to punish the impotent male.

Now, at last, she had the means to hand. To destroy him utterly, to see him exposed, reviled, imprisoned. He wondered if she would do it. Even after all the years, he didn't know the answer. He got up and went to the door. The camera was useless; he would have to memorise the details of that morning's meeting. It might well be the last information that his American controller would ever get from 'Blue'.

. . . . .

'I can't tell you who it is,' Judith said. Richard Paterson had been out of Washington on Friday—sheer desperation had made her make that call to his home. She had not asked him to sit down; they stood facing each other at a distance of a few feet in the living room of her apartment. Now that he had come she was quite calm. The anticipation had been so much worse than the reality of seeing him again, that she found it possible to be cool and polite, as if they were just casually acquainted. On his part Richard Paterson seemed as eager to maintain a strict formality. He hadn't even tried to shake hands. The identity of the Russian who wished to defect was his first question; she repeated her refusal.

'Then you'd no right to drag me up here,' he said. 'I'm not at all anxious to be involved in this, and if it's some bloody fellow filling ink bottles who thinks he's going to con some money out of the West . . .'

'It's nothing of the kind,' Judith interrupted. 'I know the person very well. He's in very great danger and he wants political asylum. Believe me, Richard, nothing but a real necessity would have made me get in touch with you.'

'I'm relieved to hear it,' he said. 'My wife overheard your call and it upset her terribly. I had the hell of a time trying to calm her down.'

Judith looked at him. Indifference; total indifference. That was what Sverdlov had done for her. 'I'm sorry,' she said. 'But it couldn't wait till Monday. I had to call your home. What my friend wants to know is whether the British will receive him and whether they will promise not to hand him over to the Americans or to his own Embassy. That's what he told me to ask you. I tried the Intelligence man who's been in on this, but he's gone to England. I couldn't think of anyone else to approach.'

'I can't answer either of those questions on my own authority,' Richard said. 'All I can do is go back and refer the whole thing to the Ambassador. If this is a really top man in the Russian Embassy, then it should go to the Ambassadorial level straight away. At any rate I could see the Minister first.'

'There isn't time. Go to the Ambassador,' she said. 'My friend would take an assurance from him. You can tell him that this man would be a very valuable acquisition to Britain.' Sverdlov had told her to stress that. She hadn't understood till he explained it, that in these affairs, countries bargained for people as if they were commodities.

'If you can't give me his name,' Paterson said irritably,

'I don't see how I'm going to back that up. What section is he in—can you tell me that?'

'Military,' Judith answered. Beyond that, Sverdlov had warned her not to go. It was enough to wet the official appetite.

'Hmm. That could mean anything. You keep calling him your friend . . .' He glanced at her, slightly accusing. 'You must know his name. Why can't you trust me? It would give me something to go to the Ambassador with—it's all so damned vague, otherwise.'

'I'm sorry, but I'm not allowed to tell you. I've told you all I can; he's important, he wants to come over to us, and he hasn't much time. I know you're a great stickler for the rules, Richard, but if you tie this thing up in red tape, it'll be too late to help him.'

'I'm not particularly interested in helping him,' he said. 'I came here in case it would be a help to *us*. There's always the odd unreliable who's ready to sell himself to the highest bidder just because he's in trouble with his own side and he wants to get out of punishment. We've had this kind of thing before—soldiers coming in from East Berlin calling themselves political refugees, when they'd got drunk and gone AWOL.'

He knew perfectly well that this wasn't the circumstance but her attitude irritated him. He hadn't expected her to be so cool; she might never have been to bed with him at all. All she appeared to be thinking about was the safety of her 'friend'.

'Oh my God,' Judith exclaimed. 'My God—I never thought I'd want to see that little brute Loder, but I'd give anything to have him here instead of you. If you can't do anything to help, then can you put somebody from the Intelligence people on to me direct? That's all I want! You don't have to go to the Ambassador or get involved at all—after all, if it didn't turn out well, it might do some damage to your almighty career, though I'm damned if I can think what!'

'I'll get in touch with Loder when the Ambassador tells me to.' He went to the door. 'I don't know what you've got yourself mixed up in, Judith, but it sounds like a pretty scruffy mess this time. I advise you to remember which side you're on. I'll get in touch with you tomorrow.'

She ran after him to the door. 'There's not much time,'

she said. 'A week or ten days. For God's sake, get them to make up their minds!'

'I can't commit myself to any time limit,' he said curtly. 'I've told you, I'll pass it on at the top and I'll call you tomorrow.' He walked rapidly down the corridor to the lift, and she shut the front door.

Sverdlov came out of the bedroom. He had a cigarette in his hand which he gave her. 'You heard it?' Judith asked him.

'Yes. It was satisfactory. He will go to his Ambassador and the Ambassador will refer it to his Intelligence section. You've done very well for me.'

'How do you know? How do you know it will happen like that? Supposing Richard never does anything at all—you heard what he said about a scruffy mess—he may decide it's better not to get himself involved—you don't know how he thinks things out!'

'I know better than you do,' Sverdlov said. 'He will do what he said, because he wants to claim some credit for himself. He will go to the Ambassador and say "Sir, I have a most important Russian officer who wishes to come over to our side." It will go down on his record and he will be happy. But he won't deal with me himself. I'm glad about that. I don't like him.'

Judith looked at her watch. 'We'd better get out of here before Nancy comes back from her lunch date. Feodor, do you have to go back to your Embassy? It worries me so much in case they suspect anything.'

'They won't,' he said. 'It is amusing, really. The one who is trying to catch me in a trap, thinks I have caught you in one. He will wait to get the reward for himself, before he shoots the bolt on me. It's an old trick, but it is always working. If you have something in one hand that an enemy wants, show him there is something in the other. Then he can't make up his mind which one to take from you first.'

'Another Russian proverb?' Judith asked him. He looked less tense than the previous night, but even so the signs of strain were evident. There was a nerve by his mouth which was jumping visibly under the skin, and there were deep rings under his eyes. She herself had been unable to do more than doze during the night. Waiting for him was made into a nightmare by the fear that he might somehow be prevented from arriving, and she would never know exactly what had happened to him.

'We can go to a movie,' Sverdlov suggested. 'Then I can hold your hand in the dark.' He suddenly threw an arm round her shoulders, catching her off balance, and kissed her on the mouth.

'You don't like that Englishman any more, do you?'

Judith disengaged herself. 'How do you know that?'

'Because now you kiss me,' Sverdlov said. 'We will go to the movie and sit in the seats in the back row.'

Afterwards Judith couldn't remember what they saw that afternoon. He insisted on putting his arm around her, and though she whispered and argued with him in the darkness he refused to take it away or sit back in his own seat. All round them couples twined and necked, oblivious of the programme. Sverdlov rested his head against her shoulder, and within minutes she knew he had fallen asleep. She sat there in the darkness, uncomfortable because of the weight of the exhausted man lying against her. It was impossible, a situation far more incredible than the phoney dramatics being enacted on the wide screen. Nobody would believe it; nobody seeing them together in the darkness would imagine that the man sleeping was taking a respite from the pressure of imminent arrest and certain death.

They looked like lovers, and they weren't. They had met on a Barbadian beach and begun a relationship under the sun which was growing into something as dark as the atmosphere around them at that moment. She had gone away from trouble; in the island refuge she had unwittingly engaged herself in trouble of a kind that made a disappointing love affair, a simple widowhood, into mundane events in an unremarkable life. The man whose head was on her shoulder, was not an ordinary man; meeting him, allowing him to get as close to her as he had done, was not only a mistake in judgement which she had no excuse for making, but she sensed that as a consequence her life would never be the same again. She didn't love him; she was sure of that. Whatever she had felt for Richard Paterson her feeling for Sverdlov was not the same. It was not love. But she didn't want anything to happen to him. She didn't want him taken back to suffer and die. She got one hand into her bag and found a handkerchief. He was so sure Richard would help him. She lacked that confidence. Sitting in the dark cinema, she blamed herself for having taken an aggressive attitude. She knew her ex-lover's vanity; she should have played upon it. He hadn't liked her reference to the Russian as a 'friend'. Pride, not jealousy but even so it might affect his actions. Her mind raced backwards and forwards down different avenues of anxiety. Sverdlov made a joke of it, quoting those maddening, folksy Russian proverbs, like a poor man's Krushchev. She would say that to him, she decided, the very next time he produced another. But the nervous twitch remained, the black hollows under the lazy greenish eyes, the sudden lapse into sleep because he felt it was safe to relax for an hour or so. There was a musical crescendo and a change in the lighting; the movie was over, whatever it was, and she moved him gently, waking him.

'I'm sorry,' he sat upright quickly. 'I meant to make love to you.'

'You were dead tired,' Judith said. 'It did you good to sleep.'

'Was it a good movie?'

'I don't know; I wasn't concentrating. Feodor, why don't you move into the apartment with me until we know?'

'What about your friend—Nancy?'

'I'll tell her you've taken Richard's place. She won't ask questions; I don't enquire who she's going with; we lead our own lives. I can say you're a White Russian.'

He began to laugh until the people in front of them turned round and hissed angrily at them to shut up. The second feature had begun. He went on laughing at her, shaking in the seat.

'This is my friend Feodor Sverdlov, the White Russian! Oh my darling, what a fool you are! Come on, it is time we went back. I have work to do tonight; you will get the message from your Embassy tomorrow.'

He took her home in a taxi, where he subjected her to bear hugs and rough kisses until she forgot to be frightened for him and told him angrily to stop.

She could get no serious reaction from him about anything. He repeated the remark about White Russian several times, and started to laugh at her over again. Judith had offered to take him in to live with her. And after weeks of determined efforts to wrest this out of her, Sverdlov had declined to take advantage of the offer. It was not until she was actually in bed and trying to get to sleep that she realised it might be because he knew himself to be in greater danger of arrest than he had told her. And the presence of a couple of women in a Manhattan flat would not deter his people. He had elected to stay in his Embassy where she couldn't become involved.

Two days passed; Monday and Tuesday and still no telephone call from Richard Paterson. On Wednesday she managed to work with her usual efficiency till lunch time; she refused to take a break but stayed on in Sam Nielson's office, drinking coffee from the automatic machine in the corridor outside, waiting for the call that didn't come. She made several mistakes in dictation and had to come back and ask Nielson to repeat himself. He was working at full pitch and she had chosen the wrong day to foul up his letters. He said so. 'I'm sorry.' Judith actually stumbled over the apology. The phone in her office was ringing. She gave Nielson a startled look, half pleading and half defiant, and then ran out to answer it.

Her anxiety was such that she said 'Richard' as soon as she picked it up.

'Mrs. Farrow?'

She grabbed the receiver with the other hand. It was Loder's voice.

'Yes,' she said. 'Yes, it's me. I've been trying to get you . . . .'

'Don't talk,' he cut through her. 'Just listen and keep it cool. I know what the score is; I got back this morning and the message was passed on. I'm flying up tonight, I understand it's urgent, is that right?'

'Oh yes,' Judith said. 'Yes, terribly. Please come tonight.'

'I take it it's our friend who wants to see me?'

'Yes,' Judith said again. Never mind what Sverdlov had told her; she had forgotten it anyway. All she wanted was for somebody at the Embassy to see him and get the machinery moving.

'Okay then.' There was a peculiar note in his voice; if he hadn't been such a flat, phlegmatic man, she would have said it was excitement. 'Get him to take a walk with you this evening. Go up Fifth and pick up a cruising cab on the corner of Park; 9.30 sharp. You both get in and I'll be in it. Have you got that clear? Corner of Park, 9.30 tonight.'

'I've got it,' Judith answered. She could feel Sam Nielson waiting in the inner office, fuming while she talked. He was going to fume even more when she put through a call to Sverdlov.

She didn't go back and ask permission. She dialled the number Sverdlov had given her and was put directly through to him. He was still in the UNO Embassy.

'I can have dinner tonight,' she said. 'Will you pick me up after work—6.30?'

'With pleasure. Is it going to be a party?' She could imagine the damnable twisted grin. She was so glad to speak to him and find everything normal that she gave a nervous laugh. 'Yes, it is. I've just fixed it all up.'

'How did you sleep?'

'Not too well. How did you?' To hell with Sam Nielson; she could hear him clearing his throat angrily behind her, his papers rustling as he threw them down on his desk.

'Not as well as if I had been with you,' the voice mocked. 'Insomnia is bad for the health. We must do something about it.'

'Six-thirty,' Judith said. 'I won't be late. Goodbye.' She hung up and then she went back into Sam Nielson's office.

'Mr. Nielson,' she said, 'I'm awfully sorry about the interruptions. Something very important came up for me. But it's all right now. There won't be anything more.'

. . . . .

Loder had got off the plane, after an all-night flight, worrying about the appalling prospect of his chief's suspicion like a dog digging frantically for a buried bone. A grade one traitor, working for the K.G.B. Passing information of the most confidential nature. That Arab Israel peace move had been a real diplomatic time bomb; it should have ticked away in secret until it was due to go off in the face of Soviet influence in the Middle East. Instead it had blown up in the hand, so to speak, damning the chances of a truce between Egypt and the Jews for a long time to come. Whoever the bastard was, Loder already felt a personal hatred for him. He respected the agent working for his own side, though this attitude didn't deter him from the most drastic action against them; his complaint was that often the action wasn't drastic enough. But for the paid double agent, the traitor working for the enemy, Loder had a pathological hatred and contempt. Blackmail was no excuse to him; there was always a moment when the guts to refuse were there or they weren't. As for the ideological traitors, the atom scientists giving their secrets to the oppressors of half Europe—Loder would have put a bullet through the lot of them.

Who the hell was it this time? Was it really an Englishman, following the shameful tradition of the ones that got away, that damnable trinity of dirty traitors? Loder sat up in his plane seat, his anger growing like a pain in his insides. He came into his office looking as tired and ill tempered as he felt. And that was when the Ambassador sent for him. The Ambassador was a man who couldn't help overawing other people. He was a very tall, well built man, with a habit of looking down at anyone to whom he was speaking. It was quite unconscious, but Loder found it difficult. He wished more than once during the interview that the Old Man had been away and he was speaking to Stephenson.

The Ambassador had been brief. Group Captain Paterson had been to see him over the weekend. He had made a great fuss about a Russian Embassy official who apparently wanted to seek asylum with the West. The Ambassador had advised him that this was not really within the diplomatic province, and he had therefore told the Group Captain to forget about it; this was Loder's sphere of operations. He had made it sound as if the area in which Loder worked were somewhat unsavoury, and that a squalid deal with a Russian prepared to sell out his own people reflected little credit on his Embassy. Loder had gathered up the brief notes prepared by Paterson and gone back to his office at the run. The possibility that it might be Sverdlov was so tempting that he had to discipline himself to read every word the Group Captain had written down. His interview with Mrs. Farrow. Her refusal to give the Russian's name. Her insistence that it was urgent. Very urgent. By Christ, Loder said to himself, if it was Feodor Sverdlov, urgent was an understatement. She had assured Paterson that he was in 'great danger', the words were italicised as hers, and there was 'only a week or ten days' to get him away.

Sverdlov. It must be him. That was the reason why he

had contacted Farrow in Barbados. Not to pull her in, but to make sure of an escape route for himself. Christ. What a turn-up for the book that would be. Four hundred miles away in New York, Judith had no idea how Loder sweated while he put that call through and asked that one vital question.

'Is it our friend?' And then the God-given answer. 'Yes.' Sverdlov it was. The top man; the biggest fish in the United States. He could hardly believe it. And coming to the British, not the Americans. What a kick in the slats for Commander-God-Almighty-Buckley. He had been tormented with a tension headache all day; he swallowed more aspirin with a cup of tea, and composed a long memo to his chief in London. Then he drove out to Washington airfield to catch the airbus to New York.

. . . . .

General Golitsyn decided to go up to New York himself. He had spent the weekend considering the situation and planning what was best for him to do. The position as a whole, and his own in particular, had changed direction so suddenly that at first he had been caught off guard. Sverdlov had cancelled his return to Russia. He had spoken to Golitsyn, informing him as a matter of courtesy that he had altered his plan, and the reason was sufficiently important to outweigh his personal considerations in going back to see his wife. It concerned Mrs. Farrow; his long-laid plan concerning her was about to come to fruition, and he had hinted to Golitsyn that she was far more important than he had anticipated. There was nothing Golitsyn, as a subordinate, could say; he had been informed immediately afterwards by Anna Skriabine that Sverdlov had instructed her to make a tentative booking for Moscow for the week after next. According to her report, he was in excellent spirits. There was nothing Golitsyn could do about it, except send word back home that the suspect was not coming, and so far as he could ascertain, the reasons for delaying were perfectly valid. However, he would check this personally and refer back for instructions.

He took the plane at five, and was in the Soviet UNO office by seven. He was welcomed with deference at the airport, as befitted the nominal head of the Military Mission to the United States; the UNO Ambassador himself came down to meet him in the hall, he was shown upstairs to a luxurious suite of bedroom and private office kept at the disposal of high ranking visitors from Washington or elsewhere. The rooms reserved for the K.G.B. were in another part of the building and they were occupied by Sverdlov. The old man was tired; flying disagreed with him, even a short trip made him feel bad tempered and exhausted. It was time for him to go home and accept the armchair he had resisted for so long. But he had this one service to perform for his country before he gave in and retired.

He had to rid Russia of the Sverdlovs, with their spineless belief in compromise, their decadent flirting with the heresy that it was possible to serve the Revolution of the proletariat without the total destruction of its enemies.

When he asked for Sverdlov he was told that he had gone out. Golitsyn helped himself to vodka. He retained the humble taste of his peasant origins. The staff had sent up a plate of pickled cucumber and black bread, with a dish of salt. The old General liked his vodka with the right accompaniments. The diversities of Western cocktail canapes were not for him. Then he sent for Major Stukalov of the Soviet Air Force. Stukalov was from his home province in the Ukraine; he was a square, fair-haired man in his middle thirties, reputedly very popular at cocktail parties and on friendly terms with many of the UNO diplomats from allied countries. He was one of the best K.G.B. officers in America, and a protégé of the General. Like everyone else he came under the ultimate direction of Sverdlov. He stood at attention in front of Golitsyn.

'Major,' the General said, 'I am going to entrust a very delicate matter to you on behalf of General Panyushkin himself.' He bit into the black bread, encrusted with salt, and then swallowed some vodka. The Major's eyes had blinked at that dreaded name. Panyushkin lacked the Himmlerian horror of his predecessor Beria, but he was a man whom his subordinates feared.

He ruled his Secret Service with the autocracy of a Tsar. His orders were as absolute and his puishment for disobedience as terrible.

'I am at your disposal, General. I await Comrade Panyushkin's orders.'

Golitsyn pointed to the vodka. 'Another glass. There is nothing like vodka. Listen to me, Major. Have you got two men whom you can trust completely? I mean trust as you would trust yourself—as *I* trust you?'

'Yes, General. More than two, if you need them.'

'Two will be enough. This is a very serious matter, you understand that the order comes from Panyushkin himself? I am following his instructions.'

He waited, letting the young man stew for a minute. He trusted Stukalov, but he trusted fear of Panyushkin more than any sentimental tie, like his patronage and recommendation for promotion in the past. Fear, not loyalty to him personally, would keep Stukalov from making an attempt to warn his chief.

'Your two men are to watch Colonel Sverdlov,' Golitsyn said. 'He has come under suspicion from the Praesidium.' There was silence then; he broke it by clearing a residue of phlegm from his throat and coughing it into a handkerchief.

'I'm sorry to hear that,' Major Stukalov answered. 'He can be watched day and night by my two men. I will supervise this personally, General.'

'You will report to me, and no one else,' Golitsyn said. 'Panyushkin has placed this in my hands. Sverdlov is due to return to Russia soon. If anything happens to alert him before he goes, I shall hold you responsible, Major. You and your two men. You understand?'

'I understand, General; I won't fail you.'

Golitsyn said, 'There's a woman involved with him, a Mrs. Farrow, who works for Nielson, the Canadian lawyer. He is preparing her for recruitment. You might be the right choice as her controller after he leaves. I hear you have a way with women, isn't that so?'

'I don't know, General. But I can try to direct Mrs. Farrow, if you select me.'

'She could be very important to us,' the General said. 'If you run her successfully, you would be promoted. On my recommendation. But we will see, Major, we will see. This is in the future, after Colonel Sverdlov has gone back to Russia. Begin the surveillance as soon as he returns to the Embassy tonight. You can go now. Good night.' He chewed some of the pickled cucumbers and drank his second glass of vodka. He had a head like a boulder. He never got drunk.

. . . . .

The inside of the taxi cab was dark; Sverdlov flagged it down as it cruised conveniently along the kerbside, arriving precisely at 9.30, almost crawling to a halt as it came level with them.

He had opened the door for her, and as she climbed in she saw Loder sitting well back in the far corner. He didn't speak. Sverdlov got in next; they sat squeezed together, all three on the back seat.

'My name is Loder. I'm from the British Embassy in Washington. I believe you want to see me.'

'That is quite correct.'

It seemed to Judith that they travelled half a block in complete silence. Sverdlov lit a cigarette, offering the case to her, which she refused.

'Well then,' Loder spoke first, brisk and unfriendly. 'What's the score? What do you want?'

'Political asylum. The usual guarantees, and one extra one: no trade with the Americans. I want to go to England.'

'I see. I was told you were in a hurry to get out, is that right?'

'Yes,' Sverdlov answered. He sounded different, the same cold authoritarian who had talked to his subordinate Memenov over a drink. Judith looked out of the window; as far as the two men were concerned she might not have been there. She could appreciate that both of them wished that she weren't.

'I have to make the move within the next two weeks or I may be prevented from leaving. You have the authority to give me the guarantees I want?'

'I have full authority,' Loder said. 'But I haven't committed us to giving you asylum yet. You could cause complications, Colonel. You could be a big embarrassment in Anglo-Soviet relations. This has got to be considered.'

'I understand that,' Sverdlov said. 'But I am not coming empty handed.'

'I didn't think you were,' Loder answered. 'Protecting you from your own organisation for the rest of your life isn't going to cost peanuts. What will you bring with you, just supposing we're prepared to offer our hospitality?'

'One piece of information.'

'One? One item, is that what you're offering? Come on, Colonel, nobody's going to wear that! I wouldn't waste my chief's time making the suggestion—he'd just tell me to tell you to get stuffed!'

'One piece of information,' Sverdlov went on as if the vulgar interruption had not taken place. 'Something more useful to your country than all the lies my predecessors have told you about Soviet security methods. What do you want, Mr. Loder—the names of a dozen expendable agents working in Europe, the key to a code which will be changed twenty-four hours after I've gone—or information about who is betraying Western top security secrets at this moment? If that doesn't interest you, then stop the cab, and I will get out.'

He turned and for a moment the two men looked at each other in the semi-darkness. Loder wanted Sverdlov; he wanted him so badly that his headache had become a full scale bombardment of anxiety pains. But he wouldn't have given the bastard an inch; he would have played it indifferent and made him crawl, made him beg for safety. Within five minutes of Sverdlov getting into that cab he knew that nothing would produce that effect on this man. He was ready to come over, but it would have to be with a pretence of self respect. Otherwise Loder felt convinced that he would try to make it on his own or even indulge in a bout of Russian fatalism and take what was coming to him.

He wondered what exactly Sverdlov had to fear that he was ready to change sides. Certainly not the type to do it for money—nor was he the idealistic kind, seeing himself as the saviour of twentieth-century civilisation. Sverdlov was in danger; those were the words used. Danger from his own people. But on what grounds, for what crime?

Loder didn't really care, but it gave him a means of avoiding the direct challenge issued by the Russian.

'Of course we'd be interested,' he said. 'But there's one thing you'll have to come across with before we go any further. Why do you want asylum?'

'I believe I am going to be put on trial when I go home,' Sverdlov said. 'And then executed. As for a crime, I have certainly committed one. I neglected to change my political attitude in time. I am a moderate, Mr. Loder. There are a number of us in Soviet Government; I think we are all about to be liquidated. Beginning with my department, as usual.'

'Nice for you.' Loder couldn't resist it. The mills of God, he thought with satisfaction. Hungary is catching up on you at last, you bastard. Now you're on the receiving end for a change. 'Nothing else? They'll do their best to discredit you, so we might as well get the picture right.'

'I am not a drunkard, or a dope addict, and I like to go to bed with women, not men.' For a brief second Judith could sense that his attention had turned to her. 'I do not gamble or steal money. Mrs. Farrow will give me a character reference.' She saw him smile at her in the poor light. She had heard every word, but it was unreal; however plainly they talked, the meaning seemed to escape her, like the conversation carried on in dreams.

Loder lit a cigarette. 'You talk about a top grade agent,' he said. 'I'll need more information than just that.'

'There isn't much more I can tell you,' Sverdlov answered. 'I don't know his identity, but I have seen his reports and his photocopies; I will promise to bring original documents with me. You can probably identify him when you see what he has been providing. Like the secret truce talks between Egypt and Israel.'

Loder swallowed smoke. He stopped playing his little game.

'You can bring these papers with you? That's definite?'

'That is the bargain,' Sverdlov said quietly. 'You'll find it is a very good one. I will make, what do you call it—a deposit for full payment. He has a code name. "Blue". I have been thinking about what this means, and to me it is nonsense. But you have this saying, True Blue.' Judith started, and for a second she opened her mouth to interrupt, to remind him that she had mentioned the phrase. But Sverdlov was going on, and she said nothing.

'The Americans don't have this saying,' he said. 'So I believe our agent is an Englishman. I will give the papers to you when I am on board the plane for London.'

'Okay.' Loder said it with finality. 'We'll do a deal with you. You bring the information and we'll see you safe and snug for the rest of your life. Now, Colonel Sverdlov, how, when and where do you go? You'll have to work out your own details; all I need from you is a time and a place. We'll take charge of you from then.'

'I shall make my arrangements this week,' Sverdlov said. 'How do we communicate?'

'Through Mrs. Farrow,' Loder answered. 'You seeing her won't rouse suspicion; any new contact might do just that. Are you being watched?'

'How would I know?' Sverdlov had relaxed; Judith could tell by the sound of his voice. 'For all you know, one of our men could be driving this cab. For my sake, I hope that he isn't. Stop him at Mrs. Farrow's apartment. We'll both get out there.'

'As it happens,' Loder said, 'the driver's one of mine!'

Sverdlov took Judith by the arm, and then he asked the taxi driver what was owing, and gave him the fare. He even included a tip. Loder was invisible in the far corner.

'Attention to detail,' Sverdlov said to her. 'Maybe your Mr. Loder is right; if I am being followed, then I have to pay the taxi cab and see you to your door. And to make it seem right, I must kiss you good night.'

'It's going to be all right,' Judith whispered. 'Please stop, Feodor, let me talk for a minute. It is going to be all right, isn't it?'

'Yes, I think so. I think he is a clever man and he will not make any mistakes. And I never make a mistake; don't you know that? As for you, do you know what you are now? A letter box. A live letter box, because you're not a hollow tree or an ashcan by a door . . .'

'What are you talking about?' She tried to dodge the endless kissing. She even pushed but he took not the slightest notice.

'You're my channel of communication. My letter box for Mr. Loder.' A long and especially determined embrace followed this remark. 'I will telephone you tomorrow. Will you come and live with me in England?'

'No, of course not. Don't be silly.'

'Why are you so miserable?'

'I'm not miserable; I'm just worried. I'm not like you, I can't see everything as a joke!'

'But if it isn't funny, then it must be sad,' Sverdlov said patiently. 'If I am caught and taken home, then it will be sad. Sad for me and even for you, because I think you will be sorry. Until then, it is funny. Making love to a letter box is one of the great jokes of the world.'

When Judith had gone inside the apartment building, Sverdlov spent the next hour walking. It was a fine night; within five minutes he had left the quieter residential block off Park Avenue and was in the brightly lit and busy street itself, mingling with the crowds who poured along the broad sidewalks.

Sometimes he paused to look in the department store windows. The displays were colourful and original; he had never bothered to look at them dispassionately before, or to compare them with the dismal uniformity of the State enterprise GUM, which displayed its goods as if it were inviting the purchaser to commit a crime.

He had never minded criticism, provided it served a purpose and was not a peevish carping in disguise. He had found a great deal wrong in his own society, and rather enjoyed upsetting Elena by saying so; he had never found enough to make him prefer another country's mode of living. He was a Russian; he thought and felt and behaved like a Russian. He had never wanted to leave his home and he didn't want to leave it now. But equally he was determined not to die in it.

Traitor was a word which other people used too freely, usually to describe somebody whose opinions differed from their own. Men he had worked with would apply that word to him, if he was successful and escaped. Probably in his own mind he would apply it to himself at moments. Only a fool supposed that self-elected exiles felt no nostalgic qualm, no savage pang of disillusion. But Sverdlov knew the working of his own machine. Suspicion was followed by sentence as night followed day. The State had taken the place of the Deity and with Divinity it had also to assume omnipotence. Like God, it was incapable of error. Walking along the glittering street, mixing with the American crowds going home from the movie theatres and the restaurants, Sverdlov faced the prospect of living in exile for the rest of his life. And not only in exile, but in hiding.

An assumed name, a series of moves from one place to another, months of living under protection before it was assumed safe enough to settle somewhere permanently, with only a minimal watch being kept. And even then there was no certainty. His people would go on looking for him; it would be regarded as a crusade to find and punish him. And Loder's government would not be easy on him, not once he had committed himself to their custody. He used the word custody on purpose. In many senses the defector was the prisoner of those who offered him protection. He had no place else to go and they could exert as much pressure on him as they liked. The most obvious being the threat to hand him back. It wouldn't be easy and it wouldn't be happy. He accepted this. But considered as an alternative to months in the Lubiyanka, being destroyed as a human entity capable of reason or resistance, Sverdlov did not hesitate. He would not shuffle out like a dummy to be shot for the crime of thinking differently. He began to walk at a faster pace, pushing against the stream of the crowd. Soon the streets would be empty. The respectable people enjoying an evening out were all hurrying for the shelter of their homes before the city became a late night jungle, where violence, robbery and death were the marauders. Only the bravest or the most desperate risked the subway trains late at night.

He could not have lived in America, except as a last refuge when every other avenue had closed against him. And he had told Judith the truth when he described it as his country's major enemy in the West. The English would be tolerable. Sverdlov knew they were capable of great ruthlessness; the conquest of one sixth of the earth's surface by a shrimp sized island was not achieved without a due regard for force.

It was surprising what a man of Loder's type could do if circumstances pushed him. But the British were not a major power, and they were too clever to pretend they were. What he had to offer was more than enough to satisfy them; the traditional rivalry between the British intelligence and the CIA would ensure that they didn't break their promise and make a present of him to the Americans. As soon as he thought of going over, he had thought in terms of Britain. Probably because of Judith Farrow. He was not far from his Embassy but he was tired; he waited on the sidewalk until a vacant cab appeared. He jumped in and dropped back against the seat. She was in a separate compartment of his life. He never thought about her in connection with his work. He needed her help and he would make full use of it, but he kept her apart, unconnected with issues which were irrelevent to her and what she meant to him. It had always been so; he had tried very hard to segregate Elena from the political world in which they lived, to shut her away from his career, to keep a private compartment in his life where nothing outside was allowed to enter. But she had refused to accept this. No two people had a right to such privacy; it was an offensive cult of the individual. Individuals were part of each other because they were part of the State. It was not possible to have a relationship from which the larger issues and responsibilities were excluded.

And exclusion was what Sverdlov wanted. That was why it was possible for him to hold Judith Farrow in his arms and ridicule the fear and uncertainty of his situation by a joke. She was separate, and for those few minutes when they were together, so was he, from all of it. She was the only woman he had ever known with whom he could sustain this private existence.

He reached his offices just before eleven. His return was the first item on the surveillance report which Stukalov's men began on him that night.

. . . . .

It was not the first time Loder had exceeded his authority; it was certainly the only occasion when he felt sure there would be no protest from above.

He caught a plane at eleven, at the same time Sverdlov went through the door of the Embassy Building on 98th, and passed the short flight eating a candy bar which he had bought at Kennedy and making notes in his pocket book. Sverdlov. The top man in the K.G.B., in the United States. He couldn't believe his luck; but as if the man himself were not enough, there was the unexpected bonus, the diamond stuck in the nugget, so to speak, of his knowledge of the Soviet agent. His chief had described this unknown traitor as a major threat to the safety of the Western powers; at that moment top level security men in NATO were chewing their nails over this new development. None of them had a clue who it was; they only knew that the beast was moving through the paper jungle, and by a miraculous coincidence they had picked up its spoor. But Sverdlov could provide enough information, documentary proof which was the most impressive kind for high authority, to help them trap and catch it. Blue. True Blue. It might be a lead or it might not; he was inclined to agree with the Russian's assessment that only an Englishman would have chosen the code name. On the other hand it was a tortuous explanation, likely to present itself to Sverdlov; the truth could be quite different and much simpler. There might be a particular network using colours as their recognition; 'Blue' could be one of them. There might be Green, Yellow, Brown . . . He picked up his car from the park at Washington Airport and drove straight back to the Embassy. The night staff would be on, dozing and playing rummy till eight o'clock in the morning. Rummy, that old war-time game long out of favour, had become an Embassy staff craze. Everyone played it. Loder thought it was a dreadful game. He never played anything but contract bridge. He went up to cyphers and gave the duty officer a telegram to code and send off to London immediately. When he went back to bed he knew it was a waste of time to try to sleep. He couldn't stop thinking; his mind was going like one of those mechanical racing cars he had bought his son for Christmas. He made himself a cup of his special tea, ran a hot bath and dropped into it. Lucky Jack Loder. Someone had said that when he got the Washington post. How right they had been.

And unlike most Intelligence projects which took weeks, often months, to put into operation, this would be over in a matter of days. That meant the margin for error was reduced to the minimum. The longer the time, the more people involved, the more danger of a leak, of somebody on the other side getting a hint. He remembered the unfortunate defector who had approached the Embassy at Ankara with a proposition. Britain had delayed and hesitated, until the buck was eventually passed to the head of Anglo-Soviet Affairs at the F.O. The post was occupied by Philby, and the Russian was never seen again. He had taken the initiative, referring back for confirmation but he intended to proceed without waiting for an answer.

Once he had Sverdlov on board a plane, the most difficult hurdle would have been jumped. After that it would be the Special Branch's job to keep him alive. Loder didn't mind once they were in England. But until then Sverdlov's life was not worth a penn'orth of cat's pee. The vulgarism came into his mind quite naturally. The K.G.B. would use any method to prevent Sverdlov escaping to the West; one hint that he was trying to desert and he would be murdered. A car crash, a faked suicide, a cyanide 'heart attack'. But he knew this better than anyone. He could take care of himself. Loder lay in the steam and sloshed the hot water over his stomach. He felt exhilarated; a moment like this made all the tedious dead ends of his job worth while. Failures, unresolved problems, unanswered questions. They were all there in his official file. But nothing would count beside the one tremendous coup of his career. The safe delivery of Feodor Sverdlov into British custody in the United Kingdom.

## CHAPTER EIGHT

Fergus Stephenson went to a dinner at the Brazilian Embassy with his wife; they drove together in their private Rolls, Margaret glittering like minor royalty in the back seat at his side, wearing a white dress with a handsome Victorian necklace. She looked very impressive in evening dress, the formality unsexed her; there was no suggestion of the angry fires that smouldered under the polished upper class appearance, bright and superior as her own diamonds. She had not spoken to him since the morning she threw back the lighter. He hadn't tried to seek her out. He worked as usual and concentrated on his duties with the discipline which mad been instilled into him from infancy. He accepted the period of mental anguish, knowing that it was a price she had decided to exact, sensing also that a precipitate move on his part might tip the balance of her judgement against him. If indeed it had not already come down in that direction, and the silence was merely an additional sadism she had chosen to inflict upon him. He smoked excessively; it was the only indication that he was under strain. When he offered one to Margaret she shook her head.

'Not for me; and for God's sake be careful, you've dropped ash on my skirt!'

'I'm sorry,' Stephenson said. The car was full of her strong scent; it was a true reflection of her personality, powerful and decisive. She had often remarked that the delicate flowery scents were useless to her; they were absorbed and disappeared. He would have liked to open the window; he hated the smell.

'Tonight should be interesting,' his wife remarked suddenly. 'I hear the Brazilian Minister is on the point of resigning.'

'Yes,' Stephenson said. 'That's what the rumour is. It may not be true of course.'

'I should have thought you found that sort of thing very interesting.' She had glanced out of the window as she spoke. 'Don't you pick up all the scraps of gossip, just in case they might be useful to your friends?'

'No.' His voice was patient. He knew it was coming at last and he felt nothing. Nothing at all.

'So you only interest yourself in the top grade, I suppose?'

'That's right.'

'What exactly would happen to you if it went wrong?'

'The same as the others. Unless I got out first.'

The glass partition was up between them and the chauffeur. Even so he leaned forward to make sure there was no gap.

'I can't imagine you living in a dreadful little flat in Moscow,' his wife said. 'But it would be better than Pentonville I suppose.'

'May I ask which you have decided would be most suitable?'

She turned and looked at him. To his astonishment her face was contorted with emotion.

'I've decided what's most suitable for *me*. By God, Fergus, I've been tempted to give you what you bloody well deserve. I've spent the last two days going round and round, trying to make up my mind. Well I've made it up now: you've ruined my life in one way. You were a queer when you married me; I'll never forget the day you told me about your love affair when you were up at Cambridge—I'll never forget what I felt as long as I live!

'Maybe that's why I've been able to take this new thing calmly. Nothing could be as bad for me as that night, with you snivelling and confessing about being buggered. I could have got over most things, but not that. Never that. Now, after twenty-odd years, with the children grown up and our life settled on a certain course, after all the years of living in frightful places, moving from dreadful little postings to better and better until we're in line for a grade one Embassy—now you have to tell me you're doing something which could destroy it all.

'I could ruin you, Fergus, and don't for one moment think I wouldn't like to do it! I'd like to see you go to jail for the rest of your life. If we had the death penalty for what you're doing, I'd be happy to see you hanged. That's what I feel about *you* personally. But I'm tied to you; if you go down I go with you, and I'm damned if I'm going to let that happen.'

She opened her bag and took out a handkerchief; her eyes were dry but she patted her lips in a gesture of pure nerves.

'I've worked for my reward,' she said. 'I've spent my life helping your career because I wanted to get to the top. I want that Embassy; I want it for myself, not for you. And I'm going to see that I get it.'

'I see.' He still felt nothing; it was as if his whole system had been anaesthetised. 'Then you've decided not to say anything about it. Thank you, Margaret.'

'Don't you dare thank me!' Her face was suddenly close to him and he felt her breath. It was as if she might attack him and tear him with her teeth. It was a subconscious fear of which he had never been aware in literal terms before.

'Don't you dare say that! Don't you understand? I'd crucify you if it didn't mean the same for me! I'm doing this for myself, to protect my interests. And the children. You always said I wasn't maternal; well I am as far as that kind of filthy disgrace is concerned! Nobody's going to know, and from this day on, you're going to stop doing it, you hear? You're giving up. Otherwise you'll get caught. I caught you out, and that shows you're getting careless. I want your promise, Fergus. I want your word of honour that you'll not do any more of it.'

'I can't do that,' Stephenson said. 'I can't give that promise. I can only promise I'll try.'

'You try,' his wife said. 'And you'd better succeed. We're here now. Isn't that the Patersons driving up?'

'Yes,' Stephenson said. He was still numb, but there was a growing weary ache in his limbs. 'Is she still one of your protégés?'

'I like her,' Margaret said. 'He's such a cold-blooded swine; I think she needs someone to stand by her. I know I would have liked someone to stand by me.'

'You never needed anyone,' he said. 'You were born strong.'

'I've needed to be,' she said. 'And now I am. I'm as tough as nails. You did that for me at least.'

When the chauffeur opened the door she got out, her long spirts lifted in one hand; together she and Fergus walked up the short flight of steps into the imposing Embassy building, shaded by tall dogwood trees, discreetly floodlit. They looked so imposing they could have been extras in a Hollywood movie.

Rachel Paterson did her best to sustain a conversation with a Brazilian gentleman on her left. It wasn't easy because she found her attention constantly wandering in Richard's direction; she answered the pleasant questions about her length of stay in Washington, when her baby was expected and other trivia, with a vacant smile and some vague answers. But she watched Richard across the table. He was talking to a beautiful South American girl, married to one of the Chilean air attachés. She was laughing, showing dazzling teeth, her big black eyes flashing up at him, one slender hand touching her left breast, which Rachel thought indecently exposed. She had begun to feel jealous by degrees. When he came back from that trip to Washington she was calm and apparently quiescent in the explanation he had given her. But she lay awake thinking and bursting into fits of crying, worrying about the woman who had telephoned. He had sworn there was nothing in the friendship. He had said they never even kissed. But now Rachel watched him as she had never done before; she watched him with other women, and she saw him in an entirely different light. He was smiling down at his companion; he looked amused and animated, the woman was displaying herself before a genuinely appreciative male audience. Rachel tried to eat the food, but she felt as if her stomach had swollen until it was impossible to swallow solids. She reached out for her wine glass and took refuge in that, forcing herself to concentrate on her companions on either side, not to see her husband flirting with that half-naked nigger down the table . . . Normally abstemious, Rachel let the butler fill her glass again and again through the dinner. She followed her hostess upstairs in the wake of the senior diplomats' wives, feeling as if she were walking through a slight mist. In the enormous boudoir, decorated in a riot of Rio de Janeiro French furniture and gilded mirrors, Rachel sank down on a satin chair, and fumbled in her handbag. She felt unsteady emotionally, as if she might disgrace herself by crying in front of the other women.

'Aren't you feeling well?'

She looked up and found Margaret Stephenson standing beside her. There was only fifteen years' difference between them, but Rachel regarded the Minister's wife as a motherly figure.

'No, not very well, Mrs. Stephenson. So silly of me. I'll be all right in a minute.'

'There's a smaller bedroom through here,' Margaret said. 'Come with me; you can lie down for a few minutes.'

Rachel followed her obediently. There was a small dressing room with a canopied bed, supported by gross little Spanish cupids, clutching chiffon drapes.

'Put your feet up,' Margaret said. 'I know how awful one feels at this stage. Don't worry about it, you'll be better in a minute.'

Rachel heaved herself up and lay flat. The alcohol made her head swim. A large tear gathered and spilled out, running down one cheek.

'I'm not sick,' she said. 'I'm just so miserable, that's all!'

The older woman sat on the edge of the bed beside her. She took out her own handkerchief. 'Here, use this. Now I should sit up, Mrs. Paterson, that's right. What's the matter?'

'Richard and me,' the words came with a rush. 'I'm so unhappy. I don't know what to do. Oh, Mrs. Stephenson, I shouldn't talk to you about this—Richard would be so furious! I'm afraid I drank some wine at dinner. That's what brought it out. Please, let me stay here for a bit. I'll come down in a little while. I feel so awful! I shouldn't have said anything to you.'

'Yes you should,' Margaret Stephenson answered. 'I shan't mention it to anyone and I might be able to help you. Now listen, my dear, you come and have lunch with me tomorrow—no, damn, lunch I can't do, I'm going to some Senator's wife—come and have coffee tomorrow morning about ten-thirty. You can tell me all about it then. And don't worry, your husband won't know.'

She leaned over and squeezed the younger woman's hand. She felt closer to this stranger than to her own daughter. Had she analysed it, it was less an instinct to protect Rachel than an urge to fight her husband and all he represented. Paterson was the kind of challenge that

Margaret resented most. In spite of her sexual dependence upon them, she hated men. She hated them in the person of her own husband who had subjected her to the crippling humiliation of his own incompetence, and destroyed her self confidence by confessing that he preferred his own sex when making love. She hated the men who became her lovers because their very existence proved her failure as a wife. She hated Richard Paterson because she knew that she had met a personality capable of matching up to hers. The immovable object had met the irresistible force, and for Margaret Stephenson this was intolerable. She felt as if the amiable, foolish wife, who so obviously admired and leaned on her, was in some way an extension of herself, a representative of the whole race of women, preyed upon and failed by, men.

'You stay here,' she said. 'I'll tell the Ambassadress you're not feeling very well, and one of the maids can take you downstairs in about twenty minutes. Your husband will be waiting to take you home. And don't worry. I'll expect you tomorrow at ten-thirty. Don't lie down again, my dear, it'll only make you feel more dizzy.' She actually pulled up a pillow to support Rachel's head. 'There. Stay quietly like that until somebody comes for you. The Ambassadress will understand. She's had nine children, so she ought to.'

When she came downstairs Richard was waiting for her. In spite of her fear, he showed no sign of irritation at having to leave early. In the car on the way home he held her hand. She had decided to make an excuse and not go to see Margaret Stephenson the next morning, when he said casually that he had invited the Chilean attaché and his wife to dinner the following weekend. Rachel glanced at him in the dark; he was driving, concentrating ahead.

'She's attractive, isn't she?'

'Devastating,' he answered. 'Most amusing too.'

'I thought her bosoms were going to fall out,' his wife said.

'It would have made the dinner party if they had.'

By ten o'clock the next morning, she was on her way to the Stephensons' house on Kalorama Road.

. . . . .

'What the hell's up with you, Judy? I heard you go to the kitchen at four in the morning and you were up again at six. The way you're looking you could hire out to haunt a house!'

Nancy Nielson had chosen the breakfast both women ate together as the one time when Judith wouldn't be able to avoid her or make an excuse to rush out of the apartment. What she said was true; Judith looked drawn with lack of sleep. There was an expression of permanent anxiety on her face, and she moved through the day in a fog of cigarette smoke. Nancy, scrubbed and pink like a college girl model in a deodorant ad, watched her with hard eyes. She was an attractive girl, blonde and bouncy in manner, but the eyes were like flint.

'I couldn't sleep,' Judith said. 'Coffee please.'

'You're in another mess, aren't you?' Nancy passed the pot and poured for her. 'Who is it this time?'

'Nobody you know,' Judith said. 'And it's not the sort of mess I got into the last time. It's just worrying at the moment. It'll be all right.'

'It might help if you told me,' Nancy suggested. 'Apart from you losing your beauty sleep, honey, you're doing me out of mine. When you take to walking the damned floor all night you wake me!'

'I'm sorry. It won't be long; it's just temporary.'

She lit a cigarette; the coffee tasted strong and bitter. Nancy was entitled to complain; she was also entitled to an explanation, since she had been such a loyal friend when Judith needed friendship and understanding most, when she broke with Richard Paterson. The temptation to tell her about Sverdlov was very strong. She was unbelievably tough, with a realistic attitude that often provided a straight, simple answer to something which Judith was inclined to see as a fearful complication. But this was more than a personal difficulty, involving a man. This meant Sverdlov's chance of escaping from his own people. He had treated some aspects as a joke, but she knew him well enough now to realise that this was part of his personality, as distinctive a characteristic as Richard's incapacity to see himself or anything connected with him as anything but deadly serious.

Sverdlov would die with a sly little jeer at the expense of Fate. But she knew that he had not exaggerated his own danger, or the lack of time in which he could manoeuvre. There was no real reason not to tell Nancy some of it, and relieve herself of the anxiety which was driving away sleep and trying Sam Nielson's patience to the limit. But if there was no logic, there was certainly instinct, and this counselled her to say nothing, nothing to anyone outside Loder.

'If there's anything I could do to help,' Nancy prompted.

Judith shook her head. 'Nothing, thanks. And don't take any notice of me, Nancy, I'll sort myself out soon. Perhaps one day I'll find someone who's just a nice straightforward man.'

'Like hell you will,' the Canadian girl said. 'You're a born victim, dear. You can't have it without *love*, can you?'

'I'm not in love with him,' Judith said. 'You're wrong about that.'

'Oh for Christ's sake!' Nancy got up from the table. 'Kid yourself, but don't try and kid me!' When she left the kitchen she banged the door.

Sverdlov flew back to Washington. He walked into his office and settled down to work; he called for Anna Skriabine who sat by his desk, discreetly showing a gap between her knees, taking dictation. She had been told to watch for the least sign of anything unusual; there was nothing she could detect except that he looked extremely tired. His face seemed thinner, the cheeks hollowed out, and ugly dark patches under the eyes.

'Would you like your tea now, Comrade Sverdlov?' He looked up and smiled. He hated the soft, throaty voice, the sly sexy look that darted at him over the dictation pad. When he looked at the girl he kept thinking of Kalinin, the young man who had worked for him for three years and whom he had respected and liked for his integrity. A man of the new generation of Soviet Russians, with a mind reaching out for a little independent thought, rejecting the old tenets of blood and terror as a cleansing agent for humanity.

He thought of Kalinin as he was when he last saw him, when he was getting ready for his trip to Barbados, and as he must be now, a broken puppet in a cell in the Lubiyanka, only kept alive so that he could drag Sverdlov to the grave.

'Yes, you can bring it now. I have a letter to write to my wife.'

'You look tired,' the girl ventured. 'I hope nothing is wrong at home.'

'New York is a tiring place.' Sverdlov stretched a little and watched her with a look of approval. 'Most tiring of all is making love to pretty ladies who can't make up their minds. Tell me, Anna—do you think women are easy to persuade?'

'I don't know. It depends.'

'Depends on what?' The eyes were travelling over her; she felt as if he were seeing her as a person for the first time. It made her feel odd, almost frightened. She had gone to bed with numerous men in the course of her training and her duties, but she felt panicked by the thought of Sverdlov.

'It depends on the woman; and what you want her to believe,' she said. There was a colour in her face, and she looked extremely pretty. Kalinin wouldn't stand up well to a comparison. By this time he might weigh even less than she did.

'That you love her,' Sverdlov said. 'That's all. But when a woman believes that, she will do most things the man wants, wouldn't you say so?'

'Yes. Yes, I think that's so, Comrade.'

'Good,' Sverdlov smiled crookedly; the girl opened her lips, showing the teeth, and then for a second her pink tongue appeared.

'Then my friend in New York will soon be convinced,' he said. 'And I shall be able to get some sleep. I will also be able to go home.'

She brought the glass of tea, and turned to leave the room for the usual ten-minute interval until he called her back again. 'Anna, I've changed my mind; I want to send a telegram to my wife. Take it down to the coding officer.'

He had decided on impulse not to write; it took too long to arrive even by plane, and it would be further delayed while Golitsyn had it opened before despatch. At all costs he had to lay the faintest suspicion that might stir in that old but cunning brain, that he was avoiding going back to Russia.

He gave it to Anna Skriabine, who wrote it down and then went out, no doubt to make a hurried copy, as he thought. What he had said was simple and he hoped convincing.

'My duty delays me from returning for a few more days. Please suspend your petition until we can meet. My hope and desire is for reconciliation and I remain as always your loving husband.'

That should satisfy Golitsyn, and more important still, keep the long arm of Panyushkin from stretching out suddenly to pluck him back by force. Golitsyn's trip to New York had been reported to him as routine; it only emphasised how closely he was being watched; it also alerted him to the possibility that he might well be under real surveillance. So long as his contact was Mrs. Farrow, this provided him with an alibi; he intended to strengthen this by explaining a fictional plan to Golitsyn which would allow him the latitude he needed to make the final connection with Loder.

He thought suddenly that the mental strain he had been suffering for so long, the nervous tension, the frustrations and inward bursts of irritated cynicism, culminating in that decision to go away to the West Indies, had found a common channel. His mind was working at a speed and with a precision that had been lacking for many many months. The strain upon him was enormous, but the resources were meeting it and all the ingenuity, the brilliance which had brought him to the top level of his country's Military Intelligence, were now marshalled against his own organisation in the effort to save his life. He had called himself a survivor to Judith during that holiday on the island. Then it had been a cynical disclaimer of any true commitment. But now survival had a sharper significance. It was allied to an intense fury at the way events had turned against him, at the fate of Kalinin, at the direction in which his people were going and which must exact the lives and liberties of so many men of quality in the service of their country. On a lower level it was the simple hate he bore for Tomarov, who had protested friendship while he was trying to persuade him to return, for the bitter fanaticism of his wife, who loved a political ideal more than the man she married, for the dour enmity of Golitsyn, the sucrose deceit of Anna Skriabine. Justice for the weak did not exist; there was no guideline for humanity but the logic of expediency. He had said all that to Judith too, and meant it, in the way it is possible to mean an abstract. He knew it was true intellectually; now he felt the sting of it in actual situation. There would be no justice for him. He had been condemned by the mere fact of being suspected. Again as he said, the pendulum had swung, but like the nightmare instrument in the Poe horror story, it had a razor's edge. Expediency dictated that he dodge that murderous sweep at the expense of patriotism and at a price he had never imagined he could bring himself to pay. And there was the ultimate irony, which Judith would appreciate. It was the lack of justice, the rule of expedience which prompted so much human treachery, that gave him the right to betray them and take his chance with the enemy.

He had spent the last part of the week working out possible plans for taking refuge with Loder's organisation. The most obvious was to walk into the British Embassy and ask for asylum. With the bribe of the documents passed over by 'Blue', the British might well have agreed to this, and faced the considerable diplomatic storm and Soviet protests which would have followed their refusal to return him. But on reflection, one possibility made the easiest solution the most dangerous for him to follow. If he were being watched he would never be allowed to reach a Western Embassy. And the more he considered it, the more convinced he became that Golitsyn had put men on to him after New York. He would have done so in similar circumstances. He would also have given orders to murder the suspect immediately, by any means available, if he showed any sign of running for diplomatic cover on the enemy side. Golitsyn would have done the same.

He could not hope to go to the British direct; if his own people had any immediate indication of where he had gone for protection, his chances of being tracked down and murdered ran that much higher. He needed a time lag to get out of the United States; a day or at best two days, long enough for Loder's people to move him somewhere the K.G.B. couldn't go to first. Knowing his own organisation's efficiency made it more imperative to guard against the least mistake, to minimise risk to the point of cowardice. He was literally thinking in two halves, running and pursuing himself at the same time. Only then could he avoid the action which he judged would be taken. And in the long hours of the previous night, he had found a solution which could buy him the time he needed.

He put an internal call through to Golitsyn's office and said he would be there within five minutes to see the General.

He thought that the old man looked even older; he

seemed to have shrunk, even when he stood up and greeted Sverdlov as usual, offering him tea or the whisky which he was known to drink irrespective of the hour. Sverdlov chose the whisky; he had drunk very little since the crisis emerged. But he couldn't show any variation in his routine, any change of habit. He took the drink, and gave the General his twisted smile.

Golitsyn was very deferential; on that morning his hostility seemed veiled, as if he were making a special effort with his chief.

They talked of internal Embassy subjects for a few minutes, and then Sverdlov said coolly, 'I have come to a crisis with Mrs. Farrow.'

'Oh,' the old man said. 'That is a pity. I thought she was committed."

'She'll be committed when she brings her first report,' Sverdlov said. 'I said I thought I had got her, but there is still that little bridge to cross, the one from her side to ours. She is in a romantic mood at the moment. I shall have to take next weekend to help her cross that little bridge. Seduction is hard work, General.'

'I am too old to remember much about it,' Golitsyn said. 'Surely it has some compensations?'

'At another time I might enjoy it, but I've had to cable my wife and ask her to wait again.'

'I can understand,' the General said. 'It is not easy to choose.'

'I choose my duty.' Sverdlov spoke sharply. 'There's no question of which has the first priority. This woman has access to the most confidential reports on everything Nielson does in UNO. He has no secrets from her; she told me. She even has a set of keys to his safe, that's how much he trusts her. She deals with his personal correspondence as well as everything official. He is on social terms with the President and half the Senate. Mrs. Farrow could be one of our most important agents over here. You know the old proverb—women and horses, ride them often and make them work. If I let this woman go now, and take time to attend to my personal business, we could lose her. One weekend to convince her she is doing it for love, and then a controller can look after her for a week or two. I should get a copy of Nielson's brief from the Brazilian Maritime development after the weekend. Then she can't turn back.'

'Have you decided who is to take her over in your absence? It might be dangerous to leave her uncontacted even for a few days. Women aren't reliable in the same way as men, they have to be nursed, Comrade, carefully nursed until they've become used to what they're doing.'

'Have you a man in mind for her, as a temporary link till I get back?' Sverdlov asked him.

Golitsyn hesitated. He had chosen Stukalov for another reason besides rewarding him for watching Sverdlov; he knew the importance of replacing Sverdlov with a personable man who could establish a similar hold over Judith Farrow. It wouldn't be easy to make the transition, but he relied upon Stukalov to substitute effectively. He had picked up a girl in The Hague two years earlier, begun a discreet liaison with her and ended by subjecting her to blackmail. She had worked for Soviet Intelligence for eighteen months until she became suspect by the Dutch and finally served a long prison sentence. Stukalov had been posted elsewhere long before and his connection with the case never came out, because the girl had known him under a different name.

'What about Gregory Stukalov? He is a ladies' man—he could keep Mrs. Farrow reassured till you come back.'

'I will leave her to you to run,' Sverdlov said. 'And you will be responsible for keeping her while I'm away. You and Stukalov. If she likes him, he can take over from me completely; but one can't hurry these things.'

'No,' Golitsyn agreed. 'Patience is need. I hope you will be able to persuade Elena Maximova to forget about divorce. She is a very fine woman; it would be a pity to lose her.'

'I don't intend to lose her. As soon as I have Mrs. Farrow in my bag, I will be on my way to see my wife. I may bring her back with me.'

'I will look forward to that,' the old man said. He had Anna's scribbled copy of the telegram to Elena in his tunic pocket. So far there were no discrepancies. A weekend with the Englishwoman. It presented no problem, they could both be watched. And afterwards she would have to get used to Stukalov. Certainly she would never see Feodor Sverdlov again.

Sverdlov went back to his office; Anna Skriabine was in the outer room typing. When he came in she looked up and smiled; he smiled back and made a gesture that she should continue. He didn't need her. Alone he opened his desk drawer and took out some sheets of papers, reports which had come through in the course of the morning. He folded them flat and slipped them in his pocket. He lit a cigarette, drawing the strong smoke deep into his lungs. Golitsyn had accepted the explanation. He knew the old man very well; in the past few months he had studied him with special care. He was cunning, and in spite of the general opinion of his capabilities, he was certainly no fool. Equally he moved to a pattern, like all his generation, schooled to think and act in certain ways. There was a confident air about him, a secret smugness which he couldn't hide because he was unaware that it showed itself. He believed that Sverdlov was hooked. He was so sure of himself that he had made arrangements for one of his protégés to take over Judith Farrow and continue the work which he, Sverdlov, had begun. The suggestion of Stukalov as 'minder' confirmed this. Stukalov was one of the old man's favourites in the Service; he had taken trouble to recommend him and see that he was given jobs with the chance of promotion.

He was a young man, but he was cast in Golitsyn's implacable mould. A natural hard-liner. Sverdlov crushed out the cigarette. He left the office and in Anna Skriabine's little office he paused by her desk.

'You are busy?'

'Yes, Comrade Sverdlov. Do you want me?'

'Not at this moment.' He looked down at her; she glanced up at him, hesitant, a little uncertain. 'I am going away this weekend. I shall be back on Monday. Then I am going home. Is there anything you would like me to bring you back?'

She actually blushed. 'That's very kind of you, Comrade. I can't think of anything.'

'I shan't be away for long,' Sverdlov said. 'A week, or ten days. When I come back perhaps we will have dinner together. Would you like that?'

'Yes. Yes, that would be very nice.'

'Good,' he said. 'Good. We will have a pleasant evening. I shall look forward to it.' He went out and down the corridor. He took the lift two floors down to the filing section. Everyone stood up as he came in. The head of the section hurried towards him.

'I want the "Blue" file, number 23.' The safe containing the top security files were only opened on his or Golitsyn's instructions. Even the Ambassador himself needed a second signature in the book before it could be unlocked and the contents taken out.

'I don't need to sign for it,' Sverdlov said. 'I'm not taking anything out, I just want to look at something.' The head of filing put the withdrawal book back and went to an inner room to open the safe. Sverdlov followed him. He took the file marked 23 and opened it. He spent some minutes reading the last of 'Blue's' reports. The man had moved away, but he was still in the room. Sverdlov didn't hurry. The sheets of paper he had brought with him were in his coat pocket. He stood with the file open in one hand, the other slipped into that pocket.

'Get me 22 as well.'

Now the positions were reversed. The man was in front of him, taking out the earlier dossier. There were twenty-three in all, each contained in a separate folder, all the highly important information sent to them by 'Blue' over the last three years in Washington. Sverdlov's hands were steady. With the right he pulled the sheets clear of their clips in the file and doubled them. His left hand came out of his pocket with the papers taken from his office. The transfer was completed in seconds. By the time the head of the filing section turned round, Sverdlov was in the same position, one hand in his pocket, the half opened file balanced in the other. He closed it and handed it back.

'One moment, then you can have this back too.' He glanced quickly through the file marked 22, flipping through the pages, frowning, pausing for a second at one page, said 'Ah,' as if he had found what he wanted, and then that too was handed to the man. He waited while they were put back in the safe and the door was locked.

'Perhaps I should sign anyway,' Sverdlov suggested. He was almost at the door.

'That isn't necessary,' the man said. 'Not for you, Comrade. As you said, the files haven't left the department.'

'Good morning then,' Sverdlov said. Everyone was standing again. 'Good morning, Comrade.' With his hand in his pocket, holding the contents of the 'Blue' file against his thigh, he left the filing section.

An hour later he was in an official Embassy car on his way to the airport to catch the noon plane for New York.

. . . . .

Spring in Central Park. It reminded Judith of an old wartime movie, re-issued on television, or a Cole Porter song. The trees were out, bending under the weight of blossom, the grass grew green and great patches of spring bulbs blazed under the warm sky. It was difficult to equate the charm of that country oasis in the city desert, with the hunting grounds of thieves, rapists and killers which it became at nightfall. It was equally difficult to equate herself and Sverdlov with the other couples strolling along the walks, arm in arm, or holding one another round the waist.

He had flown up on Monday night; she had asked Sam Nielson if she could leave early Tuesday afternoon. He had agreed with a bad grace; her manner said more plainly than words that she would have gone anyway, so he had no alternative. As usual Sverdlov was waiting for her in a taxi cab; he seemed very cheerful, and kissed her without making too much of a struggle of it, giving the driver instructions to go to the Park. It was a lovely day and it would be nice to walk. The way he said this indicated that it was for the driver's benefit. Judith glanced anxiously into the man's little mirror to see whether he was watching them. His reflected face was looking ahead, not paying attention to anything but the road.

They walked together for some minutes, Sverdlov holding her arm against his side, gripping her hand in his.

'You look very worried,' he said. 'And you are not sleeping. I think you are in love with me.'

'Well you think wrong,' Judith said. 'I am worried and I haven't had a good night's sleep since this thing started, but I'd feel the same for anyone I liked. Feodor, when are you going to get out?'

'The end of this week,' Sverdlov said. 'On Friday I shall board a plane for a weekend trip to that pretty island where I met you.'

'Barbados! You're going to go there? But why—why can't you just give Loder a time and a place here and leave it to him to do the rest?' She had stopped dead in the middle of the path; he pulled her gently to continue walking.

'That's what I am doing,' he explained. 'I am giving him the time and the place, and after that he makes the arrangements for me. You'll have to come with me, Judith. Will you do it?'

'I don't understand,' she said. She felt like bursting into tears, or losing her temper with him. The strain upon her had been greater than she realised. His ambiguity made her furious.

'Why do you have to go through all this pantomine, when all you need do is walk into the British Embassy?'

'Because I'd never be allowed to reach it,' Sverdlov said. 'I am sure I am being followed. So far I am also sure they don't suspect what I am going to do. Please try and trust me, I know what I am doing. I know how this kind of operation works.'

'You're pitting yourself against the K.G.B.,' she said angrily. 'Don't forget that!'

'I'm not forgetting it,' he said. 'That's why I am making a pantomine. As far as the K.G.B. is concerned, I am taking you to Barbados to complete your seduction. I have explained that you're a difficult woman, who won't work for us unless I make love to you under the palm trees. I have said you know everything that Nielson does and can open his confidential safe whenever you like.'

'But that's nonsense,' Judith interrupted. 'Sam wouldn't let those keys out of his sight!'

'I am sure he wouldn't, but they don't know this. They think you are a most important person, and I must delay my trip to see my wife so I can make sure of you. There is even a very handsome young Russian ready to look after you when I have gone. It's all arranged. When I go to Barbados with you, it will be part of the plan I have explained to them. But you will have to come with me on the flight. After that, it is your friend Mr. Loder who takes control.'

'It seems such a risk,' Judith said. 'It seems such a terribly complicated way round. Barbados is a tiny island, anything could happen to you out there!'

'No more than could happen to me here, walking along this path with you,' Sverdlov said. 'Do you think I would be safer in New York? Barbados is a British island; there, Mr. Loder can really protect me. Here, in this city, in Washington, I am truly defenceless. Will you come to Barbados with me?'

'Yes,' Judith said. 'If that's the only way to help you, of course I've got to come. I'm cold,' she said suddenly. 'I don't want to walk any more.'

She was shivering; Sverdlov knew it had nothing to do

with the temperature which was mild and warm, but he didn't say anything. 'A little longer,' he said. 'Just to the end of this path, then we come out on the street and we'll find a bar. But we can't talk about this once we leave the Park. We can't be overheard here.'

'You really think we're being followed? Now?'

'I am sure of it. You know there are microphones that can pick up a conversation from twenty yards away?'

'My God,' Judith said. 'It's like a nightmare! Are you sure it's safe here?'

'We're walking very quickly,' Sverdlov answered. 'And there's nobody close enough to be able to listen. I'm being watched from a distance, and that's a good sign. It means they are not really suspicious. Now listen very carefully. After we leave each other, you must make your contact with Loder.'

'He's expecting me to call him,' Judith said. 'I let him know today you were coming up and I'd be in touch later on.'

'Where did you ring from—Neilson's office?'

'No,' Judith said. 'No, I thought it better not. I called from a public booth in the building.'

'Very good.' Sverdlov squeezed her. 'Very good. Now you tell him we will be leaving on Friday—on the 4 p.m. flight from Kennedy to Barbados, PANAM 238. I have made the plane booking and also booked for us in the same hotel, where we stayed before. We arrive at 8.30 and I shall go to the hotel with you unless he gives you different instructions. I shall have the papers on "Blue" with me.'

'It's so quick,' Judith said. 'There's so little time. Supposing he can't make arrangements in time?'

'I could make them,' Sverdlov said. 'He must be able to. All he will need is a plane to fly me to London. Tell him I would hope to go on Saturday or Sunday at the latest. If someone looks for the "Blue" file, and it's gone, and I'm gone, we will have trouble. Even in Barbados. Can you remember all that? The flight number?'

'PANAM 238, arriving 8.30. Is that Barbadian time or New York time?'

'Barbadian time,' he said. 'Now we are going to find a bar where we can have a drink together. We can talk about our weekend in Barbados, and perhaps you could pretend to be in love with me—it would help, if we are followed inside.'

'I'll try,' Judith said.

'Thank you,' Sverdlov said gravely. 'I'm sure you will do it well.'

. . . . .

Rachel Paterson was crying. She cried respectably, in Margaret Stephenson's opinion; she had considerable experience of weeping junior wives over the years. She had once amused a London dinner party by describing the categories into which they fell. The ones who sniffed and snuffed from homesickness, the abandoned weepers whose old mother had dropped dead two thousand miles away, the rare cases of wives who had made fools of themselves in some official capacity and had to be reprimanded. Even one nervous breakdown who had come in apparently quite self possessed and been taken from the room screaming like a banshee.

It had sounded most amusing at that dinner party, which she remembered from years back. There was nothing to amuse her about Rachel's tears.

Like Fergus, Margaret's upbringing had armoured her against shock. Contrary to the belief of those outside it, the aristocratic upbringing of their generation was harsh and demanding of self discipline. The price to be paid for their considerable privileges was an amalgam of inflexible principals which did not permit personal weakness, cowardice or emotional disaster to be manifest to anyone. Margaret sat on the Regency sofa beside the younger woman, and patted her shoulder with every appearance of kindness.

'I just can't trust him,' Rachel said. 'From the moment that woman rang up, everything changed.' She blew her nose, not too loudly, and wiped her eyes again. 'He's always been difficult, but I never thought he was after other women. Now I can't think of anything else!'

'Don't you think you're exaggerating? After all, you say this woman in New York was only an acquaintance—she had a perfectly good reason for getting in touch with him. My dear, she'd hardly make up a story about a Russian defector, if she wanted to see him? That's a little too far-fetched.'

The remark was even more significant for herself than

to Richard Paterson's wife. She had listened to the first part of Rachel's confidence with real sympathy; the way they had drifted, his lack of interest in her, his career worship at the expense of her wish for a child—it was all quite familiar and only confirmed Margaret's opinion of Paterson as a selfish swine.

She had listened to the story of the early morning telephone call; she had known about Paterson's mistress in New York, and quite illogically, held it against him. When Rachel repeated his explanation of that call, it constituted such a shock that for a moment Margaret Stephenson couldn't speak. Now, in the space of the few minutes while the other woman broke down into tears and stumbled through the story, confusing it in her distress, Margaret's acute intelligence, schooled by a lifetime of living with diplomacy, saw the point of that one frightful revelation and the possible direction in which it could lead. Then she took the shock as she had taken everything of real importance; outwardly unchanged, calm and in control of herself.

Someone in the Russian Embassy was about to defect to Britain.

Out of the welter of Rachel Paterson's material troubles, that one fact stood out independent of anything else. She took hold of Rachel's hand for a moment.

'I know he didn't stay in New York,' Rachel was saying. 'He came back and saw the Ambassador that night, he told me. So he wasn't with *her* . . .'

'Of course he wasn't,' Margaret said. 'If he went to the Ambassador that proves the story is true. Did he say this Russian was important?'

Rachel paused; she couldn't see the relevance of the question to herself.

'I don't remember really. Yes, I think he did say something about it when he came back, but I didn't take much notice. I was so shocked to discover about this girl. He swore he never slept with her—do you think he could be telling me the truth?'

'I'm sure he could,' Margaret said. If he had gone to the Ambassador, then the whole story must be correct; he wasn't likely to involve the Head of the Washington Embassy on behalf of a filing clerk. If the Russian was an important diplomat, then that increased the danger. 'I'm sure he hasn't been unfaithful,' she said. 'There's no harm in taking someone out to dinner a few times.' She was saying things mechanically, her mind racing away from Rachel Paterson's jealous miseries, racing to the ultimate conclusion like a greyhound after a lethal hare. If someone defected, they paid blood money for protection. They betrayed agents, secrets.

'I've got it out of proportion, I suppose.' Rachel went up in her estimation for having reached that conclusion by herself. Margaret glanced at her watch. Eleven-fifteen. Where the hell would Fergus be? In his office—at a meeting? 'You must take a grip on yourself.' She made her voice firm. 'You have an attractive husband, and there's nothing more foolish than going round suspecting him when he's not doing anything. It's the surest way of bringing it to his mind. You say you're worried about Senhora Fuentes Gargano coming to dinner?'

'Yes I am; he obviously likes her, and she's terribly pretty and amusing. I look such a bolster at the moment!'

'Not for much longer.' Margaret stood. It was time to get rid of her. She had to find Fergus. 'Take my advice, my dear. Write to the Fuentes Garganos and invite them yourself. Be charming to her and tell your husband you think she's fabulous, and so *nice*. I promise you, he'll lose interest immediately. Now I must send you home, I'm afraid. I have an appointment in ten minutes.'

She sent Rachel back in her own car; she shook hands and then gave her a little friendly peck on the cheek. She went to her sitting room at a run, banging the door behind her. She wrenched the telephone off its cradle and dialled her husband's office number. His secretary answered. Margaret had a short way with secretaries when she wanted to get through to Fergus; she had been resented by every girl who worked for him.

'Mr. Stephenson, please. Mrs. Stephenson speaking.'

'I'm afraid he's in conference with Mr. Hopkirk.'

'It's extremely important,' Margaret cut in angrily. 'Please tell him to call me as soon as possible.' She rang off. Damn him! Damn and blast everything about him! Rage with him for not being available was giving way to a sense of how luck had played on her side by sending Rachel Paterson along with her confidences. Pure chance, dictated by her initial whim of taking a liking to the girl. The graciousness, the odd marks of favour she had shown the air attaché's wife, the genuine sympathy when she was tipsy and miserable at the Brazilians the night before—

it had all contributed to the discovery of something which could be the total ruin of her husband and herself. There might be no danger; she forced herself to consider that and quell the furious ringing of alarm bells in her mind. The Russian, whoever he was, probably knew nothing about Fergus; he might not even know of such an agent's existence. Might. Might not. Their survival could hang on two words. Their destruction could follow if it became one. She had told her husband the truth when she said that his disgrace and punishment would have given her personal satisfaction. Her feelings towards him were cruel and vengeful to an unbalanced degree, increased to frenzy by the discovery that he had put her and all she valued most at such an appalling risk. She loved her position; she enjoyed the privilege, the sense of influence that went with the top doplomatic posts. She wanted to end her public career with a spectacular success, mistress of one of the three major Embassies, Paris, Moscow or New York. Paris was the one on which her heart was set. The glamorous shade of Diana Norwich still hung about the Borghese Palace in the Fauburg St. Honoré.

She, Margaret Stephenson, lacking the legendary beauty, but endowed with the breeding, the personality and the aura of a different kind of feminine power, was the only diplomatic wife capable of taking the place occupied by one of the most famous women of her time. It was the culmination of Margaret's ambition, her justification for the sordid marriage, her loveless adulteries, her assumption of a gangster toughness in pursuit of what she wanted.

What the hell was keeping him from calling? . . . Suddenly the strain overcame her. Paterson had flown to New York on Saturday, seen the Ambassador the same night. It was now Friday morning. The Russian might have come over already.

She was on the telephone again. 'I want to speak to my husband. Put me through at once.'

Fergus sounded surprised; he had a gentle voice which the telephone accentuated. 'Margaret? I'm rather busy at the moment.'

'You've got to come home,' she broke in on him, her tones low. 'Something terrible has happened. About your lighter.'

There was a slight clearing of the throat which became a little cough; she heard it clearly.

'Oh dear,' he said. 'All right, don't worry, 'I'll slip round in about a quarter of an hour; Eric and I have nearly finished.'

. . . . .

'Christ!' Loder said, 'Friday—you mean this Friday? That's cutting it pretty fine!'

'That's what I said.' Judith Farrow's voice sounded strained and irritable from New York. 'But that's the message. I'm going to Barbados with him, on that flight, and we'll be at the Beach Hotel, St. James. He wants to get out as quickly as possible. He's sure he's being watched. Can you make the arrangements in the time?'

'I'll bloody well have to,' Loder snapped back at her. Her attitude irritated him; she was unaware of it, but her concern for the Russian made her aggressive; she had stood up to him the first time they met, and he hadn't forgotten it. 'Is that all he said?'

'He'll have the documents with him.' She remembered that last. 'He particularly asked to get to London by Saturday or Sunday at the latest. Could it be any time on Friday night? I think he's mad to do it this way, but he says he's covered himself with his Embassy.'

'I'll bet he has,' Loder said. 'If he's picked Barbados, he knows what he's doing—nobody better. As for Friday night, tell him that's impossible. I can't lay on a plane capable of making it non-stop to London at this short notice. I can commandeer part of a commercial aircraft, but that will take twenty-four hours to get it cleared. I can get him out on a Saturday flight. Tell him there'll be protection laid on at the hotel, and to stay inside when you get there. You understand that? Stay inside till our chaps come to collect you. Okay?'

'Yes, I'll tell him. And don't worry, I'll see he doesn't leave his room.'

'You do that,' Loder said. 'I want those bloody papers, whatever happens. You're not expecting to go back with him, are you? That's not on; I thought I'd warn you.'

'You needn't have bothered,' Judith cut in on him. 'I'm going to Barbados because he needs me as an alibi. I've no intention of going to London, Mr. Loder. All I want to do is come back here and get on with my own business, for a change. That is if I don't lose my job, taking time off!'

The line went dead, and Loder allowed himself to jab

two fingers in the air. That had stung her; uppity bitch, pretending she wasn't involved with the Russian. He put her out of his mind. Saturday or Sunday. He told his secretary to get him a list of scheduled flights going to London from Barbados on Saturday, from mid-morning on. He drafted a cable to London, had it coded and sent off, requesting that a 'green' signal should be sent to the Ambassador on his behalf. This would give him full authority to do whatever he thought necessary without referring back to the Ambassador, or to Stephenson should the Head of the Embassy be away.

With the 'green' in his pocket, Loder could take over an entire VC10 if he wanted to; he could call on as many security men within the Embassy as he needed, and also expect the fullest co-operation from the internal security service of the Barbadian Government. He would probably need the Canadians to help on the island. He hesitated trying to decide if it were possible to get Sverdlov off the island without enlisting the Canadian contacts. A posse of Canadian Secret Service men standing round the Beach Hotel would look bloody suspicious; he could get a couple of men out on the flight with Sverdlov tomorrow; they could keep an eye on the hotel. He decided to dispense with Canadian assistance.

His secretary came back with the information that there was only one non-stop flight to London from Barbados on Saturday and that was at seven-thirty in the evening. There was an Alitalia at eleven on Sunday morning, making four stops, Trinidad, Nassau, Bermuda, then London, last stop Rome. Both flights were fully booked and the British night flight was also wait listed. Loder swore; the girl pretended not to hear. He must be upset because he had used some really awful language to himself. 'Get through to BOAC's top man in New York,' he said. 'Then I'll speak to him.'

The call was unsuccessful; the man Loder needed was out of town. A further telephone call unearthed his assistant, who couldn't give the authority anyway, but at least it disclosed a telephone number where his chief could be found. An hour and a half later Loder got through to him at the third attempt. Previously he had been on his way down and delayed by traffic, then to Loder's intense rage, he was asked to call back as the man was in the bath tub and a brisk American woman refused any suggestion of getting him out of it to answer the call. When he finally connected, Loder was unnecessarily curt. He needed three first class seats for the night flight from Barbados. Yes, he knew he was asking something which was practically impossible and he appreciated the difficulty of turning people out of their seats on a fully booked flight—none the less, he was not asking for the accommodation on the aircraft, but giving warning that it would be requisitioned on HM Government's authority. He would produce that authority by the next day, and unless he was assisted by the Corporation, he would not hesitate to requisition the whole aircraft. He hung up. Moments later the internal telephone rang on his desk. He was still mentally fighting BOAC when he realised that the caller was Fergus Stephenson. They hadn't lunched together for a month; Loder had meant to suggest a date to Stephenson, but when the cable called him back to London, the urgency of tracking down 'Blue' and the immediate prospect of Sverdlov's defection had driven everything else out of his mind. Above all, he was a supreme professional; this fanatical dedication to his job had contributed to his broken marriage; it couldn't allow the most valued personal relationship to claim a moment which properly belonged to his job in a time of crisis. For the first time, he refused an invitation from Fergus, who sounded disappointed. The Minister said something pleasant and rang off.

Loder ordered sandwiches and orange juice to be sent to his office; he also told his secretary he would need her for most of the evening. She complied without resentment: there was a 'flap' on in Loder's slang terminology, and she enjoyed the excitement. She had a good working relationship with him; he had never made a pass at her, which was a relief because she considered him a repulsive-looking little man. He was considerate in general, and when the pressure of work increased to the present frenzied pitch, he remembered to thank her afterwards. She couldn't have said she liked or disliked him; she was more similar in type to him than she realised. She too loved the job.

• • • • •

'What are you going to do?' Margaret Stephenson demanded. 'Loder won't see you, now what?'

Her husband had poured himself a glass of sherry; the choice struck her as infuriating. Brandy was the appropriate antidote to the kind of shock he had received. There was something so offensively sissy about that glass of sherry that she could have knocked it out of his hand. He was extremely shaken; he had come back from his office and stood listening while she told him what Rachel Paterson had said. At one moment he seemed likely to interrupt; Margaret silenced him by saying immediately that Paterson had gone to the Ambassador, so there couldn't be any doubt about the story being true. Then she had asked him the one vital question.

Could the defector know anything about him? Fergus had said quite truthfully that he didn't know. No minor official, or junior officer would have access to his level of secrets. They had nothing to fear from the lower ranks. But a senior Soviet official might well know of the existence of an agent within the Western diplomatic circle, without any clue to his identity. But once alerted, as he said, the Intelligence services would be digging like terriers. Without question, he would be in serious danger if a full scale investigation began. It had taken two years to uncover MacLean, he reminded his wife. Slow they were, but sure in the end. The first thing he had to do was find out details of the defection, particularly the position and, if possible, the identity of the Russian.

He had telephoned Loder while his wife stood waiting, biting her lips till the lower one was stinging and raw. Then she had asked the question again.

'Now what are you going to do? Your precious policeman won't see you—my God, you don't suppose . . .'

'No, no,' Fergus reassured her. 'Don't get panicky; nothing's happened yet. These things take a long time. It could be weeks before this Russian comes over. But I have to find out who it is.'

Margaret stood in the sunny room, which was considered one of her decorating triumphs. A magnificent Casteels painting dominated it, a superb flaunting peacock in the foreground of the picture. She always used it for smaller parties; someone had once pleased her by saying it was a reflection of her personality. She looked at Fergus, standing by the fireplace, tall and a little too thin, sipping Tio Pepe while the ground cracked open under his feet.

'And if you do find out?' She hadn't thought beyond a

confused idea of resignation, a return to England and then exile somewhere where there was no extradition treaty. It was all a muddle, quite without direction. But suddenly she saw the only practical solution.

'I shall warn the Soviet Embassy and have him stopped,' Fergus said. 'Apart from myself, I should do that anyway. Whoever it is, he's turned traitor. He deserves everything he'll get.'

Margaret Stephenson said nothing. He was completely serious; there was no suggestion of a joke, or any ironic reference to himself in that last remark. He meant it in all sincerity.

'From your point of view,' Fergus said quietly. 'It's this Russian or me. And you've already decided about that. So you had better leave this to me and I'll deal with it. Thank God we got the warning in time. I'm going back to the office now, and I'll see the Ambassador. Don't worry; it'll be all right.'

After he had gone, she noticed that the sherry glass was still half full. For the first time in her life she went upstairs and was physically sick.

. . . . .

'I can't believe it,' Judith said. 'I can't believe we'll be out of here on Friday.' Sverdlov had his arm round her. He had called her later that night at the apartment and suggested taking her to a club to spend the evening with him. Judith hadn't wanted to go, she felt exhausted. Nancy was out on a date; she had settled in front of the TV but after a time the banality of the programmes got on her nerves and she had switched it off. Sverdlov had sounded so cheerful that it annoyed her to hear him. As a compromise from the nightclub he suggested, she said wearily that he could come to the apartment for a drink.

As soon as he came through the door her angry feelings disappeared. Telephones were deceptive. He looked sallow and exhausted.

'What was all that about a nightclub?' she said. 'You look dead beat. Come in and sit down.'

'I didn't know I could come here,' he said. 'I wanted to see you; I thought a little music might be good for us. But this is better. Much better.' He turned her face up and kissed her.

She gave him a drink and made coffee for them. He

glanced round the sitting room. They were together on the big upholstered sofa which Nancy had ordered custom built. 'This is very comfortable,' he said. 'And you make good coffee. This is better than going out. I think we are both tired; especially you. This has been a strain for you. I'm sorry.'

'It doesn't matter,' Judith said. She hadn't wanted to see him, now she was glad that he had come. She was glad to be beside him and the arm which circled her was warm and gave a sensation of comfort. 'I just want the next two days to be over, that's all. I want to see you on the plane for England.'

'Will you miss me?'

'Yes,' Judith said. 'Yes I will miss you. But that's not important. What matters is to get you safely out of here and out of Barbados. Feodor, are you still sure that's the best way to do it?'

'It's the best way,' he said. 'Please believe that. And it's the least dangerous too. I wouldn't take you with me, if there was any real risk. Just so Mr. Loder takes care of the other end.'

'He will,' Judith said. 'Everything is fixed, he assured me of that. He's a poisonous man, but I'm sure he's good at his job.'

Sverdlov looked down at her. 'And you don't despise me for what I'm doing? You don't think I'm a traitor and a coward? It's not very English and stiff upper lip, is it, to run away?'

'Well if you feel like that, go home and let them shoot you.' She pulled away angrily. 'Sometimes you make me so furious talking like that after all the hell we've gone through in the last week—and just when everything is fixed up!' She was surprised when he laughed.

'You have become very fiery, do you know that? I love fiery women. What am I going to do in England without you?'

'I don't know,' Judith said. She was still angry; she had never been so irritable in her life. Alternatively she could just as easily have burst into tears. He seemed to know this, because he stopped teasing her. He lit a Russian cigarette and gave it to her; they sat in silence for a few moments. Then it was Judith who spoke.

'I was thinking today, if I hadn't walked out on Richard I'd never have gone to Barbados and met you; what would you have done when this blew up? Would you have still come over?'

'I am not sure,' Sverdlov said. 'I can say yes now, because that is how it has worked out. But without meeting you, I might have done the other thing; taken the easy way. Certainly I would never have let my own people arrest me. No show trial, Judith, no execution as a traitor. If I'm going to die, it won't be as a political lie for someone else to tell the Russian people. Truth has a value; I think I have learned that from you.'

'So has faith,' she said. 'I've been praying for you. And you can laugh if you like.'

'I am not laughing,' Sverdlov said. 'I need all the allies I can get. Even your non-existent God. Don't be angry again. I am glad you prayed. Maybe there is a God. Maybe there really was a Tamarind tree that defied nature because of one man's innocence. You believe these things; I don't. Perhaps believing then has made you as you are. If that's so, then I can't quarrel with them. If I said that I loved you, would you believe me too?'

'I'd rather you didn't say it,' Judith said. 'Please, don't say it.'

'All right,' Sverdlov said. 'I will take it back so I can say it another time. I am going back to our offices to get some sleep.'

'You know you can stay here,' she said. 'There's an empty bed.'

'No,' Sverdlov said. 'That's not how I want to stay with you. I will go back. Will you kiss me? For luck tomorrow?'

'Oh God,' Judith said. 'I have an awful feeling that we're going to need it.'

## CHAPTER NINE

It was the Ambassador who sent for Fergus. The coded telegram had come in from London in the early hours; it was handed to the Ambassador as soon as he came into his office, marked top priority. He read it first, before looking at the rest of his official correspondence, and when he put it down, he grimaced. It contained the kind of news that a man in his position most disliked; a major security operation was about to take place from his Embassy. His full co-operation was requested in terms that were very courteous, but unmistakably authoritarian. Loder, the clever intellectual sleuth who had been wished on him from M16, was given unlimited powers and everyone within the Embassy was requested to assist him in whatever way he asked. The request, if such it could be called, also applied to British companies and citizens who might refer any such question back to the Embassy. In other words, Loder could ask for the moon, and if he did, it was to be given to him.

The Ambassador was a career diplomat, trained in public service, intellectually and socially equipped beyond the expectation of ordinary men. He had an old-fashioned regard for his responsibilities and an intense loyalty to his colleagues in the Service. He resented anything which could bring a taint of low intrigue or vulgar scandal upon his Embassy or anyone connected with it. The request from London stated that Loder was empowered to receive a defector from the Soviet Union, and that accounted for the arbitary *carte blanche* which had been issued to him. The Ambassador knew that this accorded with the information passed to him by his own air attaché. He had sent that scurrying in Loder's direction, hoping that it was no one of importance and that the Embassy need not be directly involved. Now it appeared that whoever the man was who had decided to seek asylum, he rated the maximum priority. However much he wished to avoid it, the Ambassador could not keep the stench of espionage out of his Embassy. Diplomacy was a profession of honour and skill; he regarded spies and spying as a squalid occupation in which no gentleman could possibly indulge in peace time. Most of all he detested it because it had seduced members of his service into unforgivable treason and disgrace, thereby subjecting everyone else to the scrutiny of the Loders of the world. He dealt with the most urgent matters for the first hour, and then sent for Fergus Stephenson.

He had a high opinion of him as a diplomatist and a warm regard for him personally. He liked his wife, who went out of her way to charm, and had never made the mistake of allowing her personality to overpower his own wife in their public roles. He thought of Stephenson as a man from the same mould as himself, and it never occurred to him to omit a single detail of the 'green' telegram or of his conclusions about its significance. He had to acquaint the Minister with the facts, because he might well be called upon to act upon them. The Ambassador had accepted an invitation to spend a long weekend in California. Responsibility for helping Loder, as for anything else that might happen over the three days, would rest with Fergus Stephenson.

'I can't say how much I dislike this sort of thing,' the Ambassador said. 'I should make a personal protest. We are not part of the Intelligence organisation, and they have no right to drag us into their unpleasant escapades. It's certain to come out that this whole thing was masterminded from my Embassy, and I shall be thought to be a party to it! I shall make a protest anyway, but it won't do any good.'

'It's a very emphatic telegram,' Fergus remarked. 'This Russian must be a very important member of their team. They should have had the courtesy to let you know his name. I think that's something I personally resent—this feeling of being told to help while not being completely trusted.'

'I don't want to know anything about him,' the Ambassador said. 'When Dick Paterson started telling me about all this, I quickly cut him short. Defectors and double agents aren't my affair. He seemed rather excited about it; I suppose he thought it would be a feather in his cap to act as go-between for this Russian. I told him to turn the whole thing over to Loder.'

And it was then, while the Ambassador was talking, that the veil dropped for Stephenson. When he first heard the story from his wife, the initial shock she had given him over the telephone when she mentioned his lighter was still operating; he had been numbed by it; it was as if a part of his brain was in suspended animation. Richard Paterson knew of a Russian defector. He had taken that in, while the framework surrounding that single fact was lost in a few unimportant details of Rachel Paterson's jealousy, her breaking down in tears. He had concentrated on the fact, without realising that the key to it all was to be found in the details. Paterson had been told of the defector by his mistress, the girl friend he used to visit in New York, until he, Stephenson, had warned him off at Loder's instigation. Because the woman was mixed up with a Russian. He had discussed it all with Loder over one of their early lunches together; Loder had told him the name of the man whom he suspected of trying to recruit this girl—what was *her* name—Farrant, Farrow—that made the defector Sverdlov. Feodor Sverdlov, Colonel in the Soviet Army, assistant to the old K.G.B. General Golitsyn. The truth screeched at him; he broke out into a massive sweat all over his body. Sverdlov, the man suspected of being the real head of the Russian Intelligance in the United States. The most important member of the whole Embassy. The man to whom 'Blue's' confidential files would go directly from the controller. He felt if he didn't get out of the room he might pass out.

The Ambassador noticed nothing. He went on talking while Fergus struggled to keep calm and he managed to mutter something that could be taken for an answer.

He heard the Ambassador say, 'Well, my dear chap, I'm going off to the Vanderholdens' for the weekend, so I shall leave this wretched business in your hands. You'll have to let Loder have whatever he needs, but I needn't ask you to keep the Embassy as far in the background as you can.'

'Of course,' Fergus heard his own voice saying. 'Don't worry about that.'

He left the Ambassador's office and slipped into a general staff cloakroom on the way back to his own room. He washed his hands, damping his face with plain water, dried, and looked at himself in the glass. He looked jaundiced, his eyelids peeled back from the eyeballs. Sverdlov. No wonder London was sending 'greens' which would have authorised Loder to take over the Embassy if he felt like it. No wonder Loder was too 'busy' to have lunch so he could try to pump the information out of him. No wonder. Sverdlov was bigger than Penkovsky; he made even a defector like Dalmytsin look like an office boy. If he came over to the British he could bring down half the Soviet Intelligence networks in the West. At that moment, facing personal disaster, Fergus saw beyond it to the catastrophic consequences to his chosen ideological system. It would be a major blow to Soviet prestige in the world, apart from causing havoc in their Intelligence organisation.

Even if he himself were not involved, Sverdlov's defection had to be stopped. The arrival of the 'green' proved that it must be imminent. He couldn't delay, even though he incurred some personal risk. He had a telephone number which was to be used only in extreme emergency. The normal means of passing his information was by the dead letter method; he frequented a record shop in the city centre; his love of rare classical recordings was well known, and he had been a regular patron since he arrived from Washington. His method was simple. He went once a week as a matter of course, bought a record or a tape. When he had something to pass on, he went into the recording booth and stuck the tiny cylinder containing the film from his lighter camera into a certain hole in the soundproofed wall above the entrance. His visits were timed exactly, although they alternated each week; his contact, whom he didn't know, was sometimes in the shop at the same time. After Fergus left the booth, his contact went in and picked up the microfilm. The risk of anyone else seeing it among the multitude of perforations and at the agreed spot, well above eye level, were negligible. In the same way it was easy for Fergus to pass a message to his controller, whom he also didn't know except by a code name, Paul. But this was too slow a means of communicating his vital piece of information. He had the telephone number in reserve; he had always had one, wherever he was posted. He knew the figures off by heart.

He left the cloakroom; he was calmer now. He looked at his watch. He had two appointments that morning, one due in fifteen minutes. By all the rules of caution, he should make that call outside the Embassy, where there was no risk of its being overheard or traced. This meant delay. It was eleven o'clock in the morning; he would have to wait until midday, and leave the building. He could go to the record shop; there was a telephone kiosk there which he could use. It was a delay but not long enough to flout the careful rule he had observed throughout his double life. Never do anything within the confines of the Embassy which could be traced back. He walked back to his office. Midday; he could leave early and take the car uptown. There was no reason to panic. Friday. It would be easy for them to remove Sverdlov over the weekend; most people went out of Washington as it was beginning to get hot. He could be taken on board an Illyushin jet and flown back without anyone noticing. It had been done before. Fergus went into his office and settled down for his first appointment. He smoked a lot during the half an hour, and his fingers shook slightly. Otherwise he appeared his normal self.

. . . . .

Judith called Nielson at home that morning. She had decided what to say; Sam was becoming increasingly annoyed and impatient with her requests for time off or to leave early. He just wouldn't take another one. She tried to sound hoarse over the telephone, and told his wife a straight lie. She had an infected throat and a fever; she wouldn't be able to come in that day but she expected to be fit for work on Monday. She apologised for causing inconvenience and then rang off quickly before he could come to the phone. Nancy was away for the weekend, so there was no risk of her lie being discovered. She had spent a wretched night; she made her face up and decided that knowing Feodor Sverdlov had put ten years on her age. She packed a small bag, just enough for the one or possibly two nights she would be away. She hadn't decided how to get back after Sverdlov left for England, but there must be several flights to the States. She couldn't plan that far ahead; it didn't seem to matter by comparison. She didn't eat breakfast; coffee made her feel sour and slightly sick. She drank fruit juice and wondered whether the continuous feeling of dread was anything more than a manifestation of acute nerves. It was nothing she could define in terms of common sense. Everything was going well. Loder had the operation in his hands, and she trusted his efficiency. Sverdlov seemed confident; their first step was only a few hours away. Once they were on board the plane for Barbados she would certainly feel easier. Twice during that interminable morning she nearly telephoned Sverdlov at the Soviet New York office. Seeing him last night had given her courage; whether it was for herself or because she felt he needed her support. Judith didn't know. But by the morning the confidence had ebbed away, leaving the sick feeling of imminent disaster. She had tried to express it to him just before he kissed her good night, but there hadn't been time.

He had said he loved her. He had kissed as if he meant it. It had made her feel quite disorientated afterwards. There were two or three hours left in spite of her efforts to pass the time, by cleaning out the apartment, and even doing some of Nancy's ironing for her. But she was afraid to go out. Sverdlov might call; Loder might call; there could be a last-minute change. Even Sam might decide to check on how ill she really was. The apartment was like a prison; Judith made a sandwich which she forced herself to eat, and settled down to try to read. The telephone rang once and she sprang up, but the call was from a man, asking for Nancy. No others came through. At three o'clock she brought her bag into the front hall. Sverdlov was never late; he would be coming to collect her at any moment. They were supposed to be going away for a lovers' weekend; he had impressed on her several times that she must appear to be happy and relaxed. But he hadn't reminded her last night. His mood had been restrained, almost sad. She checked her watch again. It was ten minutes past. He had never been late before; never once . . .

A minute later the front door bell rang.

. . . . .

General Golitsyn was asleep in his chair; he had eaten a heavy lunch and by early afternoon he felt slack and weary. The atmosphere was humid and outside the windows a bright sunshine beat against the glass. He had the window shades lowered and the air conditioning turned up. Then his old body sank into the chair, the limbs relaxing, the head dropped on his chest, the eyes still open like a lizard lying apparently comatose on a rock. Then they shut, and he snored softly in the way of old men who have dozed off sitting up.

When the message came through from Fergus Stephenson, he had just woken and was drinking a glass of tea. He found it more difficult to shake off the lethargy following a short sleep; as a young man he had used the technique of cat napping very successfully. A half an hour taken in trains, cars, lorries jolting over primitive tracks, behind a desk where he had worked all night—in aeroplanes and even on horseback, in the early days of revolution—Golitsyn had been able to recharge his energy with the minimum rest. But now he dithered, he sucked his cheeks in and out, and blinked his reptilian eyes to focus. When he first got the message he didn't understand it properly. It demanded too much of him too quickly. He read it a second time, and then his assistant and his secretary heard a yell, followed by a shattering blasphemous obscenity. The assistant came in, the secretary did not dare.

He found the General standing with the message in his right hand, his face blood red, bellowing and swearing like a man twenty years younger.

Moments later Anna Skriabine, white and shaking, stood in front of him explaining every detail of the flight schedule Sverdlov had taken from Washington to New York and from New York to Barbados. He had been booked on a plane leaving at four-thirty. Golitsyn glared at his watch. It was already five-thirty. He was in the air and on his way. Quite suddenly he turned on the girl. He shouted at her. She had been told to watch, told to report every word and movement of Feodor Sverdlov. Only that morning she had come to his office and said that Sverdlov seemed attracted to her and was going to take her out. Golitsyn's hand came out and slapped her brutally across the face. She had not only failed, he roared at her, but she had been completely duped, and duped him, Golitsyn, in turn. She stood with both hands covering her face, and sobbed with fright. The old man gave her a look of dreadful menace. Then he told her to go back to the secretarial quarters and to stay there. Within the next half an hour there was frantic activity in the cable section. One of Stukalov's men would be on the way to Barbados to watch him; he had caught an earlier flight scheduled to arrive two hours before, catching a connection in Trinidad. But one man was not equipped to deal with this development. He had no orders to kill Sverdlov, only to shadow him and note his movements. He, like all the Embassy staff concerned, were completely off guard. Sverdlov's trip to Barbados was regarded as an Intelligence operation, carried out with the full knowledge of the General, openly planned and the details arranged through the Embassy. No one had imagined for a moment that it was a preliminary to Sverdlov's defection. And that it must have the organisation of the British S.I.S. behind it. The message received by Golitsyn said very clearly that he was dealing with the British Embassy, and preparations to receive him were in hand. The tone of the warning suggested urgency, but they were in ignorance of the fact that he had already managed to leave America for a former British colony. Golitsyn felt like a madman; Sverdlov had slipped away, following the boldest of all Intelligence maxims that if you want to elude a pursuer, do so in daylight with as many people round as possible. Sverdlov had got out of the States, where his seizure and disposal would have been easily arranged. He had got away to a West Indian island, where his abduction would be difficult, if not impossible, without an international scandal. And it was sufficiently remote, with an indifferent system of communication to make a top speed change of plan extremely difficult to organise. Golitsyn cabled Moscow first, giving Panyushkin the details received in the warning message from 'Blue's' controller, and asking for his instructions by immediate return cablegraph. Golitsyn's mind had seen two or three possible courses of action, but he dared not take any of them without the final approval of Sverdlov's superior. He had never even considered acting without authority. No blame could attach to him for waiting on his chief's directions.

A plane could be chartered which would fly a team out to Barbados. A single directive could be cabled to Stukalov's lone operative, ordering him to seek assistance from their meagre contacts on the island and try to seize Sverdlov, to hold him until the kidnap plane arrived. From there he could be conveyed in stages to Europe. Once in any of the East European countries, he was as good as in the Soviet Union. The old man's hands shook with rage and terror. He had initiated the arrest of Sverdlov; he had sent the secretary Kalinin back, dazed and doped by the Embassy doctor, to the experts in the Lubiyanka, who had got what they wanted.

He, Golitsyn, had begun the whole investigation into Sverdlov, worrying at his reputation like a fierce old hound digging for a buried bone. He had cast the doubts, and taken it upon himself to deliver the wrong-doer to justice. Instead, he had permitted Sverdlov to escape into the hands of Soviet Russia's Western enemies. He might punish the failure of Anna Skriabine, but the vengeance of Panyushkin was too dreadful to imagine.

He contacted Stukalov in New York, allotting a portion of the blame to him; he spoke to the Soviet Ambassador to UNO and then dragged himself to an interview with his own Ambassador to explain exactly the crisis which threatened them. It was the Ambassador who made the suggestion which the General should have thought of for himself. If Sverdlov were going to defect, he had probably taken his British hosts a present. Was anything missing from the confidential files . . . Even before the chief filing clerk appeared before them, stammering and dripping sweat, Golitsyn knew the answer. They went down to the filing section, and the Ambassador opened the safe with the General beside him. He handed him the file which the departmental chief said Sverdlov had inspected that morning. He found the sheaf of papers which had been substituted. A long memo from the personnel officer; a list of leave for the senior K.G.B. officers in Washington and New York.

The latest communication from 'Blue' was missing. That meant the defection was going to take place in Barbados. As the Ambassador had said, Sverdlov had brought his hosts a present. And as a result the K.G.B. would inevitably lose their most important agent since Philby. Golitsyn could have given a cry of physical pain; instead the silence developed round the group in the filing section, until it was more expressive than the most explicit words. Then Golitsyn broke it.

Throughout his life he had made only two momentous decisions without reference to a higher authority. When he had hidden the school teacher's books, and when he raised the red flag from the ranks of his regiment and gave the call to march on Petersburg.

This was the third and probably the last.

'I cannot wait for General Panyushkin's instructions,' he said. 'Sverdlov has stolen the "Blue" file. He must be stopped.' Nobody answered him. The Ambassador stood back to let him pass, and Golitsyn went back to his own office.

Later that night a privately chartered jet flew from San Francisco with four passengers on board. It arrived at Seaways Airport on the island of Barbados at 5 a.m. The four passengers, all men, were described on their passports as Canadian citizens. They informed the sleepy Customs official that they were making a tour of the islands. They showed the normal signs of being too rich for their own good; one of them appeared a little drunk. They drove off after a long wait, during which they complained and argued, in a hired car, giving the address of the smartest hotel on the Atlantic Coast, formerly the mansion built by Sam Lord, a slave owner and smuggler famous in Barbadian history. That was what the airport officials heard. It was only afterwards, when the investigations began, that nobody at Sam Lord's Castle had ever seen or heard of any of them.

. . . . .

It was dark when they landed at Seaways Airport. The night was very black without the lustrous moon Judith remembered, but stars glittered in profusion overhead. The gentle trade wind blew, cool and constant, moving the trees. As they crossed the tarmac there were pools of water on the ground. It was the rainy season; she had forgotten. Sverdlov was holding her arm, walking with long steps that forced her to hurry beside him. The journey by air had seemed long and a brief storm over the Caribbean had made their gradual descent uncomfortable, with a lot of bumping.

It was the worst journey she had ever experienced, even by comparison with the short trip in a police car to the mortuary to identify her husband's shattered body after the motor accident. Every face was suspect; Judith looked at the business men, who were few and scattered among the obvious groups taking a holiday, wondering which of them were travelling on behalf of the K.G.B. She had leaned close to Sverdlov, whispering.

'Don't worry,' he said. 'If there is someone on the plane, they won't do anything. Be calm; read *Look* magazine and hold hands with me.' He had been in his usual ironic mood when they met; he teased her during the journey to Kennedy International in the car. It was the first time he had used an Embassy car with a driver. In the plane his attitude changed. They settled into their seats, and for a moment he laid his hand on her arm. There was no mockery, no sly advance because he knew she couldn't rebuff him. He was gentle, with the look in his pale eyes which Judith dreaded more than the mischievous sensuality which had pursued and bedevilled her during that first trip to Barbados.

Now, standing together in the arrivals hall, passing through the Customs, giving their passports to the policeman in his white tropicals, Judith felt a sense of finality, as if the island itself were the end of the journey for them both. It was surely impossible to feel as if she had come home, to a place she had visited for two weeks, nearly as many months ago. But the soft air, the elusive tropical smell, the insistent night breeze—the broad regional accent originating in the West Country and adopted by the slave ancestors of the Barbadians as they learned English—it was all familiar. Also quite illogical; she had despised anything pertaining to nerves, and after three years in the States, the term neurotic was a description applied so indiscriminately that it had ceased to mean anything. Now her own reactions were neurotic; there was no reason in them; emotion had taken control, substituting for common sense. They were in transit, at least Sverdlov was; for a night and a day at the most. Far from having reached a safe haven, they were only on the first stage of the journey. They drove to the hotel in silence. He had leaned his head back and his eyes were shut. She thought suddenly how tired he looked; the strain of the past two weeks had aged him. Naturally lean and wiry, he was now too thin. On an impulse Judith wriggled her hand through his arm; immediately he opened his eyes and smiled at her.

'Don't worry,' he repeated. 'Now we are here, I feel everything will be all right.'

I don't. She almost spoke the thought out loud. I may be strung up, and indulging in a lot of neurotic fears, but I can't help it; I don't think everything is going to be all right and I can't explain why. . . .

They registered at the reception desk; it looked different in the electric light; even in the few weeks since they had last been there, the decorations seemed faded, the manager looked older than she remembered; the poster advertising a cruise aboard the replica of the pirate ship *Jolly Roger* still hung on the notice board, secured by only three drawing pins.

While Sverdlov signed, she turned away to look at it. Packed lunches, rum punches in the cocktail bar—the authentic atmosphere of a Caribbean privateer. Judith read it with a sense of horror. It conjured up a mental picture of hearty business men, their stomachs suspended above their hideous Bermuda shorts, getting drunk amid the foney canon balls and the mass produced pirate cutlasses in the 'authentic' bar. There would be screaming, ill-disciplined children and bored wives. Sverdlov was beside her.

'Don't tell me you want to take a trip?'

'No thanks.' She turned to the desk, shook hands with the manager and signed the register. 'No thanks, I don't think that's my idea of fun.'

She felt the man's eyes looking at her, making his own assessment of what she and her Russian friend considered amusing. Christ, Judith said inside, if only you knew what we had come for, you nasty-minded, leering . . .

The bungalow was identical to the one she had stayed in before. The same large open plan living room with a dining table and chairs, a kitchenette leading off, a narrow passage to the entrance door, the suspension staircase leading to the bedroom and bathroom on a floor above. The glass sliding doors were closed; they could hear the sea rushing up the sandy beach, and the muted chorus of the cicadas in the trees. Sverdlov tipped the man who had brought their luggage, and then came up to Judith.

'Would you like to swim? It would be good for us both.'

'No,' Judith said quickly. 'No, Loder said you weren't to leave the bungalow! You've got to stay inside.'

'For two days? I'm not to go out for two days? . . .

'Feodor, for God's sake don't argue. That's what he said. Keep indoors till someone comes to put you on the plane!'

Sverdlov started up the stairs, leading to the bedroom.

'I am tired and I'm hot,' he said. 'I am going to swim in the pool where I first saw you.' Judith ran after him.

'Stop being such an obstinate fool! Why can't you do what Loder says?'

She heard him moving about in the room above, changing out of his clothes. She was shaking with fright. The bungalow was safe; Loder wouldn't have given the instruction without reason. Why couldn't Sverdlov be sensible and stay out of sight; why did he have to invite risk? She ran up the stairs after him. He met her at the top; he was in his swimming trunks with a towel round his shoulder.

'If you're worried about me,' he said, 'come too.'

By the time she got to the pool, he was already swimming, lazily moving through the water on his back. 'It is very warm,' he called out. 'You'll enjoy it.'

Judith gave him a look of fury and dived in.

He came up to her, and under the water he closed his

arm round her body. They were near to the side; he held on to the rail with one hand, keeping them suspended.

'I know what I am doing,' he said. 'I am being watched by my own people for certain; someone has followed us here. My only hope of getting on to Mr. Loder's plane alive is to act naturally. To behave as if I am having a weekend with you. Stop trying to kick at me.'

'I don't care what you say,' Judith whispered; he was holding her against his naked chest, 'Loder said you were to stay inside . . .'

Sverdlov suddenly let go of the pool's edge and they went under the water. He brought her up immediately, and gripping her body with both arms he kissed her.

'I know better than Loder,' he said. 'Much, much better. I've never been so close to you as this. Swim back and I'll tell you how I used to come down here and hide and watch you swimming all alone in the middle of the night . . .'

He insisted on having a drink before he would go back to the bungalow. There were two single beds in the room ond the floor above. His case was open on one of them. Sverdlov came up the stairs behind her, and at the bedroom door she turned. In the pool, he had locked his legs around her's, gripped her in both arms, and plunged her under the water. If he got through that door before she had time to recover, she hadn't a hope of getting him out again. 'No,' she said. 'Please, Feodor. I didn't come with you for this.'

She didn't shut the door on him; she waited for him to go of his own choice. For a moment they stood and looked at each other; they were both wet, the beads of water slowly running down his chest, gathering at his feet in a trickle; she felt cold, as if the bathing suit had been stripped off and she stood naked.

'If I asked, would you really say no to me?'

'Don't ask,' Judith pleaded. 'Please don't ask. I'm cold and wet and I'm scared to death . . .'

He put his hand round the back of her neck; she remembered that he had done that before when they were on the island. His mouth was quite warm. The kiss was a communication; not now, because I am tender with you and I know how to wait. But the time will come; we both know that.

'Go and have a hot shower,' Sverdlov said. 'If it makes

you happier, I will order some food sent up. We will stay inside tonight, as Mr. Loder said.'

Down by the bar two men sat drinking beer and smoking, apparently absorbed by the peace of the tropical night. They had moved into the hotel the previous day; they hadn't booked, they had just arrived and after a private interview with the manager, they were given the bungalow next to the one booked by Sverdlov. The manager hadn't even bothered to explain that it was already taken by a middle-aged Canadian couple who came to the hotel at the off season period every year and regarded that particular bungalow as their own. He just studied the credentials they showed him, put a brief call through to the Commissioner of Police at their suggestion, said yes, certainly, yes of course, any help they required, and then hung up. When Judith saw him staring at her and Sverdlov when they registered, she completely misinterpreted his look. He also engaged two extra staff, both Barbadians, who were assigned to clean the two bungalows and take this duty away from the maid. This caused much comment among the hotel waiters, because they were only half full and there wasn't enough work to justify a full complement. They were further surprised when one of the new recruits began weeding the flower beds outside the bungalows; all the gardeners on the island were women; by the end of the day the manager was reduced to giving the disposed maid, the head waiter and the garden girl, who suspected she was about to be sacked, an extra week's wages and the instruction to keep their mouths shut or lose their jobs. As he understood the arrangement was only for the weekend, the manager felt he could just rely on them to do as they were told. The night that Judith and Sverdlov arrived he lay in bed beside his mistress, who was sulky because he hadn't wanted to make love, and wondered secretly whether he might sell his story to one of the U.S. newspapers after it was all over. Whatever 'it' was—he didn't know why two British security men were watching the Russian, or why he had a couple of Barbadian Special Branch men working under his windows on one pretext or another. Until the weekend was over and everything had gone through without trouble, he didn't want to know. He turned over to sleep.

By early morning, with the sun full up, and the seasonal

rain clouds gathering black on the Western coast, a small yacht slipped round the promontory which sheltered the insland's most exclusive hotel and gave its sandy beach protection from the ocean swell. It proceeded under sail, although there was a small but powerful motor. The wind carried it at speed, cutting through the choppy blue water. It was about a quarter of a mile from the St. James hotel when the sails were slackened and hauled down and the yacht dropped anchor. Two men dived over the side, and began swimming, calling to each other and laughing. A third figure began to fish. From a position on the mast-head, a fourth, stockily built, with greying close-cropped hair, studied the bungalows through a pair of field glasses. At half-hour intervals he changed places with the fisher-man who took over his watch. The swimmers had come back aboard and were sunbathing on the deck.

To her surprise Judith had slept very deeply. At Sverdlov's insistence, she had gone upstairs to bed ahead of him, quite soon after they had eaten. He had ordered a bottle of whisky, which upset her, and suggested that she go ahead and get to sleep. There was no suggestion on either side that when he came upstairs he would disturb her. When she woke the bed was empty and had not been slept in. Panic overwhelmed her. She sprang up and ran to the stairs.

'Feodor! Feodor?'

'Good morning.' She was halfway down when she saw him. The couch in the living room had extended into a bed. She had forgotten it had a double function. Sverdlov had slept covered by his coat.

'I thought you had gone out,' Judith said. She came down the stairs; the shock had given her a headache. Sverdlov got up and came towards her. At the same time she realised two things; her nightdress was flimsy, her breasts were clearly visible underneath it, and the whisky bottle by the telephone was three-quarters empty.

'I am not drunk now,' Sverdlov said. 'But go and put something on, so I can't see you like that.' She ran back upstairs; as she dressed she heard him moving round the kitchenette. When she came down again she was dressed in trousers and a shirt; he came out into the living room with a tray of coffee and a bowl of fruit.

'You slept well,' he said. "I went up once and looked at you. You needed it; you were very tired.'

'And you got drunk,' Judith said. 'Why did you do it—what would have happened if anything went wrong and you were in a stupor?'

'I never get in a stupor.' He drank coffee. His hair was on end and the shadows under his eyes were like pits.

'It's very stuffy in here,' she said. 'Let's open the sliding door and get some air.'

He came up behind her as she struggled with the catch. 'You look very pretty asleep,' he said. 'Kiss me good morning and don't be angry about the whisky. It kept me away from you.'

Aboard the little yacht, the grey-haired man was adjusting his binoculars; he twisted the knob quickly to bring the two figures by the glass doors into focus. The man's figure became clearer as he separated from the smaller one; behind the shield of glass it was impossible to see his face in detail. The watcher waited, very still. Then he sucked suddenly at his upper lip. The glass door was opening, slowly sliding back. He made a slight adjustment and for perhaps two seconds, the man in the lens became magnified and perfectly in focus. He lowered the glasses and spoke quietly to the others on the deck.

'It's him. Second bungalow from the end.' The man who had been fishing laid aside his rod. He took the glasses and looked through them for a minute. 'The doors are open,' he said. All four were in a group now, each stared through the glasses in turn. 'Very careless,' the grey-haired man said. 'Very, very careless. Launch the dinghy; we must hurry.'

. . . . .

'It's raining,' Judith said. 'It looks as if there's a real storm blowing up. Look, there's a little boat out there—I'm glad I'm not on that!'

'Are you a bad sailor?'

He followed where she pointed out to sea; the little yacht was bouncing among the rising waves like a toy. 'I don't like it when it's rough. My husband adored sailing; he never minded the weather.'

'You know,' Sverdlov said, 'you never talked about your husband. About the English lover, yes, but not your husband. Why not?'

'Because I feel guilty, I suppose,' Judith said. 'Look, the wind is blowing this way—we'd better close the doors.

I'll do it; I feel uneasy about you showing yourself too much.' He let her do as she wanted; he didn't want to argue, or to increase the strain from which she was obviously suffering on his account. He sat back on the sofa bed, which they had readjusted, and watched her push the sliding door closed. It ran smoothly but the last three inches of track were slightly bent. It required extra effort to snap it in place. Judith pulled, and believed she had connected the ratchet with the slot.

'Why guilty?' Sverdlov said. 'Tell me—what did you do?'

She came and sat beside him; they smoked, and she let him put his arm around her.

'It's more what I didn't do,' she said, 'I told you he was killed. We'd been married three years. But for the last two, I wasn't in love with him. I haven't much of a record, have I—him and then Richard . . .'

'I'm not complaining,' Sverdlov said. 'You suit me. If you loved him for one year, then he had something; he must have been happy.'

'He was very happy.' Judith watched the rain battering against the beach, kicking up the sand like bullets. 'He enjoyed everything he did; he was a completely uncomplicated man. At least that's what I kept telling myself afterwards, so he couldn't have realised how little contact we had. Life was a big laugh, one party went on to the next, non stop. When I think back on it, it was hell on earth after the first eight months, a year. If he hadn't been killed, poor lamb, I'd have left him.'

'You won't be allowed to leave me,' Sverdlov said. 'Look at the rain; do you remember it rained the first morning we talked, out there? I told you not to sit under the poisonous tree.'

'The Manchineel,' she said. 'I remember. I wanted to read my book and lick my wounds and you wouldn't go away. You're the most persistent man I've ever met. Tell me something—are you sorry it's turned out like this? Having to live in exile, hiding and running.'

'I am not hiding,' Sverdlov smiled. 'I am only waiting for the rain to stop and then I'm going for a swim. As for being sorry . . .' He shrugged, and then he squeezed her. 'I am Russian and we believe in Fate. In fact we invented it, like fairy stories. That way if anything goes wrong, it is never your fault. It is Fate. I am not glad to go and live with Mr. Loder, but I *am* glad not to be in the Lubiyanka at this moment. A lot of people I have worked with won't be so lucky. When will you come to England? A month?—you can give Nielson time to find another secretary.'

'Feodor, I'm not coming. You know that. Stop joking about it. I wish we'd hear something from Loder. He promised Saturday night; why hasn't there been a message?'

'It will come,' Sverdlov said. 'And I am ready. I have what I promised in my case over there.'

'That file you talked about,' she said. ' "Blue". I remember you asking me about that the night we talked to Peter Memenov. True Blue. I think you're right; it could be an Englishman; with a very perverted sense of humour. Where are you going?'

'The rain has stopped,' Sverdlov said. 'I am going upstairs to shave, and then we are going down to the pool, and I will make love to you in the water. Don't say I'm not to go, or that Loder said I must stay inside. When I am in England he can treat me like a prisoner. But not before.'

He went up the stairs, before Judith could begin to argue. Then the telephone rang.

'Mrs. Farrow?'

'Yes. Who is that?' Upstairs the shower began to work; she could hear the water hammering in the bath and the unmusical sound of Sverdlov singing.

'There is a seat on the plane leaving at seven-thirty tonight. Tell your friend to be ready by six o'clock. We'll come and pick him up.'

'Oh thank God,' Judith said fervently. 'Thank God. I was beginning to think something had gone wrong. Look, he won't stay in the bungalow—there's nothing I can do, he just won't. He's going out in a few minutes to swim in the pool . . .'

There was a pause at the other end. The man's voice which had given the message grew muffled; he had his hand over the mouthpiece while he spoke to someone else.

'Did you explain this was part of the instructions?'

'Yes,' she said. 'I said everything, just as I was told. But he wouldn't listen last night either. He'll be down in a few minutes. Dammit, now the sun's coming out . . .'

'All right, Mrs. Farrow. Not to worry. We'll keep an eye on him.' It was an educated voice; young sounding, with a brisk authority in the tone.

She turned away from the telephone and looked down on the beach. It was dark with rain, pockmarked and pitted with the force of the downpour, but the sun was coming through the clouds, set like a burning jewel in a patch of brilliant blue sky. Three men were strolling down by the water's edge; they had a beach ball, which they were tossing at each other, making practice passes. Judith turned back. The shower had stopped, and so had the singing. Relief surged in her; the plane was fixed, Loder's men were close by, there was only another six hours to wait, and then he would be safe. She went up the stairs and banged on the bathroom door.

'That was the telephone,' she said. 'Everything's ready. You'll be collected at six and taken to the airport.' Suddenly she leaned against the door; she felt physically weak. 'I've been in such a state,' she said. 'I've been so terrified for you. Thank God, it's nearly over.'

'We will have a good lunch,' Sverdlov called through. There was relief in his voice. He was as relieved as Judith. 'We will have champagne. Get ready quickly and come down. *Dushinka*—you've been very brave for me.'

Suddenly the door opened and a hand came through; water dripped from it.

Judith caught hold and for a moment they gripped. Neither of them spoke. Of all the things she was to remember afterwards, that moment of silent communication was the most painful.

She went into her room, shut the door, and sat on the bed. She heard Sverdlov come out of the bathroom, and go down the stairs. With an effort, Judith began to change into a swimming costume. In a few hours he would be on the plane for England. Loder's men were close and keeping watch. Sverdlov had been right; her fears were exaggerated and unnecessary. There was absolutely no reason why, at that particular moment when they seemed safer than ever before, they should return with such a blinding impact that she almost ran to the door and screamed for him to stop—stop . . .

Outside the bungalow a wind was shaking the trees, whipping the surface of the sea into a froth; the sun blazed down, a few bathers ventured in for a swim close to the shore. The little yacht anchored out at sea was riding the slight swell. As Sverdlov came down the stairs the sliding door inched back along the aluminium rails, moved by the vibration, and the wind came through the gap like a hand. It moved an inch or two, guided by the wind, gaining momentum from its own weight as it slid backwards.

On the beach below the bungalow, the three men went on playing beach ball; the figure of Sverdlov was clearly visible as it crossed the room from the staircase. It was only a glimpse, because the downstairs living room went back under the overhang of the bedroom above, and from outside it was impossible to see anyone distinctly once they had moved under its shadow.

The door had stopped moving. It was open about a foot. The beach ball thudded into the arms of one man; he let it drop on the sand; he formed part of the base of a triangle, a single man stood as the apex, his legs braced apart, head tilted backwards. He was well built, with a tough muscled torso, but his hair was grey and cut close to the skull. Suddenly his right arm swung, his body moved with the throw; something small and heavy hurtled the twenty feet from the beach to the bungalow and disappeared in the narrow gap between the glass door and wall.

Judith was at the bedroom door; she heard a bang, like a firecracker. The whole of the room beneath seemed to dissolve in a blinding yellow flame. Above the instantaneous crackle of an unearthly kind of fire, enveloped in a heat so intense that it was as if a volcano had erupted in the room below, she fell back, her screams shredding the mid-morning quietness, before the triumphant roar of all-enveloping fire drowned everything.

. . . . .

It was Fergus Stephenson's custom to read all the American and English newspapers before he left for his office. He had breakfast in his study, and it was a frugal meal of crispbread, bitter marmalade and tea. While he ate he began with the English papers, which were easy to manage with one hand, and then proceeded through the bulky Americans. He read quickly but without missing any item, however insignificant, which pertained to political, economic or social events in the world. The paragraph in the foreign news section was well placed, with a black type headline.

'Soviet citizen burned to death in holiday hotel.' Stephenson put his cup of tea back on the tray. It was not a long report; few details were available at the time. It was a straight statement of the known facts as far as they could be established. A Russian tourist registered as F. G. Sverdlov had been the victim of a fire in the bungalow St. James hotel on the fashionable west coast of Barbados. An Englishwoman domiciled in New York had been rescued and was in hospital on the island. Mrs. J. Farrow.

The cause of the fire was unknown, but it was thought to be due to an electrical fault. The bungalow had been completely gutted and the adjoining buildings severely damaged. That was all. Stephenson looked at the date. Three days previously. A Russian tourist. F. G. Sverdlov. His warning had got through in time. He marked the paragraph. His secretary went through the papers in his office and cut out the marked sections for reference. He poured more tea into the cup, but it tasted tepid and stale. He was sorry about Judith Farrow; he hoped her injuries were not too serious. By mid-morning, he had time to put a call through to Loder's office and invite him to lunch.

They met in a pleasant uptown restaurant. It was not a place frequented by diplomats; many of the city's top political journalists were gathered there. Fergus spoke to several of them, calling them by name. He had always made a special effort to be communicative and pleasant to the Press. He was extremely popular among them.

They sat at a corner table with a view of the beautiful wide avenue from the window; the atmosphere was air conditioned and comfortable. He thought Loder looked sallow and depressed. There were patches of sweat under his arms.

'I saw the report about that Russian being burned to death in Barbados,' Fergus said. 'It was the same couple we were talking about a few weeks ago, wasn't it—Dick Paterson's girl friend?'

'Yes,' Loder said. The menu was put in front of them; he ordered melon and chicken in the basket. He detested the vast American steaks, sprawling across the plate; he maintained that they tasted of cotton waste and sawdust. He heard Fergus ask for an omelette and lobster salad.

'It sounded an odd business,' Stephenson returned to the subject.

'That's putting it mildly.' Loder sawed away at his

melon with a spoon. 'I'm afraid it was a real balls up. On my part.'

'Oh? I'm sure it wasn't,' Fergus said gently. 'Can you tell me what happened?'

'No reason why not.' Loder shook his head. He seemed glad of the chance to talk; glad too of the sympathy shown by the Minister.

'I'd got it all wrong; Sverdlov wasn't trying to recruit Mrs. Farrow. He wanted to defect to us. Everything was fixed up; they went to Barbados together as a blind. He was going to be flown to England from there.'

'Good Lord,' Fergus said. The second course was in front of them, but Loder went on talking.

'He was the Russians' top man over here, it would have been a fantastic coup to get him. But someone must have tipped them off. They were all set up for him on the island.'

'And that was the fire,' Fergus said. 'It wasn't an accident.'

'Accident?' Loder gave a laugh which was humourless and sour. 'There's nothing accidental about napalm. That's what they used.'

Fergus shuddered. He wished Loder hadn't told him that. 'I can imagine. What about the girl?'

'Burned,' said Loder. 'But bloody lucky to be alive. She was in the upstairs room. Our chaps smashed the window in and got her out.'

'Where was Sverdlov?'

'Downstairs. He hadn't a snowball's chance in hell. Napalm's bad enough in the open. Just think what would happen in a confined space . . .'

'I'd rather not.' Fergus drank some wine. He looked pale. 'What a frightful thing.'

'You once said it was a dirty business,' Loder remarked. He cut into the food but without appetite. 'That's not a bad description. I'll have to go and see Mrs. Farrow; I think I owe it to her. I'm not looking forward to it much.'

'You did your best,' Fergus said. 'I'm sure it wasn't your fault.'

'You could try telling that to my chief,' Loder said. 'This chicken is good.'

'I like the food here.' Fergus helped him close the subject. They stayed almost two hours, talking about books and an art exhibition which had opened to a controversial reception in New York. Loder muttered with some shyness that he might well go up and see it. When they left the resaurant it was agreed that Fergus should take a day and go with him. He went back to his office in a calm mood, eager to get on with some work, and genuinely looking forward to the excursion with Loder. Unlikely candidate as he was, the gap in class and background made less and less difference to Fergus's choice of him as a friend. It was years since he had met anyone with whom he could relax and enjoy the same interests. He rang for his secretary and began a long dictation. He felt so different from the past two weeks; fear had affected him more than he realised. Now his mind was clear and his energy had returned.

Sverdlov was dead, and his knowledge of 'Blue' had died with him in that frightful holocaust. Napalm in a confined space. He shut the thought out of his mind. Years of living a deception had taught him the discipline that the past could never be allowed to come back into the present. For a man doing what he did, there could be no private indulgence like taking out a memory to gloat or grieve. Nothing could exist but the present. He didn't even think of telling his wife what had happened. She had never spoken of it since, and he felt instinctively that she would never mention it again.

For all her insensitivity, this was something she would prefer to forget. As he could now forget it. The danger was past. He was safe.

. . . . . .

The room in St. Patricia's Nursing Home was quiet and shaded; for nearly three weeks Judith had looked out at the view through the window. An attractive garden was laid out, with green grass, constantly watered against the scorching sun, orderly beds of bright crimson Callas, and a beautiful misshapen frangipani, exuding its scent on the gentle wind. Beyond the garden a sheet of bright blue sea sparkled in the sunlight; twice she had seen a cruise liner inching its way along the horizon. There were storms, when the sky darkened and the rain swept in lashing torrents against the windows.

At night the view changed to one of lunar stillness. There were no lights outside; the sea and the garden, the frangipani and the palm trees on the beach existed in moonlight; when the moon was covered they disappeared. By the side of the window there was a tall tamarind tree, its graceful branches floating in the wind. It carried a mass of pods, all heavy with ripe seeds. At Judith's request, the nuns had moved her bed so she couldn't see it through the window. When she was well enough, she got out of bed and sat in a chair. She didn't read; she refused the wireless which was sent up to her. She spent the time of recovery from her injuries staring out at the garden and the sea. The burns on her legs had healed; they were second degree. There was a deep gash on her right arm where she had cut herself on the window trying to get away from the fire, she would carry that scar for the rest of her life. Her memory of that morning was confused; her mind rejected details because the sensation of horror was too vivid to be borne. It had been over very quickly, so she understood afterwards, though the moments while she screamed and clawed at the louvre windows barricading her into the room, seemed immeasurable in time. Heat and smoke were pouring upwards from the inferno on the floor below; the fire was roaring like an animal, licking and spurting up the walls and the stairway which was a mass of orange flames. Judith was nearly unconscious when the two Barbadian police on duty outside the bungalow had smashed the window in with an axe, and dragged her out. Her clothes were smouldering, her legs burned by the fire spouting through the floor of the bedroom. Two minutes after she was lifted outside, the roof collapsed and the whole bungalow opened like a volcano mouth, belching a huge tongue of fire into the sky.

She was taken to St. Patricia's in preference to the new hospital in Bridgetown. It was easier to keep a guard on her room and a discreet watch on visitors to the private nursing home. But by the time she was ready to leave, they had all gone. Nobody intended harming her. She was of no interest, alive or dead; they had got Sverdlov, and the British withdrew their security men. A single Barbadian constable remained on duty in the grounds. It was no more than a gesture.

Nancy Nielson had flown over the first week to see her. She had sat by the bed, holding Judith's hand, giving her messages from Sam Nielson, repeating the same futile clichés about taking things easy and not worrying; trying to ease the suffering of someone who could not be comforted. Judith felt the physical pain through a haze of analgesics. Nothing invented by medical science could dull the agony in her mind. She had appreciated Nancy's coming and her sympathy. It was good of Sam to offer whatever she needed; kind of her friends to send messages. Even the hotel manager appeared one day, with flowers. She appreciated that people were sorry about what had happened to her and wanted to help. But there was nothing they could do.

Nobody could bring back the man whose voice was clearer in her mind than the comforting tones of the living, or restore the touch of the hand which had held hers, without either of them knowing it was the last contact they would ever make.

He was dead. He had gone down the stairs; she had heard his tread crossing the floor. Seconds later the lethal little bomb had bounced through the door and spattered its blazing death all over the room.

A strange man had come to see her in the nursing home; he hadn't given her his name. She had a vague impression of having spoken to him once before. He asked if there was anything she wanted, or any arrangements she would like made for her return to the States. She shook her head. Nothing. She wanted nothing. He told her how she had been rescued; he explained that a bomb had been thrown through the open sliding door. The dreadful speed and ferocity of the fire was explained by the use of napalm. She didn't ask the only question which mattered. There wasn't any need. She knew the answer. He hadn't said anything either. He had held out his hand and said, 'Goodbye, Mrs. Farrow. I'm sorry.' When he had gone she remembered that he had the same voice as the man who had telephoned about the plane seat, moments before it happened.

Now she was well enough to leave. The nuns had shown their understanding of her wish to be left alone and of her disinclination to go into the outside world. They had offered her a room for as long as she wished. It was as if the calm and cheerful Scottish Sister Superior knew that her body had healed that much faster than her mind. But permanent escape was impossible. When Judith knew this, it was time for her to go. Nancy Nielson was coming over the next morning to fly her back. She was going to stay with the Nielsons for a week or so, at Sam's insistence.

She hadn't the energy to refuse them; also obstinacy within the shelter of the nursing home was one thing. She might be only too glad to let Mrs. Nielson take full responsibility. Judith leaned forward in the chair. It was five o'clock. Quite soon the first grey shadow would creep up from the sea; like someone pulling a shutter from below, blocking out the sun. She remembered thinking of the dusk on Barbados in those precise terms, the first night she had come there, running away from Richard Paterson. Running from a trivial, shallow adventure with a married man, imagining herself hurt, unhappy. The comparison with what she felt at that moment was so contemptible that she made a thoughtless movement, and the gash on her arm gave her a sharp reminder not to jerk about. Nothing in her life had penetrated her like the death of Sverdlov. The loss of her father—the accident which killed her husband—nothing had opened every nerve as the horrific murder of a man she had neither lived with nor admitted that she loved. It was not possible to cry for him; he would have made fun of her tears. The grey line was growing darker and rising faster. It would soon be the West Indian night. Until one of the sisters came and switched them on, Judith was content to sit without lights. There was a knock at the door. She called out to come in; she didn't turn round.

'Hello, Mrs. Farrow. Mind if I turn on some light?'

It was Jack Loder. He flicked the switch by the door and the room filled with light from the enclosed glass bowl in the ceiling. He came towards Judith and held out his hand. She looked worse than he had expected; she glanced up at him and didn't move. The hand dropped back to his side and plunged into a trouser pocket; he coughed with embarrassment. Then Judith spoke.

'Get out of here,' she said. 'I don't know why you've come, but get out.'

'I understand how you feel.' Loder perched on the edge of her bed, his stubby fingers interlocked on his knee. One foot, in a highly polished light brown shoe, was swinging backwards and forwards. 'I thought I ought to come and see how you were getting on.'

'Thank you,' she said. 'Well you've seen, haven't you? I'm not feeling very well, so would you please go away now?'

He got off the bed; the concilatory pose had vanished.

'It wasn't my fault,' he said suddenly. 'It's no good blaming me. I did my part. It wasn't me who left the door open for them!'

'No,' Judith agreed. 'No, *I didn't shut it properly*—oh God, don't you think I'm going mad knowing it was all my fault!'

'We lost the "Blue" file,' Loder said. 'That went in the fire too.'

'Stop talking about your bloody *file*! What do I care about a *file*!' She began to cry. Loder had seen a number of women crying and he had never met one who could do it without making themselves ugly in the process. Judith Farrow's body heaved, she was bent double, her face hidden. It was a brutal manifestation of grief, and it made him uncomfortable.

'Don't cry like that,' he said. 'He wasn't worth it; you never really knew him at all. He got what he deserved.'

She raised her head. 'You bastard,' she said.

'He was K.G.B. himself.' Loder lit a cigarette. 'He was going to get a dose of his own medicine, that's all. Just think of what he really was, and you won't cry a bloody tear for him.'

'I don't care what he was,' she said. 'He was burned to death! Isn't that enough for you?'

'I'm sorry you got mixed up in this business; you can call me anything you like if it makes you feel better. They tell me you've made a good recovery, and you're going back to the States tomorrow.'

'Yes,' Judith answered. She leaned back in the chair; the outburst had exhausted her. She wanted him to go away, just to go away.

'If you've any decency,' she said, 'you'll leave me alone now. Please.'

'Okay.' Loder had finished his cigarette; he found an ashtray and rubbed out the stub. He went over and touched her on the shoulder. 'I brought something for you,' he said. 'Here.'

It was an envelope; she tore it open clumsily, she could hardly see what she was doing. Something rolled out on to her skirt. Judith picked it up in her fingers. It was black and shining, oblong shaped.

'Where did you get this?'

'He said you'd know what it was.' Loder sounded somewhere in the distance.

'It's a tamarind seed. Where did you get it?' The white face stared up at him; the voice was a whisper.

'From a friend of yours in London.' The ugly, freckled face was dour, unfriendly. 'Here, don't pass out on me for Christ's sake! Pull yourself together!'

'What friend.' Judith said. 'What friend in London—only one person in the world would send me this . . .'

'That's right.' Loder was smoking again. 'I told you not to cry about him. He isn't dead, Mrs. Farrow.'

'I don't believe you,' she said. 'It isn't possible . . . I heard him go downstairs. The next minute that thing burst . . .'

'You remember one of my chaps telephoned and you said he wouldn't stay under cover? Well, they were getting worried; there was a yacht hanging around and it didn't look right in that storm. So they decided to pull him in and keep him hidden till they took him to the airport. When he came down those stairs, Mrs. Farrow, my two men were waiting for him; he never knew what hit him. As they got him out of the door that bomb came over the balcony.

'There were only seconds in it or they'd have been killed too. But they always say the devil looks after his own.'

'Oh my God,' Judith was saying, over and over again. 'My God . . .'

'We gave out he'd been trapped inside,' Loder went on. 'His K.G.B. pals think he's dead, and "Blue", whoever he is, will think he's safe. The heat's off him now, and all we want is information.'

'I can't believe it,' she said. She opened her clenched hand and looked down at the little brown seed.

'He's safe,' Loder said. 'But he's not happy. He wants you. We've promised him all the comforts of home, but there's no obligation, you don't have to go.'

Slowly Judith pulled herself up; she held on to the back of the chair for support.

'I never liked you, Mr. Loder,' she said. 'But I never thought you were a fool.'